1% MURDERS:
THE ADAIR CLASSROOM
MYSTERIES
Vol. I
BY T.W. MORSE

Copyright © 2018 by T.W. MORSE

All rights reserved. This book or any portion thereof may not be reproduced or used in any manner whatsoever
without the express written permission of the publisher
except for the use of brief quotations in a book review.

Printed in the United States of America

First Printing, 2018

eBook
ISBN: 978-1-5136-4223-9

Paperback
ISBN: 978-1-5136-4224-6

Adair Classroom Mysteries
Naples, Florida

https://adairclassroommysteries.sitey.me/

--For Rebecca--
Without her I am lost.

1% MURDERS:
THE ADAIR CLASSROOM MYSTERIES
Vol. I
BY T.W. MORSE
PROLOGUE
CHAPTER 1
- LOGAN -
THE NOT-QUITE-BROKEN ADAIR FAMILY
CHAPTER 1.5
- ULYSSES -
THE NOT-QUITE-BROKEN ADAIR FAMILY, CONTINUED
CHAPTER 2
- ULYSSES -
THE PINK HIGH SCHOOL IS NOT A PRISON?
CHAPTER 3
- ULYSSES -
FLUORESCENT BULBS MAKE A LIT STUDY HALL
CHAPTER 4
- ULYSSES -
JUST A GUY AND A GIRL
CHAPTER 5
- LOGAN -
WOW, A RED VELVET TRACKSUIT?
CHAPTER 6
- LOGAN -
THE NEW AP GETS THE FULL NELSON
CHAPTER 7
- LOGAN -
AN UNLIKELY DATE?
CHAPTER 8
- ULYSSES -
SHENANIGANS ABOUND
CHAPTER 9
- ULYSSES -
OFFICE COMMOTION

CHAPTER 10
- ULYSSES -
WAIT, WAIT... JUST A SLAP ON THE WRIST?
CHAPTER 11
- ULYSSES -
MY BEST FRIEND IS MY GIRLFRIEND?
CHAPTER 12
- ULYSSES -
PENNY UNIVERSITY
CHAPTER 13
- LOGAN -
AWKWARDNESS FOLLOWED BY A DUET...CHECK, PLEASE!
CHAPTER 14
- ULYSSES -
PIZZA, DRUGS, BASKETBALL, AND TRACKSUITS. OH MY!
CHAPTER 15
-ULYSSES -
WHO KNEW BASKETBALL WAS MURDER!
CHAPTER 16
- LOGAN -
THE 1% MURDER
CHAPTER 17
- ULYSSES -
A CAFFEINATED WAR ROOM?
CHAPTER 18
- LOGAN -
THE COACH NEEDS A NEW PLAY
CHAPTER 19
- ULYSSES -
KNOCK, KNOCK AT THE GALLANT HOUSE
CHAPTER 20
- ULYSSES -
IT'S A HOLEY ESCAPE!
CHAPTER 21
- ULYSSES -

A NOT-SO-PRIVATE READING NOOK
CHAPTER 22
- LOGAN -
IT'S A TRACKSUIT INTERROGATION
CHAPTER 23
- LOGAN -
THE DETECTIVE IS A REAL BRUTE
CHAPTER 24
- ULYSSES -
IT'S A MEATBALL CONCERT
CHAPTER 25
- LOGAN -
THIS CARPOOL SUCKS!
CHAPTER 26
- ULYSSES -
GG&W?
CHAPTER 27
- LOGAN -
PINEAPPLE EXPO MARKERS + MURDER BOARD = DEAD ENDS
CHAPTER 28
- ULYSSES-
WAKE, WAKE, DON'T TELL ME
CHAPTER 29
- LOGAN -
REDHEADS AREN'T FUN AT WAKES
CHAPTER 30
- ULYSSES -
CUBAN SANDWICHES AND MAFIA CONNECTIONS
CHAPTER 31
- LOGAN -
I DIDN'T LIE TO THE SHERIFF. I ONLY LIED TO THE DEPUTY
CHAPTER 32
- ULYSSES -
PROMISES CAN BE BROKEN—A LITTLE

CHAPTER 33
- ULYSSES -
WHO IS THE REAL MARY CLIFTON?
CHAPTER 34
- LOGAN -
P.E. TEACHERS WORRY TOO MUCH
CHAPTER 35
- ULYSSES -
ASSISTANT PRINCIPALS SHOULD NEVER STEAL
CHAPTER 36
- LOGAN -
PRINCIPALS SHOULDN'T LIE
CHAPTER 37
- ULYSSES -
X MARKS THE HIT
CHAPTER 38
- ULYSSES -
HELL HAS NO FURY!
CHAPTER 39
- LOGAN -
CONCUSSIONS ACCOMPANIED BY SQUEALING ARE NOT GOOD
CHAPTER 40
- ULYSSES -
AN UNEXPECTED FAMILY REUNION
CHAPTER 41
- ULYSSES -
THE GALLANT MURDERS
CHAPTER 42
- ULYSSES -
A SHOT IN THE DARK—AND YOU WANT TO LISTEN TO QUEEN?
CHAPTER 43
- LOGAN -
A TRACKSUIT REVENGE
CHAPTER 44

- ULYSSES -
IT PAYS TO PAY ATTENTION IN SCIENCE
CHAPTER 45
- ULYSSES -
HELLO DOLLY!
CHAPTER 46
- ULYSSES -
NEVER BACKING DOWN

PROLOGUE

THE FAMILY'S HOME

The white house with green trim swayed, appearing hollow in the downpour, yet still standing tall against the abyss of conservation land. Having lost its power, the house stood ominous in the night. The robust home was imposing as the winds beat against its clapboard siding. Each raindrop pelting the ground bathed the lonely child. The child began to creep in from its hiding place. Ripped white pajamas and total darkness would not deter the child from the truth. Walking around the wraparound porch to the front entrance, the sound of the glass was diminished with the waves of wind and searing rain.

An entryway, once ornate with fine Brazilian wood and intricate wainscoting, now was adorned with leaves and debris from the ferocious storm. The windows of the house, once welcoming, were now blown in and threatening every step of the child's petite footsteps. The child's footsteps crunched over the shards of glass. The rain had been blowing in all night, creating puddles on the floor that now turned red from the lacerations on the child's feet. The wind screamed through each open window while the child, barely dressed, shivered from the humid, damp air.

The darkness of the stairwell awaited the child as it climbed, shivering, bleeding, following the large muddy boot prints. The child only briefly glanced up to see the photos of the family through the years along the way. The child stopped at one framed photo near the top. It showed a strong blond man, wearing summer golf apparel, which included a straw fedora. His dimpled, protruding chin led up to kind, loving eyes that gazed upon a woman with a simple polka dotted summer dress. The woman bore a soothing, motherly smile directed toward two young children who sat at the parents' feet. Each child hugged the other in playful admiration, as only toddlers can do.

The wounded child continued to cautiously climb the immense staircase, quietly expelling sobs that were lost to the wind and rain attacking the house with ferocious precision.

The Brazilian floorboards switched to a darkened carpet at the top of the curved stairs; the footprints were no longer visible. The carpet was a soothing relief to the child's shredded feet. The child peered over the hallway banister to the opened entryway below. The wind was calmer here, as the windows were still intact. Hung above the entryway was an ostentatious glass chandelier, twinkling as it danced in the blowing winds. The child hesitated at the landing. The murmurs coming from the hallway sounded muffled in the storm, but the child knew a different kind of tempest waited ahead.

Three doors lay in the child's path, but only one had a broken handle. Only one contained the murmuring — growing louder. Murmuring coming from the first door, a muffled gurgling sound, was now increasing. Definitely not the wind, the child nervously thought. The child touched the door ever so gently, and with the smallest of ease, it swung open. A crack of thunder blasted as the door opened, and a mere second later, the room came alive with a flash of light. The child jumped! The sobs and sniffles grew intense as the lightning's illumination of the room exposed its dark secret. In the few seconds of illumination, the child saw the gigantic bureau turned over on its side, clothing scattered on the floor, and jewelry spilling all over the carpet. Chairs were thrown and splintered against the walls.

    The child inched further into the room, following the sounds like a series of bread crumbs, moving debris, slipping on a silk handkerchief that lay on the floor, stumbling around the fallen chairs. The sound was now all around the child, heavy gasps, short then quick. The child was stunned, shaking. Pain from the glass magnified as the floor transitioned from the bedroom's dark soothing carpet to the master bath's cold, white, marble tile.

    The marble's gray veins, shooting in every direction, were now a deeper color. The child inched into the bathroom, slower now. No external windows were present, and it was difficult to see. The child was navigating the surroundings only by memory. The moaning changed to intermediate light breathing. The child didn't know what to think - or do. Calling out could be dangerous. The child's eyes were adjusting slightly to the darkness, seeing silhouettes in the massive shower ahead, silhouettes that should not be there.

The child crawled on the floor, inching closer to the open glass door of the massive shower. Then the breathing and moaning stopped. The child stopped moving.

The massive house started to win against the storm. The child's eyes quickly shut as the power surged back on, blinding the child as it lay on the giant marble bathroom floor, frozen in time. All the chrome and recessed lights were left on prior to losing power, and the bathroom burst with electricity.

Outside in the bedroom, the TV cranked on and the child could hear a familiar Disney Channel cartoon. When the child's eyes opened, the darker veins of the marble were no longer gray; they were painted over with a dark crimson. The floor was all the child could process. The child could not look up to the opening of the shower. The cold marble was a safe place; looking down was safer than the realization of what was in the shower. Finally, a crackle of thunder rang through the night, shaking the house and causing the child's eye to look up. Exposed before the child was a vivid and demonic scene. In the massive white marbled shower lay three bodies. The marble was no longer white; it was now a deep crimson.

The bodies were pale, white, all dressed in their night clothes. Their skin was flayed, and a knife with a dark curved black plastic handle protruded from the larger of the three victims. Their bodies lay contorted, with mouths open in horror, looking out into oblivion. The bodies' blood was trickling into the shower drain, trailing from the white marble where the child lay in horror. For a moment the scene was too difficult and surreal to comprehend. The child started hyperventilating; no breath was coming, just gasp after gasp with no air getting through. After realizing the meaning of this sight, the child erupted with a deep, soul-crushing wail. It echoed and throbbed through the house and out into the night, "NO!!"

    The screams were enveloped by the storm and ultimately silenced by a firm hand that latched over the child's mouth.

CHAPTER 1

- LOGAN -

THE NOT-QUITE-BROKEN ADAIR FAMILY

Waking up is still difficult, even after five years, but Ortiz's whimper is vexatious. "Shut it, Ortiz!" He continues the whimpering. "Shut it! You have to be the neediest dog in Florida."

Like clockwork, my cell phone comes to life precisely at 5:30 a.m. The hypnotic piano tunes of "She's Got A Way" by Billy Joel work their way out of my phone and into my ears. I touch the screen before the lyrics are sung and rub my eyes, as an image of Jillian and I dancing to that very song at our wedding flashes through my mind. It was a lifetime ago. The memory begins to fade while I shower. I shave my beard with the electric razor, leaving nothing but a closely cropped goatee. I look in my vanity mirror and pick at my gray hairs, which now greatly outnumber the brown on my head. I always jokingly blame my son, Ulysses, becoming a freshman as the reason my hair is now practically gray.

The sink is covered in beard trimmings. As I clean, I look to the other side of the double vanity, remembering Jillian's dream of having a sink all to herself. Every place we lived together only had one sink, and sharing a sink was difficult to say the least. The other side would've been Jillian's, but she never had the chance, and it sat there untouched, clean, empty. My side is a mess of contact solution, allergy pills, and toothpaste. The facial trimmings add to the fray. It has been that way for five years now; the faucet was never even touched or turned on. I blankly stare at the sink, with a growing urge to turn it on after all these years. It is a perfectly good sink, but never used since we moved into this tiny apartment. Finally, tired of this distraction, I scoot quickly over, turn on the faucet, and yank it off after a brief moment. Water had burst out, and then quickly extinguished. I sarcastically blurt, "Great job, Logan, your shrink would be so proud. You turned on a sink. You must be ready to date now!"

I'm not; I don't feel the urge. The pain of her loss lingers everywhere, even in the freakin' bathroom! I start to tear up again while my thin fingers fumble with my wedding band hanging on a chain around my neck. I quickly think of Ulysses and stop myself, remembering to be strong for him.

There's something to be happy about; today is Friday! I am a teacher, and teachers, more than students, love Fridays. For me though, it is also Bow Tie Friday. I quickly struggle to tie my ruby red bow tie. It is my personal tradition to always wear a bow tie on Friday. It helps to take the attention away from my frayed blue shirt and wrinkled chinos. I am going to try and bring the bow tie back in style, if it ever was. It is truly a neglected accessory. Since I am such a great trendsetter, maybe more people will wear them. I am a little delusional — I know. I'm trying to bring back the words swell and nifty, too. I'm not sure they're trending though — yet. Actually, I get teased by the teachers who are way older. The teasing is mainly because of my grumpy nature, love for jazz and Sinatra, and, for obvious reasons, my style. My regular use of the words swell, groovy, and "great googlie mooglie" doesn't help the situation either. I think it's funny, but sometimes I'm called grandpa or dad by the faculty and students. I may be 39 but have a 79-year-old's personality. I'm okay with that though; I think of myself as vintage. Although lately I feel closer to 79 than 30.

    I leave my room while pinning the Mangrove High School teacher badge to my brown belt, which is a required accessory, unlike the bow tie. It reads, "Logan Adair, social studies dept., teacher." The picture on my badge shows an oval face sporting a long beard and crooked grin. Picture day was a bad day.

    I quickly glance outside; it is going to be another hot sunny day in Southwest Florida. I wish Ulysses and I could go to one of Somerset's many Gulf Coast beaches rather than school. Yeah, even teachers like to skip once in a while. It's Friday though, so at least I have my weekly trip with Ulysses and friends from work to Somerset's local coffee shop, Penny University. On Fridays we cancel carpool, so we can grab some sandwiches and coffee after school. I am especially looking forward to this Friday; it's Penny University's first open mic night. People are going to play instruments, sing, and even read poetry. Ulysses and I may go against our better judgement and perform some rock classics. We both play guitar, and we are always eager to try out some new tunes. I may love Sinatra and jazz, but classic rock is my first love. My shrink says it's a good outlet, especially since Ulysses can take part. Jillian would've been so proud.

    I snag Ortiz's leash, clasp it on, and he pulls me down our seventeen steps to his favorite green patch. I can hear the Hernandezes' baby giving her parents their daily wake up call. Ortiz is done, and we bound back up the steps.

    I scoop his kibble into his favorite Boston Red Sox bowl. As he munches happily away, I grab the egg carton and loaf of wheat bread from the fridge, plug in our worn electric griddle, then tap on Ulysses' door. "Time to wake up!"

    I hear a muffled, "I'm up, I'm up!" A few seconds later, some AC/DC echoes through his bedroom wall.

    "Nice," I blurt out, as I bob my head with the rhythm coming from Ulysses' bedroom. I boil some water in the electric tea kettle and proceed to prep the French press coffee maker, allowing the grinds to steep, while I finish cooking the eggs over easy. I add some strawberry jelly to the toast.

    I switch on ESPN from our galley kitchen, fifteen feet away from our living room flat screen. The living room, furnished with a worn crimson red futon paired with two pleather club chairs, has an array of pictures littering the walls. A dented table with four chairs occupies the dining area, with two stools lying in wait at the bar to the galley kitchen. Our place is basically one large room, so I can watch my baseball highlights from anywhere in the main living area. We have a slider at the back of the dining area, leading to a screened lanai with a small red ornate bistro set. I usually frequent the lanai for breakfast, but it is very humid this morning, so I settle for the safety of our central air.

    I eat at the kitchen table, glancing up to see Ulysses' cooked eggs still on a plate at the counter, getting cold.

    "Eggs getting cold!" I yell through his bedroom door on the other side of the kitchen, as I sit down with my coffee, freshly poured from the French press.

    My coffee cup is a monstrous beast, three times the size of a normal cup, dwarfing my hand as I lift it to my mouth like a dumbbell. The mug has Winnie the Pooh and other Hundred-Acre Wood characters barely visible over the faded blue backdrop. It once was bright blue, with colorful characters, but many dishwasher cycles changed that. Jillian gave this to me on our seventh wedding anniversary while vacationing in Walt Disney World, when we first considered moving down to Florida permanently. The memory leaves a smile on my face that remains until I am startled by a persistent Ortiz, wanting to go back out for round two.

    "Take Ortiz out! And hurry, we need to go in fifteen minutes," I yell to Ulysses as I slip back into the fresh memories of Jillian.

CHAPTER 1.5

- ULYSSES -

THE NOT-QUITE-BROKEN ADAIR FAMILY, CONTINUED

My mind springs to life, as my cell phone's alarm chirps annoyingly alive in my ear, spoiling my dream of Hannah. Dreams should be recorded so people can review them at leisure, dissecting the meaning and weirdness of our subconscious. I can only remember bits of this particular dream of Hannah. It involved her and me running on the beach.

You would think a dream that includes the girl of my literal dreams would be of us frolicking through the sand and passionately kissing in the dunes, but nope. In this dream, we were running from masked ninjas! Masked ninjas? Shouldn't have stayed up late with Dad last night, binging the second season of *Daredevil* on Netflix.

"Ulysses. Ulysses, time to wake up!" my dad says through my door from the kitchen.

Yes, you guessed right, my name is Ulysses.

Ulysses Robert Adair. I hate my name. My dad, a Civil War buff, named me after Ulysses S. Grant, great Union general and president. My dad got to name me, and, if I was a girl, my mother would have had the opportunity. She used to say my name would have been Emma, after my great-grandmother. Unfortunately, my father won this agreement and failed miserably in his task. Ulysses is such an old man name. I picture some crabby old man with a corduroy suit, hobbling around with a cane. All my friends, and even some of my teachers, call me U.

I yell out my door, "I'm up, I'm up!" I am exasperated by all that is in my head as my feet hit the cold faux wood floor. I slowly stretch my long body, as I lose all prior remembrance of my dream. Reluctantly, I transition into my morning routine. "Thanks, Dad!"

It wasn't a typical dream. For years I have become used to nightmares, reliving the car crash my mother and I were in, night after night. I'll take ninjas any day after enduring that nightmare for five years. She and I crashed on our move down to Florida from Maine. Dad was in the moving truck, several cars behind, and we were in our old minivan. Mom's death happened so fast; I only remember fragments. They come back in sharp, painful blurs. After the crash, it took a long time for me and Dad to recover mentally, a lot longer than my physical injuries. But we lean on each other, and we've learned to function in our new normal. He's my best friend, and we found out a lot about ourselves after the crash. We grew close, especially in this new strange place in Florida. But I still miss my mom, probably always will.

"Hey Siri, play some AC/DC." "Dirty Deeds Done Dirt Cheap" pulsates through the mini speaker dancing on my desk. It inspires me to drop to the floor and start my morning workout of fifty push-ups and crunches. My cold floor is littered with an unusual amount of dust and hair, reminding me to vacuum after school before Dad notices. I finish the workout and pop up to examine my shirtless body in front of my flimsy white mirror that hangs on my closet door. My pajama pants are getting tighter and the length is getting shorter. The material, once white, is now a bit gray and fraying. Pulling the waistband down I examine the four-inch scar on my upper thigh. Stroking the scar tissue, I wince at the memory of the crash and the weeks of rehab. I start flexing my biceps and abs in the mirror, showing off my thin muscled body to nobody but my fat brown guinea pig, Jedi. He is not impressed, and he scurries back into his purple plastic house.

Right on cue, Dad yells again, "Eggs are getting cold, double time!"

I check my phone; it explodes with snaps from Hannah and Conrad about today and later tonight. I have to ignore them because I am running late. I quickly throw on pink striped boxers, khaki shorts, and one of my prized Christmas presents from my rich Uncle Alan, a Vineyard Vines polo shirt. This particular one is bright blue. Dad and I cannot usually afford Vineyard Vines shirts. Reason 1: Dad is a teacher and widowed. Reason 2: Dad, being from Maine, is a tightwad. It's a Maine thing, only true Mainers would understand. Dad is so tight with money; he owns clothes that predate me.

He always lectures me saying, "Why pay eighty dollars for a shirt with a little tiny whale, when you can buy 6 shirts with no whale, for the same price and material? The only difference is one has a tiny stitched whale!"

Dad doesn't understand what a teen in Somerset, Florida, has to deal with in the twenty-first century. He thinks of the wealthy families as duchy elitists, but when I wear these shirts I feel like I belong here.

Uncle Alan is Dad's brother who works in Boston. Did I mention he was loaded? I'm his only nephew, so I score big at Christmas and birthdays. I finish getting dressed by throwing on some Old Spice, which I know the ladies like — I hope.

I look around my room and know my dad, touched with a case of OCD, would freak if he saw the condition it is in, so I quickly start to pick things up. This doesn't take long because my bedroom is an eight by eight box. It has a single bed, bureau, tiny desk and outdated soccer posters plastered to the walls. An overused and repurposed black spray-painted coffee table stands at the foot of my bed, where an oversized brown guinea pig plays hide and seek with himself in an equally oversized cage.

I smell-check each piece of clothing that is on the floor, throwing articles that pass into the closet. The ones that don't pass litter the top of my hamper in a pile that balances to stay upright. I finish by quickly pulling my sheets and my Union Jack comforter into place.

I run a brush through my brown puffy, curly, unruly hair. I can thank Mom for my hair; her hair was long and curly. She often struggled in the morning, like I am now, trying to get a less Elvis look. Dad always says my hair looks a little bit like Elvis. I comb at it again, and again, but it springs back at me with a vengeance, often curling down my forehead like Clark Kent.

My attention is once again pulled away by little paws scratching at my door. I open it to unveil our Boston terrier, Ortiz. He swaggers his chubby black body into my room, suspiciously eyeing Jedi, who, in return, retreats into his purple plastic home. Ortiz sits in front of me, looking for attention.

Dad calls after him, "Take Ortiz out, please! And hurry, we need to go in fifteen minutes."

Ortiz looks up intensely, knowing what Dad just ordered, wagging his tail ferociously. It always appears that Ortiz has a wide, smug, toothy grin on his face, right now more than ever.

I walk out of my bedroom and across the condo in five steps, passing by Dad in the dining room. He is watching ESPN in deep meditation, drinking from his enormous coffee cup. I slip on my aging tan Sperrys, grab the leash from the hook, and pin Ortiz to the ground, exposing his white belly as I clasp the leash to his collar. He leads the way out the front door, practically sprinting the entire way down our seventeen steps to the ground floor.

We live in a tight two-bedroom condo in Somerset, Florida. Somerset is one of the wealthiest zip codes in America, but unfortunately, we don't see much of the wealth. We are in the part of the city where the lower to middle class live. Condos and small duplexes litter this part of Somerset; there's a lot of Section 8 housing as well. The condos where we live are called River Creek. They are pretty nice. We have a pool and a fitness center.

The complex runs behind the Goodlette River; it is probably the cheapest waterfront in Calusa County.

The apartment next door on our floor is vacant, and the Hernandezes live below us on the first floor. The Hernandezes are a nice young Hispanic couple who have a newborn - a loud newborn. Walls in River Creek are thin, even the ceilings.

We have an end unit on Dragonfly Way near the front gate. All Somerset street names sound like a yoga studio, even in the less desirable parts of the city; I don't get it. Dad and I are happy at River Creek, since it is close to the beach and many restaurants.

We've lived here for five years now; Mom was supposed to live here too. River Creek is a series of seven cement buildings, all covered with stucco painted in browns and tans as to appear Tuscan. I'm not sure why people want Florida to look like Italy, but I'm not complaining. I made a vow to never complain about Florida. Next time my friend Conrad complains about the heat, or how we have nothing to do in Somerset, I'm going to knock him out, throw him in a crate, and mail him to Maine in the middle of January. I was born in Clark, Maine, and we lived there until we couldn't take the cold anymore and moved down here. I don't want to call out Maine, it's great in the summer, but during our last winter up in Clark we had 110 inches of snow! 110! Clark, Maine, is also home to seven antique stores. Not sure why they need seven, but, sure, whatever. I love Florida! The constant sun, the beaches, the stores, and malls. I'll even add the weirdos and the gators to the list.

I do have some great memories of Maine,

especially since they are basically all memories of my mom. Like the times we traveled down to Boston, catching a game at Fenway Park to watch our beloved Red Sox. Memories of Mom and I building a snowman after Dad snow-blowed the driveway, or a cup of cocoa with Mom as she read mysteries to me by the wood stove. Ortiz once again yanks me away from my deep thoughts. His business is done and he wants to go back in to see his favorite person — Dad.

Ortiz's tiny black paws zoom back up the seventeen steps to our apartment. I open the door and Ortiz bursts in, jumping on Dad in pure elation. Dad scratches at Ortiz's ear and throws one of his tennis balls across the room. Ortiz shoots from Dad's lap and through the house in a couple of strides, catching the ball on one of its first bounces. He then holds it between his canines, as he lays down near the front door in triumphant satisfaction.

"Eat!" Dad instructs. "We have a long day ahead of us, and you need protein if you want those muscles to grow."

"Fine, fine," I mumble from the side of my mouth. Dad's ringtone for me is the Swedish Chef from the Muppets because he claims I mumble a lot. I'm in denial. Dad is washing his breakfast dishes, while I smear my favorite BBQ sauce on my two eggs and do my best impression of a speed eater. I then pop a waffle in the toaster and gulp down a glass of OJ.

My dad looks at me quizzically; I smile, saying with a full mouth, "What?!"

"You ready?"

I slather peanut butter across the newly toasted waffle, grab a banana, and throw my plate in the dishwasher. "I'm ready."

"Okay, but did you pack your math work? If you have another missing assignment, O'Leary will want to meet with me!"

Mr. O'Leary is my honors geometry teacher, and he is in Dad's carpool. We mutually agree that Mr. O'Leary is the biggest tool in the tool bag. The guy hates me, and he always looks down at Dad.

"I packed it, and I'm trying to turn him now. He's coming around, too; he only hates me a little. You can bring me today, right?"

I usually like biking to school, but our guitars are in the back of the car and we always look forward to Penny University. Lately there are new reasons to like it though.

"Yeah, no carpool today. I'm looking forward to tonight; maybe we can play some of those Eagles songs we rehearsed."

"Too new, we better do some of the songs we're used to."

You guessed it, Dad teaches at my high school, Mangrove High. He got a U.S. history position five years ago. I don't mind having my dad teaching at my high school, especially since he's a pretty laid-back teacher. His students generally like him, unlike O'Leary: He's the devil. Just thinking about him gives me chills. I look over my shoulder like he knows I'm thinking about him and he'll magically appear, like in a cheesy horror movie.

"Can you go lock up Ortiz while I get the car and A/C going?" Dad asks as he grabs his work bag and pours the rest of his coffee from his big mug into his to-go mug, which reads "World's Okayest Teacher," before slipping out the door.

I throw Ortiz's tennis ball, now oozing with slobber, into his metal wire crate just inside Dad's bedroom. The crate is filled with a cushy bright golden bed and a couple of chew toys to keep him entertained throughout the school day. Ortiz scampers in, and I latch the door behind him.

"Works every time." His face looks sad and pathetic, not smiling at me anymore. "I'll make it up to you after school, I promise."

I run to the door, grab my faded red L.L. Bean backpack, and snatch my lanyard with my house key attached. I lock the door as I exit, racing down the steps, and yell, "Buenos dias," to a groggy looking Mr. Hernandez as he reaches for his morning newspaper. I practically somersault into our Silver Prius. "Smooth," Dad comments.

"I know — right?" I grin back.

CHAPTER 2

- ULYSSES -

THE PINK HIGH SCHOOL IS NOT A PRISON?

The Prius drifts through the streets of Somerset while the satellite radio plays a Jimmy Buffet tune, and Dad sings along. He is always singing.

As we drive through the streets to school, the restaurants and condos near River Creek blend together, passing us like the light humid breeze breaking through the open windows, encircling us in warmth. The roads of Somerset are pristine, the grass perfectly manicured, the giant palm trees remind you of where you are as they dot the medians in perfect symmetry. Nothing is out of sorts in this 1% city.

As we get closer to Mangrove High, the condos and restaurants slowly recede, giving way to multi-million-dollar gated communities lined by ten-foot privacy walls and towering fountains that play peekaboo through the security gates. The wealth is exuded on every corner, making our Prius awkward among the Porsches and Maseratis coasting by us.

I focus my attention on my phone, exchanging texts and snaps with Conrad and Hannah.

We pass a few reclaimed and recently flipped warehouses near our downtown. Probably once used for processing fish when Somerset was a fishing village in a bygone era. Now they appear lost among the brand-new condos and ritzy banks on every other corner. One warehouse in particular is painted bright slate blue with a weathered, rusty tin roof. The warehouse wears an oversized marquee facade, covered in large Broadway Edison bulbs that read "Penny University Cafe" in a bold, exaggerated, cursive font. I can't wait till tonight! Hannah's parents own and operate Penny University. She also is now old enough to work there. As we pass I start to think of her, and these thoughts become a daydream.

Hannah and I share two classes together, U.S history and geometry. Ever since seventh grade I've been wanting to ask her on a date. Two years seems like an eternity, at least an eternity for a teenager. I always lacked the courage to act.

Dad is reading my mind as he turns to me, with his lopsided grin, and says, "So — when are you going to ask Hannah out?"

"Seriously, Dad? How? How did you know what I was thinking? I don't know. I'm waiting for the right moment. Seriously, how did you do that?" He always does this, not just with me but everyone.

"Elementary, my dear Ulysses. You were zoning out when we drove by Penny University while a romantic tune by Buffett was on, and you sighed to yourself. You don't have to be Sherlock Holmes to deduce that train of thought. She's working tonight. The moment may pass by; you better act quick. I think it's her first night working since she turned fourteen, so now she's getting paid. She told me in class yesterday. She'll be so impressed to hear you play tonight."

"Hopefully," I murmur, frustrated at how Dad could read my mind so easily. "Did it take forever for you to get the courage to ask Mom out?" I ask.

"Mom actually asked me out."

"You never said that!"

"You never asked. It happened a couple of decades ago while I was waiting tables at the Kennebec Resort, back in Maine. It was during the summer of my sophomore year in college.

"I was walking out of our kitchen with a huge tray full of food when I bumped into a resort guest standing right in front of the entrance to the kitchen. I only saw a blur of bright orange before my tray went flying in the air and all over my customer's lap. The fish dish went one way, the steak went flying another, soup sloshing everywhere, a complete crazy mess. If I was lucky, the tray and the food would've gone on the floor, but no. My luck had it spilling right on the lap of my two customers, who happened to have been the couple who owned the resort! While they were celebrating their anniversary!"

"No way, so how did Mom ask you out?"

"Let me finish, U."

"I thought your first date was at the carnival?"

"It was, but Mom asked me."

Now my curiosity was building.

"How?" I ask.

"Let me finish!"

"Ok, ok."

"So I started to say sorry to the owner, I think his name was Horner, yeah Mr. and Mrs. Horner. I profusely said sorry, but he barked at me like I was a stupid simpleton, calling me some nasty names, so my anger grew. I may as well have turned green and had gamma radiation running through my veins. I called him a pompous douchebag! I never want this repeated, Ulysses, I was embarrassed, juvenile, and unprofessional."

"I know, Dad. So did you hit him?" I make the motion with my fist and start giggling.

"No! The reverse actually. Mr. Horner said, in many curse words, that I was finished at his establishment, and he had me escorted out of the resort."

"That's great, Dad, that you like to share your most embarrassing moments with me, but I thought you were sharing how Mom asked you out, not reliving Logan Adair bloopers through the years."

"Who do you think I bumped into?" Dad says smiling.

"No way?"

"Way!"

"Dad, nobody says that anymore."

"It's not hip?" Dad asks.

"No, and stop saying hip!"

"Okay, so I was sitting out on the curb in front of this massive white nineteenth-century Victorian resort on the down east coast of Maine with no ride home because my shift wasn't over. I was now jobless for the foreseeable future, and that's when I heard the most delicate English-accented voice behind me saying 'I'm so sorry!' She came up beside me and sat on the curb next to me, wearing a bright orange jumper that hugged her tiny frame.

"'Wait a minute, you're the person I bumped into!' I was so livid, but as soon as I saw her and heard her voice, my frustrations vaporized. She pushed back her tight curls showing off her soft, white adorable face, sprinkled with freckles on the bridge of her nose. I was in love at first sight. She took my hand and placed her other hand on my chin, making me look into her intense brown eyes. Time stood still. The summer breeze paused. Even the crickets stopped chirping. Fireworks went off and Gary Wright's 'Dream Weaver' let loose in my mind. She, once again, in a very serious tone said, 'I'm so miffed at your boss for sacking you like that. He's such a wanker!' Speaking what seemed like an accent straight from Downton Abbey or more like Monty Python. All I could say was 'Ah — it's all good.'

"She introduced herself as Jillian Stephens. I introduced myself and then she said in the most serious delicate voice, 'Do you like — carnivals?'

"That's how she asked me to the local Fourth of July carnival in Clark. She was studying abroad at University of Southern Maine. She was eating at the resort with friends. She was bending down in front of the kitchen exit door, trying to take a picture with her newly bought flip phone. Then I burst out of the kitchen with the tray, sending her, and my dishes, flying.

"She saw the exchange with my boss and felt

mortified that she got me fired. Her friends were, of course, her best friends, your Aunt Sally and Uncle John. They were going to the carnival the next day, and she didn't want to be the third wheel again. The rest was — history."

"Mom was so cool! I miss her."

"I do, too. How about we play a Beatles song tonight? They were her favorite."

I nod in agreement, "Yeah, sounds good. How about 'The Long and Winding Road'? It was their last hit and will be our first!"

"Sounds like plan, Stan."

"Dad, seriously, you can't say stuff like that, especially when I'm talking with Hannah."

"I know. Don't worry, I won't hurt your game. Remember I'm your wingman!"

"Dad! Dad — no! Subject change? Over the weekend, what do we have for homework?"

"Just have to study for the quiz on Monday."

Having Dad for U.S. history is great. He is hard, but it is always good to have the inside info and constant reminders. We approach Mangrove High School, which stands a few blocks from downtown Somerset and about three miles from the beach. It's rough, having the smell of the salt water fill the air during school, knowing the Gulf of Mexico is a stone's throw away.

Dad pulls into the faculty parking lot. Several football fields could fit into Mangrove High's asphalt jungle of a parking lot and have plenty of room to spare. All spaces are labeled with numbers so the students don't snag any of the faculty spots, or vice versa. Dads parking space is 221. He is so proud of his space, being an avid Sherlock Holmes fan. 221B

Baker Street is the London address of the famed literary character. Dad used to read me Sir Arthur Conan Doyle's original Sherlock Holmes stories, otherwise known as the cannon. We both love mysteries, even Mom did. Mom preferred Agatha Christie, though, and often read some of her classics to me before bed. I got the best of both literary mystery worlds. As a family, we loved all things mystery. We played Clue; we completed escape rooms, often getting out of them in record time, I might add. I think that's what kept Dad and I so tight, our love of the unknown.

We approach Mangrove High in our little Prius. Mangrove is a huge three-story, bright flamingo pink brick building; brand new sports stadiums abut the pink monster. It is no more than thirty years old. Really new compared to my hundred-year-old school back in Clark, Maine, but everything in Florida is new.

It is far better than my middle school, which resembled army barracks, and felt like them, too. That was the dreaded Somerset Middle School.

Somerset Middle School's hallways are open aired, wrapped around ten separate concrete one-story buildings, surrounded by a high perimeter fence. If it isn't an army barrack, then the next closest comparison is a prison. I'm not sure if the fence is to keep the public out or to keep the students in. I love Mangrove High, though. Especially because for the first time going to school I am treated with respect and not like a little kid. I could go on all day about how bad Somerset Middle was. Maybe I am a little jaded because it was my first years in Florida, adjusting to Mom's death.

Mangrove allowed me to have a fresh start—no uniforms, unlike the prison over at Somerset Middle. The freedom and focus of high school is so much more refreshing than middle school. When I think of Somerset Middle, Pink Floyd's *The Wall* rings in my ears. I don't want to be another brick in the wall. Conformity sucks!

Mangrove High's entrance is plastered by a twenty-foot manatee: our mascot, Manny the Manatee. He smiles down at everyone that enters, like a billboard car salesman. Dad bursts through the double doors eager to start our day and move on to the weekend.

Mangrove High's hallways are covered with turquoise lockers, still shining in the bright Florida morning sun, which stretches from the skylights above, giving a peaceful serenity and the calm before the storm of students who will invade in a short time.

Another oversized Manny the Manatee sign hangs in front of the double doors that swing into the main office, near the front entrance, reminding us with a word bubble coming from his mouth, "Don't do drugs!" Sure thing, Manny. Our manatee version of McGruff the Crime Dog, keeping kids clean one lame mascot at a time. I have never known any drug user to actually stop using drugs because the Manny sign compelled them do so. If anything, he may have driven kids to start using drugs.

Drugs are sometimes a problem at Mangrove, especially since about 70% of the student body come from homes with the top 1% of incomes. Hot parties where drugs are rampant are happening every weekend, especially since most of their parents jet set on the weekends, taking trips to their second homes in Aspen or Vail, or weekend trips to Miami. While the parents are away, the children will play and play hard. I hate that scene and avoid it at all costs. I stay away from most of the 1% influencers at Mangrove.

According to a newspaper article I read recently, Florida families that make over $377,000 of income a year qualify as the 1%. Meaning 99% of Floridians don't make anywhere close to $378,000, especially if your dad's a widowed teacher. Somerset, and of course Mangrove, is home to a majority of them, and a lot of those made far, far more than the $377,000.

Somerset exudes wealth. Some of the houses down at the beach are for sale for ten million to twenty million dollars. For the most part, at Mangrove High, students leave their entitled attitude at the door. So the average kids, including me, are able to stand shoulder to shoulder with them. American public schools - yeah!

The long corridor lay in front of us with the enormous staircase leading to the expansive second floor, littered with signs of every upcoming event and club. Signs read, "Go Manatee Basketball! Send Everglades High back to the swamp!" Wow, harsh. There's a big game tomorrow night against Everglades High School, our rivals.

Conrad, my best friend, is one of their rising stars. Some of the old cross-country signs are still hung, now partially covered by chess club and drama club signs. Cross-country is my sport. We had our last meet a week ago. I came in second at districts. Dad was so proud. He freaked out at the finish line, jumping up and down with pure elation. Running and music help me and Dad cope. When I run, my mind becomes clear and I can concentrate on the present; it brings clarity to a very busy teenage brain.

I separate from Dad, who heads for his classroom, and I start toward the before-school study hall in the cafeteria, so I can find Conrad.

"Ulysses, meet me at my classroom at quarter to three. I have to go home first before we go to open mic night," Dad yells down the hall.

I yell back, "Can I meet you at Penny U? I was going to walk over with Hannah and Conrad after Conrad's basketball practice."

Dad smiles and says, "No problemo," and winks at me before fading into his classroom near the front office.

CHAPTER 3

- ULYSSES -

FLUORESCENT BULBS MAKE A LIT STUDY HALL

Mangrove High's cafeteria is expansive. Waxed floors gleam from the extra fluorescent lighting, leaving no shadows. They remind me of the office from the opening scenes of *Joe Versus the Volcano,* Mom's favorite movie. We watched it over and over again when I was a kid. Maybe our school is preparing our retinas for future dead-end office jobs like Tom Hanks' character in the movie. The morning study hall has several students clinging to a few of the dozens of cafeteria tables that line the expansive room. All the students are either in deep thought or joyously conversing before the arduous day ahead.

It doesn't take long to spot Conrad. His blonde hair shines in the fluorescent light of the cafeteria, giving an albino appearance of pure white hair. He sits studying his geometry; his gaunt face looks more frustrated than ever. That is the face he makes whenever he's completing Mr. O'Leary's geometry work. Conrad always has to do the morning study hall because of basketball. He hates it, but it was the only way his dad let him play.

I've known Conrad Wright for five years now. He was my first Florida friend. His parents are divorced, like many Somerset families, and he could relate to my broken home. His dad is a lawyer, and a rich one, according to Conrad. I guess if he's that rich, he must be pretty good at what he does. Conrad is in geometry with me and Hannah, but this year we don't share any other classes. He has Dad in U.S. history, but a different period than me.

He lives in a large, white, Art Deco home on the beach. The place is a mausoleum. Nothing could ever be touched in his house, and it gives Conrad a nervous demeanor that never goes away. I would hate to be nervous in my own home. Conrad's mom is a famous model, never living in one place for very long. She pays Conrad's father a huge alimony check every month so the beach house can remain a museum.

I plop down opposite Conrad. As I do, the sound of his teeth grinding causes me to cringe, undoubtedly a result of O'Leary's lovely homework. "Today is the day!" I excitedly exclaim.

Conrad looks up at me with a queasy expression that quickly morphs into a wide smile as he asks, "Hey, U! What's so special about today?"

"I'm asking Hannah out, today! I've waited long enough! I'm walking to Penny U with her after your practice, and the deed will be done there. You comin' with?"

Conrad parts his white hair hanging over one side of his face. "Sorry man, I'm actually getting tutored by O'Leary after practice. Practice is going to be short, just a shoot around because of tomorrow night's game. O'Leary said he is staying late and he'd be 'happy' to tutor me." He made the air quotes around "happy" and looks like he could pass out from the horror. Other than O'Leary, Conrad's dad and his house are the only things that get him this nervous.

"What the hell, man, you volunteered for this? Are you crazy! I would rather have all my toenails pulled off than go in and get extra help from O'Leary!"

"I know. I'm already feeling anxious, well, more anxious than usual anyway. My grade is starting to slip, and my dad says if it goes below an A I'm off the team!"

Conrad's dad only dreams of one thing, his son becoming a lawyer like him. He doesn't like me that much, but I've never known him to really like anyone; he's a bit of a jerk.

"I gotcha, man. Meet you at Penny U later?"

Conrad loves basketball. Not sure what he would do if he couldn't play anymore. Conrad's dad belongs to the Somerset Beach Club, and they have a great indoor basketball court. We spend many hours shooting around. I don't care for the game — the solo sports are for me — but it's fun when I'm with Conrad. His frame screams basketball player: tall, lanky, fast, with a mean jump shot. He is the only freshman that got any playing time.

Conrad staying behind sounds pretty perfect after all, this way I can talk to Hannah alone. Conrad breaks me from my thoughts and back to our conversation by saying, "Sure, as long as Dad says it okay. Hey, look who it is!"

CHAPTER 4

- ULYSSES -

JUST A GUY AND A GIRL

I spin around and see Hannah Reyes coming into the cafeteria. Hannah moved here shortly after Dad and I arrived. Her family moved to Somerset because Mrs. Reyes, Hannah's mother, inherited from her uncle two warehouses near downtown, which they transformed into Penny University Cafe. I was the one assigned to show Hannah around when she arrived to Somerset Middle School. Ever since, we've been tight friends.

When I gave Hannah the tour of the school, I joked with her, comparing Somerset Middle to a prison, "So this is the prison barracks, that's the office where the warden beats you, over there is the cafeteria where they serve you slop. Beware, there's always of possibility of getting a shiv in the back."

She found my corny humor funny. Hey, it worked for Dad with Mom; it may work for this guy and girl.

The fluorescent bulbs of the cafeteria pulsate off

of her, exposing every unique feature. She has deep brown hair tied back into a tight ponytail at her shoulders, showing off her wide forehead that shimmers in the intense light. Her mocha Cuban skin glows with pink round cheeks that lie below her thick black glasses. Her wide eyes dance beneath the lenses that are separated by her sharp nose, which arches under the bridge of her glasses. Speaking and laughing with her girlfriends Sarah and Isabella illustrates her presence and poise, unmatched anywhere in school.

She is known to be sweet one minute, but if angered, she is capable of giving out a severe tongue lashing. This is especially evident when she overhears students talking trash about her or one of her friends. In those moments, she lets her feisty Cuban heritage loose. Today she looks hot in her knee-cut white shorts and lavender polo shirt that hugs her tiny, slim figure. She chose to go sockless under a pair of dark brown leather Sperrys that had seen better days. They accentuate her smooth dark legs, which hypnotically drew me to her. She broke away from Sarah and Isabella, sliding in the seat next to Conrad and across from me.

"Hey, Ulysses, Conrad! Are you guys excited for tonight? We've got a couple of poetry readings going on before you and your dad. I think you're scheduled for 6:30. Conrad, you stopping by? I personally can't wait! Tonight's my first night waitressing. My parents can now pay me! I can earn some extra money for the class trip to London next winter."

Hannah keeps talking while Conrad and I just stare in disbelief, nodding in foolish silence. Hannah sometimes goes on and on, without waiting for responses to her questions or even taking a breath.

"Conrad, what's with with Mr. O'Leary's math assignment? I mean come on! Why assign so much work? Do you think he'll have a pop quiz today? Probably not, but just to make sure, I studied a lot! Did you guys?"

She finally takes a breath and Conrad is about to reply when she jumps up and yells to Sarah and Isabella, "Wait up! Talk to you guys later, got to go. See you in history, U! Are we still walking together to Penny U after Conrad's practice?"

Words stumble out of my mouth, "Ahh yeah, yeah, yeah, sounds per-per-perfect."

She cocks her head and smiles innocently as she skips over to her girlfriends, giggling and throwing their heads back as they scamper out of the cafeteria.

Conrad is the first to respond after the whirlwind of Hannah's energy leaves our table. "Smooth, U! Obviously, she has access to limitless coffee at her parents' cafe, but she may want to switch to decaf."

I am thinking the same thing and wonder how many shots of espresso she had this morning. Hannah's tiny energetic demeanor is hyper enough, even without coffee.

Conrad continues, "U, Hannah may only think of you as a guy friend, rather than a boyfriend! Don't get your hopes up, dude; there's other fish in the sea!"

I am confident Conrad is wrong. "Nope, that's not how it will go down today. Ever since I've laid eyes on Hannah, I've dreamed of her. Last night ninjas were chasing us in my dream."

"Ninjas? Why ninjas? What did you have to eat before bed?" he says in an irritated, tired tone, sounding like a surfer from California.

"Nothing. I don't know!" I snap.

"It could've been a sign not to ask her out," he counters with the same annoying tone.

I don't want to hear this trash coming from my best friend. "Piss off, Conrad! I'm not telling you my dreams anymore."

"I had a dream last night that I scored a hundred points against Everglade High, and after the game everyone hoisted me on their shoulders chanting my name, 'Conrad!! Conrad!!'" Conrad proceeds to make cheering sounds with his hands cupped against his mouth.

"Wow, why don't you make it more about you?" Conrad can sometimes piss me off, but I am running on adrenaline. Nothing is going to keep me from asking out Hannah after school. What if she says no? Now Conrad is in my head. He is back to working on his math as I get out a water bottle from my backpack. It drips with moisture from the humid air as I nervously gulp most of it down and glance at the clock to notice the first bell is close to ringing. Second thoughts fill my mind as I perseverate on things to come.

CHAPTER 5

- LOGAN -

WOW, A RED VELVET TRACKSUIT?

My classroom is a small, windowless, manageable space. Thirty desks curve in a makeshift lecture hall layout. Jefferson and Washington posters stare at me while I unpack my laptop. The worn-out carpet doesn't make a sound as I trample on. The eerie quietness of my classroom often rattles me. It is uncomfortable. Classrooms are usually loud, like a mall or a sports stadium, so when there is no noise it often is unnerving, especially during tests and prior to the bell. My desk is decent, but it's too large for the room. The synthetic material gives it the appearance of real wood, but it's not fooling anyone. It is covered in piles of ungraded and graded packets, almost consuming the surface and nearly knocking over my wooden engraved sign, which displays "Mr. Adair" in ornate cursive lettering. The sign was gift from a fellow teacher a decade ago and is now held together with Gorilla Glue. I think you can guess why. My desk is littered with different color pens, highlighters, and a couple of picture frames. One frame is of Jill and I holding Ulysses on the day he was born; the other is a picture of me, Jill, and Ulysses at Disney World in front of Cinderella's Castle six years ago, the year we decided to make the move to Florida.

    I crack open my computer as I sit in my oversized, frayed, black computer chair, comfortable and fully immersed in my morning routine of emailing parents and grading mediocre class work, when my door bursts open. Bob comes strutting in. Bob is wearing a bright red velvet Adidas tracksuit, with the trademark white racing stripes running down his arms and legs. His fashion sense clearly hasn't evolved from the mid-eighties, when dressing like a gym teacher or hip-hop group was cool.

    Bob Nelson is my best friend and our school's physical education teacher. Don't call him a gym teacher because he would be the first to correct you. Bob also coaches the varsity basketball team here at Mangrove High.

    Bob is a short African-American man with barely any neck, a defensive tackle chest, and a Natty Light beer belly. He resembles an out of shape Ninja Turtle, and in his red velvet tracksuit, he has the appearance of an inverted chocolate-covered strawberry. His black freckles take up residence under his eyelids, giving his cheeks a wide appearance as if he is storing nuts for the winter. Bob reminds me of the hamster I owned as a kid. He wears a retractable key chain around his track pants. Bob claims his keys open every door in the school; why the school would do this baffles me! Bob is trustworthy, he just makes poor decisions.

Like when he broke his leg and had to use the golf cart to get around the fields. One day he was driving too fast and lost control of the cart, flipping it through the football field concession stand. Another incident was when he walked on the basketball court the day they were refinishing the parquet floor with lacquer, getting his feet stuck and ruining the surface.

Bob is an acquired taste. He is also single and always eager to get me back in the dating scene. He always uses internet dating sites; I'd be surprised if there was still a single Somerset woman who has not blocked his profile. He is a good, trustworthy friend, though. Any woman who could get past his goofy demeanor would be very lucky to have him.

"Hey, Bob, how did last night go?" I can tell Bob had another big date. According to him, they are all big dates.

Bob sits on top of one of my students' desks, swinging his immaculate red and white Nike Cortez sneakers to the front, almost knocking over a replica of the Liberty Bell.

"How do you know, how do you always know?"

"First, you didn't come over or call me up to hang out last night. Second, you're all smiles, and you're wearing your favorite red velvet tracksuit."

"Logan, let me tell you something! This girl was fine! Mm! We went to Mario's on 41," he says in a deep Barry White impression.

"Good food," I interject. "What was her name? Holly? Molly?"

"Dolly," he says in a very stern voice, lowering his nose down at me.

"Right, Dolly." I smirk from the side of my mouth. "So how did your date with Dolly go?"

"For your information, it was great; we talked all night. Dolly is an entrepreneur and a..."

I cut him off and wittily ask, "What does that mean?" I open my email and start to multitask the conversation and my emails simultaneously. "What kind of entrepreneur?"

"She sells things online."

"Like what?" I fish around, knowing Bob is slow to take the bait.

Bob lowers his head and sighs. "She sells alopecia accessories online."

"What? No way! This is too good to be true. She sells wigs online?"

"Yes!"

"Seriously, man, you couldn't just say she sells wigs to bald guys? Where do you find these girls?"

"Those are her technical terms; she was on the Instant Connection website. She makes good money, better than our salaries!"

"Wigs?" I can't hold my laughter in and let out a massive belly laugh.

"Leave a lonely brother alone! I'm seeing her again after tomorrow night's game. We have a connection."

I glance up at Bob's closely cropped hair and wag my finger at his head. "Can she do anything for you?"

"Laugh it up, bow tie white boy! You're not getting any younger; you need to join me out there. Bro, you would kill on this dating site! When you going to be ready to hop back on the horse?"

"Soon. I'm more concerned with Ulysses. I don't want him to think I'm replacing Jillian."

"Logan, U is a strong kid. You guys are both

ready. He say anything to that little Hannah Reyes girl yet?"

"No. He says it's going down tonight after your practice."

"Nice! That's my boy!" As Bob is speaking, I find an email from Principal Barron. It reads as follows:

"URGENT: All faculty report to the Media Center at 7:15 for a quick meet and greet with our new assistant principal."

"Wow, Bob, did you know about this?" I say.

"What, the faculty meeting? Yeah, I saw the email. Let's hope the AP is better than Mr. Peters. What a sink he was."

Mr. Peters was our last assistant principal, and he literally was always looking for trouble. I know his job was to address discipline at school, but Peters would be annoyingly aggressive about it. He would sneak around the school with his clipboard and high-water pants, catching students and faculty in frivolous behaviors like it was the end of the world and we had master criminals attending school. He wore a bushy mustache that made him look like he had a dead squirrel on his face, and every time he caught you doing something, the squirrel would twitch like road kill. I felt bad for the students when Peters was here. They hated the guy with a passion, often pranking him: TPing his car or gluing his supplies to his desk.

Bob hated him, too. Peters' squirrel would twitch every time he wore a brightly colored track suit to a faculty meeting. He told Bob more than once, in his condescending tone, "Teachers need to look professional, not like a sloth, hungover and too tired to find a proper outfit."

All the discipline wore on Peters. Last month, he up and quit and had a nervous breakdown, at least that's what Ms. Simmons, the principal's secretary, told everyone. She heard he is working at a rental car agency in Miami. She is our reliable gossip queen this year, keeping us informed and entertained with her stories of our new principal, Mr. Barron.

CHAPTER 6

- LOGAN -

THE NEW AP GETS THE FULL NELSON

The time is 7:13, so I point to the clock and Bob and I proceed across the hall to the media center. My classroom location is sweet, across from the main office and the media center. Bob and I joke our way over to the media center, watching all the inquisitive teachers filing in with a combination of eagerness and dread drawn on their tired Friday faces.

The media center is an enormous space, reminding me of the days of yore when students needed to read real paper-bound books instead of digital copies on their phones or computers. It resembles the media center from the classic '80s film *The Breakfast Club*, minus Judd Nelson and Molly Ringwald, although our principal acts very similar to Principal Gleason from the movie. Comfortable, cushioned chairs dot the walls, while long wooden tables are accompanied by hard sturdy chairs that often make my butt fall asleep.

The teachers collapse into the hard chairs among

their pre-designated cliques. Outdated literary posters of books, probably not read by students or teachers, decorate the whitewashed walls. Bob and I find twin heavy, hard chairs that my spine will remind me of later. Bob sits down in disgust, like he would rather be searching the dating sites back in his smelly locker room office. He puts his feet up like he owns the media center, but Bob would only crack open a book to impress a girl.

    On the other side of me sits Mrs. Carol Swanson, an honors English teacher, close to retirement and a heart attack. Her short round body just fits in the chair. I look over at her and politely smile.

    "Good morning," I say halfheartedly. Her sausage fingers are stained with the cigarettes that are eating at her heart. Her large face, affected by high blood pressure, is chalky white from excessive makeup and sprinkled with strays of blonde feathery hair along her chin.

    The weird thing about Mrs. Swanson is that she is always smiling. You would think, after a few decades of teaching, her smile would have decreased or faded away, but you'd be wrong. Mrs. Swanson dresses like a typical middle-aged teacher. Why do all older teachers dress the same? Especially middle-aged teachers, they all dress like they shop together. They're probably attracted to cheap sales at TJ Maxx or Walmart. Their dress usually involves jean skirts, striped blouses with ruffles, and suede strappy sandals two sizes too small. They finish off their horrid ensemble with chunky turquoise stone jewelry. Why chunky turquoise jewelry? Nobody knows. It's like Bigfoot or Nessie. It is the same fashion sense for older teachers up in Maine as well. I shouldn't be throwing stones because male teachers hardly ever dress any better. I wear frayed clothes and a bow tie, for Christ's sake. I blame teacher salaries.

I notice a bus ticket sticking out from the side pocket of her bright red, oversized purse, a purse big enough to hold a freshman, leading me to believe she and Mr. Swanson are on the rocks and she is staying at a nearby hotel. She confirms my theories when she unclasps the ginormous red purse for some breath mints, exposing her booty of Marlboro reds and stolen shampoo bottles labeled Somerset Motel. Damn! Right again, but I feel a little pity for her troubles.

She starts to speak to me in her snooty tone, "Oh, Mr. Adair!" I've worked here five years and she still doesn't know my first name. She always has to be formal! "I cannot fathom a better assistant principal than our beloved Mr. Peters," she says, pausing to wipe some of her excessive crimson lipstick from the corner of her tiny curled lips with a napkin that was tucked away beneath the ruffles of her blouse. "He held this school together and was such a proper educator. These kiddos need a firm hand, don't you agree, Mr. Adair?" she finishes, pompously pointing her nose further into the air.

My remaining pity for her quickly dissolves away.

I hate the word "kiddos," argh! Students, kids, but not kiddos, especially in her know-it-all voice, and in reference to a guy everyone will remember for being a jerk. It is so funny, all the young energetic teachers find each other, and all the difficult and mean ones do the same.

"Yeah, this generation needs a good flogging

once in a while!" I sarcastically blurt out, thanking God that Ulysses doesn't have Mrs. Swanson as a teacher.

"Excuse me! What did you say?" Her voice changes to a deep perturbed baritone tone.

I don't have a chance to answer as at that second Mr. Barron marches in. Following in his wake is his doddering, elderly secretary Ms. Simmons, newly hired this past summer, and behind her is a striking young redheaded woman, smiling energetically at his room full of strangers. The redhead is so striking that Bob instantly comes to life, sitting straight up like he has a had a cattle prod in his back. He suddenly is looking interested at a faculty meeting, which is a first.

Principal Barron heads for the podium at the front of the group. Ms. Simmons meekly stands behind him while the new woman, who I deduce is the new assistant principal, stands at Barron's side. Principal Barron tries to stand as tall as he can with both Simmons and the new assistant principal towering over his Napoleonic frame. His slicked back salt-and-pepper hair exposes his worn leather face, beaten down by decades of responsibility for 1,500 students, year in and year out, and their helicopter 1% parents. His addiction to the tanning booth doesn't help the situation either. He often looks like a leather football with two sunken, protruding eyes. He always wears suits that look like they were past due for alterations. Standing at the podium, he resembles an old Jersey Shore beach bum.

Principal Barron is stern and sleazy, a combination that is not endearing for a principal. When he speaks, his voice carries. He is often loud and assertive, sounding like the New Jersey transplant that he is. We're all transplants in this area of Florida. Today, Barron seems nervous. He is clenching his jaw, and I notice a thick layer of sweat above his small, duck-like lips. I've never seen him rattled before, but he does indeed look rattled. He begins to speak with an assertive, know-it-all, Napoleonic voice.

"Today, I have the distinction to introduce our new assistant principal. She comes from Brunswick, Georgia, and came highly recommended. She will be a nice breath of fresh air after the quick departure of Mr. Peters."

Quick is right, I think to myself; Mr. Peters just left a letter saying he was done in education and wished everyone well.

Barron continues on, "I would like to introduce to you Mary Clifton."

Barron proceeds to clap and everyone joins in, especially the frail Ms. Simmons, who looks ecstatic. She is probably happy that she doesn't have to take on the extra office work anymore.

Bob leans in, whispering loudly and spraying spit in my ear, "Dude! Dibs."

I frown at him, wiping my ear. "Seriously, the AP?" I lecture back.

Barron continues, asking Mary if she would like to say a few words.

A tall, athletically built, tomboyish woman cautiously approaches the podium and addresses the faculty. "I am happy to be a part of the Mangrove High family, and I hope to get to know every one of you in the weeks to come, especially all the kiddos."

I cringe.

"I would like to thank Mr. Donald Barron"— Ms. Simmons gives a quick, startled glance at Mary as the audience of teachers giggle — "I mean Thomas Barron."

Mary herself appears embarrassed at the mix up with the new boss' name. Mr. Barron also looks flush for a second. Mary giggles like a young school girl. She definitely carries herself differently than any assistant principal I've ever worked with.

My thoughts quickly return to Bob, now eager as a school boy to meet Mary. She finishes speaking, and the meeting wraps up. Bob rushes off to meet our new AP, while I follow behind him. As we rush away from our seats, I can hear Mrs. Swanson clicking her disapproval of the new AP to the other faculty hens.

As Bob races over, he says to me in his smooth Barry White voice, "I need to talk with that lady. She's goin' to get the full Nelson! Mm, yeah, that's right!" Bob grunts.

"Hey, wait up, you better not get us fired! What happened to the alopecia entrepreneur?" I say as I trail behind him.

"New prospects, Logan! New prospects," Bob confidently says as we approach the new AP, Mary Clifton.

CHAPTER 7

- LOGAN -

AN UNLIKELY DATE?

Mary Clifton is beaming. The attention the teachers are giving her is overwhelming, and she is doing her best to put on a brave face. Teachers often work on islands, so when they are off their islands, they can often act like jackals. The jackals are trying to make good first impressions with the new boss, getting in her good graces prior to observations and contract-renewal season. They continue pushing and shoving to say hello in order to advance their individual agendas. Mary remains bubbly while appeasing the needs and questions they push on her. She definitely plays to the audience really well.

Mary stands tall, especially compared to Barron. Her shoulders are muscular, and she has well-defined biceps exposed below a sleeveless, full length navy Polo dress. I believe her to be possibly ex-military by her physique, but she carries herself with much less discipline. She appears giddy, demonstrating silly mannerisms, something the military would have drilled out of her long ago. She must be an athlete or into CrossFit. Mary's eyes are bright, commanding, and active, surveying everyone who approaches her while trying to remember their names.

As Bob and I draw near, I can see her red hair is not natural as I notice dark black eyebrows above her active eyes. The shade was too dark to be natural. Bob now seems more eager than ever, pushing through the young teachers like our seniors do to the poor freshmen. The teachers all part as a small hand shoots out in front of us, greeting mine.

"Good morning!" Mary excitedly projects in a heavy Georgian twang over the now thinning crowd. "Nice to meet y'all; what do y'all teach?"

I take her hand. It is not as I expect: Her small hands are firm around mine but covered with hard calluses. Their condition is similar to mine being a guitarist. But my calluses are only on my left fingers because, if you're right handed, you use your left fingers to hold down the strings, which leaves them calloused. She wears a gold antique watch on her left wrist, leading me to believe she is right handed. Her calluses are on her right hand, the one I was shaking; these calluses also are not on her fingers, but on her palms. What would a mid-thirties, seemingly single woman (no wedding band) be doing with such extensive calluses on her hand? The first logical idea to come to mind is rock climbing.

"My name is Logan Adair. I teach U.S. history. That's a firm handshake you have there. I noticed your calluses on your hand. Do you climb?"

Bob nudges me hard.

"Logan! You don't talk about a lady's calluses! You have to excuse my friend here; he is a lonely man with no manners. My name is Bob Nelson. I am a teacher that shapes young minds through physical education."

Bob is grinning like the Cheshire cat and sucking in his stomach at the same time. I think he may pass out.

"That is what I used to teach!" Mary exclaims loudly with an equally wide grin back at Bob. She takes both of Bob's hands with hers and quietly says in a hushed tone, "P.E. teachers are the rock of the school. Getting kids healthy and active is the stepping stone to greatness."

"I totally agree," Bob blurts out in an equally hush tone, startled by the attention and contact.

My mouth is wide open in pure shock. Whatever Bob has for a neck is now the same color as his tracksuit.

"Logan here likes to observe everything, but misses out on some things, like basic manners!"

Mary giggles uncontrollably for a few seconds exclaiming, "That is so charming! To answer your question, yes, I do climb. I guess we live in the wrong state though; Florida is so flat! The tallest mountains are the roller coasters at Disney."

Bob laughs with an over the top laugh that was beneath him.

"It's so beautiful here in Somerset; I cannot wait to explore the area and get to know all of you and the students," she says as she winks at Bob.

Bob, sounding more like Barry White than ever, says, "If you need a guide?" I raise an eyebrow but he continues, "I was born and raised in Southwest

Florida. I could show you the ins and outs of this swamp."

"Oh my God, I would love that!" She sounds now like a college sorority girl. "I was looking for something fun to do since I am now unpacked and Mr. Barron has had me complete all the in-service trainings. I wanted to celebrate but I don't know anyone."

She actually sounds like she is flirting with Bob, batting her eyelashes, twirling her hair, shifting about; not very mature for an AP. This won't end well for poor Bob.

"Me and Logan are going to the local cafe later tonight. It's called Penny University; they have an open mic night on Fridays. Logan here is playing his guitar, and a lot of us are stopping by."

Mary is now beaming and getting closer so Mr. Barron couldn't hear them whispering. "That sounds great. Mr. Adair, you play in a band?"

"You can call me Logan. No, I'm not in a band. My son and I both play acoustic guitar. Just for fun. He also attends Mangrove High. He's a freshman, and his name is Ulysses."

Mary gushes, "Wow! You must be so proud."

Bob interrupts as he is losing the attention. "How about I pick you up at 6:00? After the show, I can tour you around."

"I would love that." And ever so lightly, she touches Bob's arm. "Love the red velvet," she interjects as she leaves with Mr. Barron, rushing out to the hallway ahead of the droves of students who are starting to invade the school.

If Bob's head could blow off, it would have. The Barry White voice is gone, and he squeaks, "Did you see that? She touched me, she likes my tracksuit! She taught P.E. She was diggin' me, man!"

"What the hell was that! She came on a bit strong, don't you think?" I blurt out.

"You jealous? She was digging me and not you?"

"Don't want to burst your bubble, but what about Dolly?" I remind him.

"The hell with Dolly, make room for Mary." He proceeds to strut out of the media center saying, "Mary. Mm, oh yeah." He finds his Barry White voice again as we spot her in the lobby as we exit the media center. Bob does a two-finger salute as a wave, and she gives it right back.

"Slow down, she's practically our boss. I think we've got rules about this," I whisper in his ear.

The Barry White voice comes back, "Logan, Logan ... Come on, come on. She may be the one! Mary. Mm."

"I know, big guy, I know," I say condescendingly, but I definitely witnessed something between them, either that or she's just crazy weird. It isn't the first crazy AP, and it probably won't be the last. Still, that was weird.

"I'll meet you at Penny U after practice. It is on!" Bob yells as he practically floats to the gymnasium before the bell rings. I walk, confused and a little nauseous, to my classroom door, where I greet my first-period students as they stand waiting patiently for my arrival.

CHAPTER 8

- ULYSSES -

SHENANIGANS ABOUND

Every other day, dreaded geometry is at the beginning of my day. Starting off half of my school days with Mr. O'Leary sucks. One good thing is I sit next to Hannah. How can such an evil place have such beauty? The universe must be trying to balance my existence. Hannah looks at everything with such positive energy! I, on the other hand, look at only the darkness, except when she is around. She sometimes helps me with my homework, often giggling when I don't get something correct. She made me love math; O'Leary, not so much.

We were just introduced to the new assistant principal, Ms. Clifton, on the video morning announcements. Wow, she doesn't look like a typical assistant principal; she reminds me of the cheerleaders at Conrad's basketball game. I bet Dad is going to hate her.

Mr. O'Leary starts class by yelling, "Class! Class,

enough!" O'Leary screams a lot, and he only knows one volume, loud. Correction: Sometimes he goes really loud. He could be the only one in the room and his voice could carry, making your head throb, after even the shortest conversation. His voice rattles and scratches through the classroom.

Dad says O'Leary reminds him of the judge from that eighties movie, *Who Framed Roger Rabbit*. The judge, like O'Leary, often gives me nightmares, sometimes joining the ninjas. Mr. O'Leary has a way of getting under your skin, not just his voice, but his sarcasm. His demeanor is horrendous. Even Hannah doesn't like him, and I have never known anyone she didn't like. Sure, she can get upset and start yelling at you in Spanish; she's intense, but she doesn't hate you. He continues to lecture; sometimes he can go on for the entire class period without anyone else speaking.

While I am admiring Hannah, Conrad — who sits on my other side — elbows me, and whispers, "Stalker! Earth to stalker."

"What?" I hiss.

"Here!" As he shoves a handout onto my desk, Mr. O'Leary leers at me in disgust. His sunken, baggy eyes focus on me with pure hatred, making his forehead wrinkle below his partially bald head. "Problem, Mr. A—dair?" Taking the painstaking effort to over-pronounce my name, that really irks me.

"Nope, all is good for Mr. A—dair," I quip back.

He narrows his eyes and clicks his mouth in disgust before continuing on with his lecture about theorems. I drown him out. I look at the worksheet Conrad handed me. It contains a series of parallelograms with different measurements that I need to find the areas of. Easy enough, you can do this, Ulysses. Area equals base times height. I proceed to go through and answer all the questions on the worksheet, breezing through with no problems.

I look over to Hannah and she is almost done as well, but when I look over to Conrad, he is struggling big time, wearing an expression of pure dread, turning paler than usual. He is probably thinking how his dad is going to kill him if he doesn't bring up his grades, or about Mr. O'Leary's after-school tutoring. I notice he is making major mistakes on his handout. So like a good friend, I lean over and give him some advice. Right at that very instance, Mr. O'Leary comes rushing over, with his extra loud voice screeching, "Ulysses Adair! No talking! Eyes on your own paper!"

I calmly quip, "Yeah, I know. I was just trying to help. I'm not cheating." I am cool and collected because I don't want to give O'Leary any ammunition.

O'Leary snarls back, his nostrils literally curling up, screaming, "One more word out of you and it will be a detention!"

I nod obediently. I don't need to embarrass Dad by getting a detention from O'Leary. What the hell, I was just helping out a friend. Hannah and I both finish O'Leary's handout and sit staring into space; everyone else is still working. Of course O'Leary doesn't have anything for us to do when we finish, making the time in geometry crawl. The minute hand on the classroom clock seems stuck on the four, and yes, my generation can still tell time with analog clocks, sometimes. Geometry doesn't end until 8:35, fifteen more minutes!

Mr. O'Leary is at his podium. I can see he is thoroughly enjoying grading everyone's homework with his red pen, shaking his head in disgust. The only thing around to entertain me are his lame math posters cluttering the classrooms walls. The morning Florida sunlight bursts through the wide bay windows, saturating the room, suspending the dust particles in the air. Outside the clouds sway in the powder blue sky. I look at the clock, it is still 8:20... What the hell!

Hannah sits upright, finished and reading *Of Mice and Men* for Mrs. Swanson's lit class. I'm glad I have Mr. James. He is cool, unlike Mrs. Swanson. Hannah likes her, but she likes everyone. Sick of this silence, I finally break it.

"Psst! Psst!" I'm trying to get Hannah's attention. She turns to me with a surprised look.

"You're going to get in trouble," she spits back quickly, putting her nose back into the book.

I shrug. "Do you like the book?" I whisper.

"What?" Hannah whispers softly.

"Do you like *Of Mice and Men*?" I am whispering louder now.

"Yeah, I like Lennie and George's friendship, and Lennie's so sweet."

I raise my eyebrows. I guess she hasn't gotten very far. "My dad made me read it last summer. It's a great book."

I don't want to burst her bubble, so I change the subject. "Can you believe this worksheet? Easy. Right?" She is finally dragged into the conversation.

Still whispering, Hannah said, "I know, it is much

easier than last night's homework."

I add a little more enthusiastically, "Especially numbers four and seven, come on! They were right off of the homework. You'd think O'Leary would not reuse his questions!"

As I say that, I notice Mr. O'Leary dart from grading his papers at the podium to four rows back, where I sit, in one swoop, like he flew or levitated through the room.

He stands over me with his burgundy sweater matching his eyes. His nostrils are snarling, resembling a bull being prodded. He screeches in his loudest judge tone, "Mr. Adair! I have had enough of your shenanigans!"

I'm not sure what shenanigans are, but it sounds nasty. At that moment, he snatches my worksheet and rips it in two.

"If you're going to be rude and talk in my class! Then you deserve a zero!"

I am simultaneously mortified and pissed.

O'Leary continues, "Ms. Reyes, do you need a zero as well?"

I stand up to take the attention of off her. "She wasn't talking!" I blurt out. "I wasn't cheating; why do I get a zero?"

He leans in closer to me now. "You think you can do what you want because your dad works here?!" His screech rises to its highest octave.

At this point, the whole class is staring in awe, some with mouths gaping open. Hannah wants to say something in my defense, but I scoot in front of her, blocking her from O'Leary. I move to stand up, rising to my full height, making me a few inches taller than O'Leary.

"First, nobody under fifty knows or uses the word shenanigans! Second, you're just jealous of my dad because he is not a jerk like you!"

My legs are shaking now, regret quickly creeping through my body. I hear a wave of gasps and oohs throughout the classroom. My skin tone is now resembling Conrad's, and my stomach feels as if it's dropped to my shoes. O'Leary stands startled and speechless for a moment. His face begins twitching, then the color of his face matches his sweater.

He lifts his long thin arm, uncurling equally long boney fingers, and speaks from the side of his mouth with pure hatred. "GET OUT! Go see our new assistant principal. She can now deal with you."

I turn in momentary hesitation, but I slowly grab my backpack and slump out of the room. Hannah and Conrad look at me as if it is the last time they will see me as I begin a death march to the office. Still, until the door slams shut behind me, I don't fully comprehend my situation. My stomach is now swimming in my shoes. I continue my march down the expansive stairs to the office, hitting my head during the journey: "Stupid, stupid! Nice job, Ulysses!"

I pass by Dad's class. He is in the middle of a lecture; he looks up and our eyes meet. He can read the horror on my face. He knows I am headed towards the office during O'Leary's period, which means trouble. All I can do is shrug back at him and slink into the office.

CHAPTER 9

- ULYSSES -

OFFICE COMMOTION

The office has a large, thick metal door with several coats of turquoise paint, making it appear thicker than it really is. The top of the door has a smudged glass partition labeled "OFFICE" in large thick lettering. A wave of the office air conditioner slaps me as I meekly enter: Even the A/C knows I screwed up. Why do school offices have their A/C blasting? It always resembles the Arctic, even back in Maine. You definitely wouldn't know we had tropical temperatures outside these walls. I frigidly plop down at one of the available overstuffed blue chairs that looks as old as the school.

I've only been in the office one other time. The first time was when I met with Mrs. Raines, my guidance counselor. Her office is down the corridor, along with the curriculum coordinator's office. In front of me sits a huge counter with different colored papers stacked in every corner. Motivational posters hang all around me; they're just as effective as Manny the Manatee when it comes to motivation. Behind the counter sit two enormous desks with crazy Dr. Seuss-like stacks of papers, and behind them are three doors. The door on my far left belongs to Deputy Diaz, our SRO (school resource officer). It's closed, which means he's probably patrolling the hallways. The middle door belongs to our little principal, Mr. Barron. According to Dad, he started at our school last year. The third door, on my far right and unlabeled, belongs to our new assistant principal. They probably did not have time to put the new label up prior to hiring Ms. Clifton.

One of the two huge desks sitting in front of the counter belonged to Mangrove's administrative assistant, Mrs. Lafayette. She is shared by everyone in the office except the principal, but her desk sits empty. Rumor has it Mrs. Lafayette has the flu and has been out for two weeks. Too bad, I like Mrs. Lafayette. Her absence leaves Principal Barron's administrative assistant, Ms. Simmons, to occupy the other large desk and to complete all the office work by herself. She is filing at an extraordinarily large cabinet between the SRO's and principal's offices and does not lift her head to acknowledge my entrance. She must have not heard me come in. So I sit in silence, thinking about how I let Dad down and embarrassed myself in front of Hannah and the rest of the math class.

I stare at the floor tiles, starting to count them, when I hear shouting coming from Principal Barron's office. The shouting resonates throughout the office, but at my distance, I cannot make out what the argument is about. I can tell it is indeed yelling, but the words are mostly muffled. I'm able to make out an occasional word of one of the two yelling voices. I catch "letter" and "doorstep," then another word becomes clear, "gallant," then a thud and crash end the argument. It sounds like something heavy hit the floor and then silence. I am sitting on the edge of intrigue. I am just about to ask Ms. Simmons what is going on, as she's standing motionless by the door, when suddenly the door bursts open. The gaping doorway reveals Principal Barron on one knee hurriedly picking office supplies up off the floor and a tall man with soft, wavy, thinning straw-blonde hair turning in front of the opened doorway. His movement blocks my view of Barron as he fills the doorframe. Damn! It is Conrad's dad!

Mr. Wright strides out of the office's outer area, pompously strutting just like he would in court. When he moves, he has a rich, cocky, intimidating swagger; no wonder Conrad is so scared of him. As he approaches me, his long face and small mouth are accentuated by his bright white suit and brighter pink tie. His suit clings to him like a second skin.

He sees me with my mouth gaping open, and his small mouth contours into a menacing grin as he says in his raspy voice, "Hey there, Ulysses. Hope you're not in any trouble."

He chuckles to himself and continues to stroll out as he tucks a large, bright blue piece of paper into his inside breast pocket. He is about to close the door and exit when he turns back to Principal Barron, adjusts his tie confidently and hisses, "Remember what I said, Barron!"

Barron, now standing, nods silently while slowly closing his door.

What the hell was Conrad's dad yelling to Barron about? His grades? I am about to think on it more when Ms. Simmons spins on her heels from the file cabinet, staring at me with giant green eyes. Her hair and wrinkles give her a scary grandmother demeanor.

In an ancient, frail, shaky voice Ms. Simmons says, "Can I help you, Ulysses?"

"Ah, yeah... I mean, yes ma'am. I was sent out of Mr. O'Leary's geometry class," I shamefully admit.

She clicks her mouth in disgust. "Your father will not be happy, Ulysses! Since your father is a teacher, you should set a good example for others here at Mangrove High!"

When she is done preaching, she begins to grin, showing off her dentures. She proceeds to dial on her phone.

"I have a Mr. Adair here to see you. No, it's the son," she adds sternly, looking at me, wearing that grin again that stretches her old face but her green eyes flash in disgust. Half her face appears happy while the other half shows disgust.

She continues, "Yes, all is good. It was exactly like you said, you're off to a great start, Ms. Clifton. Oh yes, Ulysses: He was sent out by his geometry teacher, Mr. O'Leary. Yes, correct, that O'Leary."

Wow, Mr. O'Leary is already known as "that one" by the new assistant principal.

Ms. Simmons drops the receiver, grinning with her wide beady, green eyes and exuberantly says, "She'll see you now."

Those eyes follow me from the chair. I can't look away from her; her eyes penetrate me and continue to follow me all around the office like an owl, turning her head in unnatural angles. What a creepy old lady!

CHAPTER 10

- ULYSSES -

WAIT, WAIT ... JUST A SLAP ON THE WRIST?

When I enter our new assistant principal's office, a muscular energetic woman prances over to me with a beaming smile and a She-Hulk body. She takes my hand and shakes it like she could shake it off.

"Nice to meet you, Ulysses. You look just like your dad. I met him this morning; he seemed so nice." She waves for me to sit at one of the two wooden chairs facing her desk.

I nod in agreement and manage a quick, "Nice to meet you, too?" Not sure if that is correct, but I went with it. Ms. Clifton's office has bare walls and a bare desk, which is fitting since she looks as if she could probably could kill a bear with her bare hands. The entire space is bare except for one picture behind her desk. Sitting lonely on a large shelf is a single picture of a baby held by, I presume, its mother and father.

"Your father mentioned you're playing tonight at this Penny College?"

"University," I reply.

"Excuse me?" she quickly interjects.

I hate the when people say "excuse me." "Pardon" or "what did you say," but "excuse me" seems to always have such an offensive connotation.

"The place I'm playing. It's called Penny University."

"Okay...Well, I'm going tonight. I'm meeting Mr. Nelson there. I can't wait."

Say what! Ms. Clifton is coming tonight to see me and Dad play? And she said Mr. Nelson like he was Romeo or something. Is this the same Mr. Nelson that sobers up on our couch and accidently ate Ortiz's dog bones? What the hell!

"Your dad and Mr. Nelson invited me; it should be a blast!" she exuberantly exclaims like she is going to a Justin Timberlake concert.

I can't believe this woman is our new assistant principal. Maybe she'll forget the reason I'm even here.

She exuberantly projects further, "So, what kind of music do you and your dad play?"

"Classic rock," I reply quickly.

She then suddenly changes her expression and demeanor to stern and solemn, "Okay, let's get down to business." She swivels her chair from side to side like a toddler sitting in a spinning chair for the first time.

"Just kidding, I can't play bad cop. So, Ulysses, what the hell happened?" She suddenly changes her demeanor back to the Justin Timberlake groupie.

Taken aback by Ms. Clifton's candor and

language, I begin to recite my story, not leaving anything out. I even explain who Conrad and Hannah are and, of course, the history with Mr. O'Leary and my worksheet. I try to not leave out a single detail. She sits typing on her laptop, which is literally on her lap, while she puts her feet on the corner of the desk.

"The referral he emailed says you were cheating on a math worksheet."

"That's a lie!" I shout as I rise in disgust.

"I know," Ms. Clifton says as she waves for me to sit down.

"You do?" I shockingly clarify.

"Yes, silly. Ulysses. You want to know why? I've known guys like Mr. O'Leary my whole life. He was clearly just mistaken. We all have these moments. Teachers get so used to seeing bad behaviors they start to see it everywhere and jump to conclusions. I've met your father, and I have a gut feeling about you. You're not a cheater." She gives me intense eye contact but swivels in my direction.

"I'm not!" I proudly interject.

"Good! Good, you should always be confident in who you are. We'll appease Mr. O'Leary and give you a verbal warning; you don't need this shit on your transcripts," she cockily says in a high-pitch giggle.

Did she just say "shit"!? Ms. Clifton doesn't seem like any administrator I have ever encountered. She is either crazy or really unprofessional, or a bit of both. I bet Dad is going to hate her. Also, if Mr. O'Leary finds out I got off with just a slap on the wrist, he'll freak. Being a freshman is hard enough, now I'll have a vengeful geometry teacher always on my case.

"So, your dad seems very smart." She is speaking once again like a teenager, twirling her hair innocently. "I hear he observes things. According to everyone at school, he knows people's secrets before they do."

"Yeah, I can never get away with anything. He is hyper observant, noticing things nobody else notices, probably more since Mom died," I blurt out without even realizing.

"Oh my God. I am so sorry to hear that!" She once again demonstrates her best impression of a valley girl, but with a Southern twang. "So he's like Sherlock Holmes?"

"No, no, nothing like that. He's just good at reading clues and observing human behavior and patterns."

"Your dad's friend Mr. Nelson, what's his story?" she inquisitively inquires.

"Ah...ah," I stammer. Why does she care about Mr. Nelson? First it was the third degree about my dad, and now Mr. Nelson? I collect my thoughts and continue past the ahs. "I don't know, they're usually inseparable. He is always at our place. We all hang out a lot."

If you count drinking, watching Red Sox games, and passing out on our couch while Dad and I jam on our guitars as hanging out, then sure...

"Is Bob, I mean Mr. Nelson, seeing anyone?" she sheepishly asks me, still twirling her hair. If she was chewing gum and holding her phone sending snaps, Ms. Clifton would've been mistaken for a student.

I picture Mr. Nelson passed out on my couch and reply, "Mr. Nelson, no, not at all." Luckily, the bell rings, and this super awkward conversation can be over.

Ms. Clifton smiles instantly and pole vaults out of her swivel chair, putting her large She-Hulk arm around me. She presses her dimpled chin into her chest and whispers loudly into my ear, "I'll speak with Mr. O'Leary and smooth things over with him, but word to the wise, stay quiet about our little talk, okey-dokey, kiddo."

I wince at the "okey-dokey" as her Hulkish arm presses me harder to her equally hard body. "Yeah, sure thing." I struggle out feeling as if I just avoided an anaconda squeezing me slowly to death.

"I like you Adair men! We're all goin' to have so much fun here!" she proclaims, once again revealing the twangy cheerleader voice, as she takes my hand in a vice grip of a handshake before she sends me off to class.

As I leave her office, Ms. Simmons is at her desk sharpening a pencil while looking at me with her beady green eyes, continuing to sharpen the same pencil as it gets shorter and shorter until I open the door and leave. As I escape that creepy grin, I hear her frail, elderly voice call, "Have a good day, Ulysses."

That was weird! Why did she care so much about Dad and Mr. Nelson? I don't want her to know how well I can read people's body language, and I read a lot in that office. One thing is Mr. Barron and Mr. Wright were both showing fear, why? I'll speak with Conrad about what I witnessed, see if he knows anything. That was weird as hell. Why were they arguing? Did Mr. Wright shove Mr. Barron? I know Mr. Wright is a rich, pompous lawyer but shoving a principal? I can't stand Mr. Barron, but he doesn't deserve to be shoved by a parent, seriously! And is Ms. Clifton into Mr. Nelson? Come on! I better face the music and get off to Dad's U.S. history class. This school just became seriously messed up!

CHAPTER 11

- ULYSSES -

MY BEST FRIEND IS MY GIRLFRIEND?

After Conrad's basketball practice, Hannah and I gather our school bags and vacate Mangrove with breakneck speed. As we march from the school, the warm blanket of humidity wraps around us on our journey. The humidity rarely lifts from our area of Florida. Throughout most of the year, it's either humid or pounding rain. Some people hate this heavy, moist humidity, but I don't mind it. Coming from Maine, I cherish any temperature that doesn't include a wind-chill factor.

The walk from Mangrove to Penny University Cafe is just a couple of miles. Hannah's family's coffee shop and deli has become a local center of the arts for teens in Somerset. We start out in silence; then suddenly Hannah breaks it. With the amount Hannah talks, I am surprised the silence lasted as long as it did.

"Was your dad mad about what happened today in O'Leary's?" Hannah asks sweetly.

I told Dad everything during lunch today, filling him in on O'Leary yelling and the comments he made. He wasn't pleased with O'Leary and probably will be bringing it up with him personally. I also relayed everything that transpired in the office from the fight between Mr. Wright and Mr. Barron, also Ms. Clifton's comments concerning Dad and Mr. Nelson. He was definitely miffed that I got in trouble, but he was more enthralled with the events of the office.

"It was fine," I reply nonchalantly, now thinking of a way to ask out Hannah without looking like a total moron.

"Ulysses, you've been acting strange when you're around me lately. I'm not just talking about today; it's been going on for a few weeks. What's your deal?"

We pass by streets filled with gaudy homes. These homes could swallow up most standard size homes and have room to swallow several more. Homes that stand tall and powerful in this plentiful city. On each street we pass houses that stand knee deep in wealth and greed; their assessed values could equal some small nations' GDP.

"So...?" Hannah beckons, awaking me from my distractors.

I start to reluctantly explain myself as she looks genuinely concerned. "Well, ever since we started at Mangrove, I see our friendship changing. I've had the urge to change it."

"What do you mean, change it?! Ulysses Adair, we will always be friends; you better not become friends with any of those basketball jocks Conrad pretends to like?" she quickly chimes.

Once again it is hard to get a word in. I'm a little

irritated I am cut off, but then continue, "No, don't be stupid, what I was going to say was..."

She cuts me off again: "Stupid, who are you calling stupid?!" She is very irritated. Her face becomes flush, but not from the humidity, "¡Soy lo mejor que te ha pasado a Ulysses Adair! ¡Eres el estúpido gringo por hacer realidad eso!"

It's never good when Hannah starts yelling in Spanish. I can make out "stupid white guy" and my name. I should've taken Spanish instead of French.

My frustration starts to increase, and I blurt out, "I'm in love with you! That's why I have been nervous around you, and that's why I cannot talk around you! Since we started high school, I've wanted to be more than friends, but I never had the opportunity. I cannot imagine my days without sharing them with you, and I go to bed thinking of you and wake up from dreaming about you. I love the way you tie your hair back because your parents won't let you cut it, and the way you wear those big black glasses to hide your beautiful face from the other boys. Your brown eyes look down, and your face smirks when you're embarrassed. Your cheeks turn red like they are now, and you always listen to my rants; nobody listens like you do. I love you, Hannah Reyes!"

When my monologue is finished, she stands motionless, frozen like a lawn ornament. She transforms from a disgusted expression, spouting off Spanish, to complete bewilderment. Relief floods my body as the tension that has been building for so long escapes. Now my stomach is back in my shoes, reunited once again since their time together in Mr. O'Leary's class. I feel a little faint when out of nowhere Hannah grabs hold of me, wrapping her hands tightly around my neck. She buries her head into my chest, hard. Her smooth, silky hair is against my face, smelling of flowers.

She mumbles, "Estas loco," and kisses me hard on the lips. The kiss is long, and I experience pure bliss! Her lips are so soft, making me want more. It is something right out of an Ed Sheeran music video. Hannah tastes like strawberries. For the first time since mom died, I feel truly alive again. My best friend is now my girlfriend!

CHAPTER 12

- ULYSSES -

PENNY UNIVERSITY

Penny University is right behind downtown Somerset, near the docks. Hannah and I finish our trip by holding hands. Her hands, like the rest of her, are soft and creamy. We approach the cafe elated and bursting with energy. We are now an item! It is Hannah's first day working for her parents, and my first gig with Dad. I'm so excited, my feet are barely touching the ground as we walk. Penny University's parking lot contains only a few cars, though it's still early. The facade of the cafe has a huge antiqued, rusted sign with large letters, of varying fonts and sizes, all lined with bright Edison bulbs that read "Penny University Cafe." Several bright red picnic tables dot the metal decking. The whole look has an industrial vibe, in juxtaposition to the 1% homes and offices that surround the cafe in their Tuscan, French and Spanish styles. There are several strands of enormous bulbs lining the tin roof entrance that hangs over the decking. More bulbs wrap poles in the parking lot in soft light, inviting patrons to follow the procession into the large converted warehouse. It's a really cool establishment!

The dark, slate navy siding is newly painted, and the tin roof contains streaks of rust. The color and facade blend so well together they look like a picture in a magazine on industrial living. Chalkboards rest beside two bay windows, laced with white hurricane shutters. The chalkboards contain a list of today's specials, from wraps and Cuban sandwiches to salads and BBQ, all eclectic but delicious. One sign even reads *'poetry and live music tonight!'* All the lettering is fine, ornate, colorful cursive. The thick, royal blue door, brushed with a rich lacquer made to shine and withstand the abusive sea salt air, looks heavy to open, but it opens with ease.

As we enter, I see Hannah's parents, the owners of Penny University. Mr. and Mrs. Reyes are mixing coffee concoctions behind the long clear display, which is full of pastries, pies and other assorted baked goods. The smells rolling along the polished cement floors make Hannah and I gravitate toward some post-school snacks. My stomach begins the usual gurgles and grumbles. Behind the counter are more huge chalkboards displaying the varied menu options.

Hannah once told me her parents chose the name because the first coffee shops, formed during the 1600s in London, were nicknamed Penny University. The story I heard from Hannah was that her dad's old-fashioned Cuban family did not approve of him marrying the love of his life, a white brunette from Arcadia, Florida. In turn, Mrs. Reyes' family came from a long line of Florida cattle ranchers, commonly referred to as crackers. Her family didn't approve of her marrying a Latino man. Like Romeo and Juliet, they broke away from their families and the rest was history. When Mr. and Mrs. Reyes opened Penny University, they wanted a coffee shop that upheld the ideals of the first ones in London. They wanted a sanctuary, a place to exchange ideas, knowledge, and express individuality through the arts, away from the archaic thinking of today's society.

    They inherited this prime real estate from Mrs. Reyes' uncle, who did not disown her and lived in Somerset. When the news came of their inheritance, they picked up their lives, moving from neighboring Fort Myers, and started their dream business while living in a two-bedroom apartment above the cafe.

    Inside, a mashup of industrial style and bohemian decor is everywhere. Worn crimson couches and brown leather chairs fill the expansive warehouse, while metal bistro sets and hammered metal tables fill in where they can. The walls are covered by artwork, mainly of Cuban inspiration, but there are also several pieces by Haitian artists and inspired by the Harlem Renaissance. All the work is illuminated by expansive windows, draped in crimson curtains. The long warehouse cafe is brought to life by enormous, ornate hammered chrome lanterns, held up by massive beams twenty feet above our heads. Quiet and cool reading nooks occupy the corners with metal pipe bookcases holding dozens of novels and board games. In the center of the expansive warehouse lies an empty, highly glossed, polished parquet circular stage, seeming almost out of place.

Toward the back of the cafe are two garage doors made of glass, probably a remnant from when this place was a warehouse. They lead to more bistro sets, picnic tables, and bright strings of lights before sloping toward the pier, littered with sailboats and yachts, on the Gulf of Mexico.

This really has become a second home for me and Hannah. Since it opened last month, we've come here after school every day, completing our homework and helping her parents set up. The cafe is very inviting. They serve great deli sandwiches, wraps, fried plantains, Cuban coffee, and don't forget the amazing fries. Being close to downtown and providing a new hangout for Mangrove High students, Penny U is turning into a success.

"Hello, Mr. and Mrs. Reyes!" I say energetically.

They return the greetings, but their happy expression quickly looks confused once they notice our hands tightly woven together. Hannah notices their confusion and asks to speak with them privately in the kitchen. I can hear Spanish being spoken through the swinging door they disappeared through. Moments later Mr. Reyes comes out with a large Cuban sandwich and a side of fried plantains, pushing it in front of me while swinging a towel over his shoulder.

"Eat, Ulysses," he hisses with his Cuban hitman voice, hissing his r's and s's. "Be good to her," he rasps, looking at me intensely while he backs into the kitchen, raising his eyebrows in presumed expectation.

I gulp, hard. "Ah, yes, sir. I will," I say as he retreats.

I was never afraid of Mr. Reyes, but now I am reevaluating that position. The smell of the sandwich overtakes me, and I start to rip through it. Mrs. Reyes and Hannah come out of the kitchen, both smiling. They probably enjoyed watching Mr. Reyes intimidate me. They giggle and talk while occasionally glancing over at me. Hannah eventually joins me with a salad.

After Hannah and I finish eating, we begin helping her parents set the tables for the many patrons they have coming in the next few hours. They are very friendly and welcoming to me, joking with me and Hannah, making me feel like I belong.

CHAPTER 13

- LOGAN -

AWKWARDNESS FOLLOWED BY A DUET...CHECK, PLEASE!

The rain hits my Prius, making it feel smaller than it already is. I have just taken out and fed Ortiz after racing home from work. Now I am managing the typical early evening rain blast during hurricane season. My Prius is practically floating down Route 41, just a couple of miles from Penny University. I am in deep thought about the weird day at Mangrove. Ulysses described his encounters with AP Mary Clifton and the fight between Principal Barron and Conrad's dad. I continue to have reservations about Ms. Clifton: What was her story and why does she want to be close to Bob? I mean, it's Bob for Christ's sake. I already need to have a heart-to-heart with Mr. O'Leary after U got the boot from his class. I can't be too mad at Ulysses; O'Leary is a dink. I think I'll be driving myself for a few weeks, since he runs the carpool. My mind wanders back to Clifton. Is Ms. Clifton truly interested in Bob? He told me before he left that he was going to pick her up and bring her tonight. She seems fake, like she's putting on an act. How did Barron end up hiring her? They seem like polar opposites. I've never seen an AP flirt like that.

I pull into the parking lot of Penny U as the rain is finally coming to an end, and my Prius can breathe a sigh of relief. Parking is hard to find, but I catch a space in the back, grab our guitars, and proceed inside. To my horror, among the packed cafe, I can see Bob and Mary Clifton sharing a four-top table. Mary is practically in Bob's lap, and Bob looks like he is a ventriloquist happily pulling her strings. Half the school is here, along with parents and staff. The cafe is large, so the crowd disperses and it doesn't feel overcrowded. Modern pop songs are drowning out the crowd noise; something by Pink or Lady Gaga is ringing in my ear.

I drop our guitars next to the table occupied by Bob and Mary and nervously sit next to Bob. "What's up, buddy?" I ask quizzically.

Mary answers first, "Hey, Logan!" She responds like we've known each other for years instead of a mere twelve hours. "We just ordered some fries, if you want in on that action. Bobby and I just arrived. We had to run fast because the rain was so hard."

Every word spoken sounds like she's known Bob and me for years. To make matters worse, Bob is falling for this act. Completely oblivious!

"Yeah, the rain just stopped. I'm going to wait and eat after the performance. Have you guys seen Ulysses?" I feel a bit desperate in my desire to get away from this awkward scene.

Bob takes a break from giggling with Mary, and,

once again in his Barry White impression, says, "He's over with Hannah Reyes behind the counter. I think they are an item now, I taught that boy well. Mmm..."

"That is so adorable!" Mary excitedly expresses.

"Thanks," I interject and quickly flee to the counter, away from the Bob and Mary show. As I move, I dodge and greet people along the way. It is hard surfing the crowd since I know everyone here.

Ulysses is behind the counter helping Hannah prep different orders coming out of the kitchen. He sees me and beams with happiness. I know instantly that he and Hannah are now an item. I gesture for him to meet me at the end of the counter.

"So? It looks like she said yes. Wicked good job!"

"Dad, are there no surprises with you? It was chill. I've been helping the Reyes family with the prep for tonight. This place is packed!"

"I'm proud of you, buddy! You're not nervous, are you?" I am becoming a bit nervous, but I know Ulysses and I have been playing guitar together since he was ten. Jill and I used to play together as well, and now music is one of the few things U and I have to remind us of her.

"I'm not nervous, I feel awesome!"

"Your guitar is over at Bob's table. We go on in about a half hour. Did you get something to eat?"

"Yeah, Dad, Mr. and Mrs. Reyes have not stopped feeding me!" he says as a side-dimple-ridden grin runs over his face.

"Nice! That's their way of saying they like you."

"They must really like me then! I've had a Cuban sandwich, fries, plantains, and a slice of Mrs. Reyes' famous key lime pie. At this pace, I may never go hungry again. How's it goin' with you?"

"Well, my best friend is hanging on our boss, whom he has barely known for a day, in a room full of his peers and parents! Did you see how Ms. Clifton is hanging on him? You don't think that's odd?"

"You're just jealous. She is pretty cute, for an AP, I mean. She did get me out of a pinch today."

I look wearily at Ulysses. "Bob does look happy, but don't you find her weird?"

"I think all administrators are weird, Dad. Don't be so worried about her; I would be more concerned with Mr. Barron's fight with Mr. Wright. That's some drama, huh?"

"So you couldn't hear a thing? What did Conrad say?"

"I haven't had a chance to talk to him, but he's coming tonight. The only words I heard was something about a letter and the word 'gallant.' I think it was gallant, I can't think of another word that sounds like that."

"Gallant doesn't ring a bell. And you say Mr. Wright pushed Mr. Barron?"

"Yeah, and when the door swung open, Mr. Barron was on the floor recovering things from his desk that were strewn across the floor."

As we speak in whispers, Hannah comes over to us and asks what we were talking about. Ulysses fills her in.

Hannah interjects, "They said the word 'gallant'?"

"Why, Hannah? Do you know what they were discussing?" I quickly respond before Ulysses can.

"Yeah, I overheard Mr. O'Leary speaking to Mr.

Barron last week before school started. They were discussing the old house that was once owned by a family named Gallant; O'Leary had just bought it. Mr. O'Leary mentioned he had bought it for practically nothing and was renovating it, or something. Then Mr. Barron mentioned he knew the previous owners and would be interested if Mr. O'Leary found anything in the renovations. I distinctly remember them saying the name Gallant several times. Barron was very interested."

"U, that's the big run-down house we run by, over by the conservation. That must be it."

Hannah beams. She just gave us a huge lead in our little mystery.

"So why was Mr. Wright arguing with Barron about O'Leary's fixer upper?" I think out loud.

Hannah shrugs, but Ulysses adds, "I say we investigate. Mr. Wright also mentioned a letter. Maybe he did work for this Gallant; he is a lawyer."

"Maybe, but I'll inquire about the house when I speak to O'Leary concerning your geometry incident today."

"It really wasn't his fault, Mr. Adair. Mr. O'Leary has it out for U," Hannah passionately defends Ulysses.

"I know, but both of you should be extra careful around him from now on." As I speak, Mr. Reyes takes the stage to introduce tonight's first performer.

"Tonight is a mucho special evening," Mr. Reyes rasps into the microphone. "Penny University will now make the tradition of having open mic night every Friday night. My wife and I are proud of Somerset's new cafe, and we want to open it up to the arts of Somerset and invite individualism and creativity. After all, that is what Penny University is all about. Well, I better finish up. Mrs. Reyes is giving me the sign to wrap up. So, our first performer tonight is a teacher at our very own Mangrove High School. He is going to share some of his original poetry with us tonight, Mr. Samuel James."

When Mr. Reyes finishes, the entire cafe erupts in applause and a tall, lanky man, adorned in a seersucker suit, takes the stage with a thin black and white composition notebook at his side.

It is nice to see other teachers perform tonight. I'm glad I'm not to be the only one putting myself out there. I am also glad to see Mr. James and not Mrs. Swanson, although she is sitting with a bunch of the older teachers near the back patio, and yes, they are also dressed in jean material and adorned in the same chunky turquoise jewelry.

"Please tell your parents thank you for allowing us to play here tonight, and congratulations on all the success," I tell Hannah as I wink back at Ulysses and rejoin the train wreck about to happen between Bob and Mary.

"Logan, Mary here was just going on about her rock-climbing adventures. She climbed K2 last summer. I'd like to go climbing sometime. The YMCA has a rock wall with our name on it," Bob says with a giggle and a boyish smirk, making his gushing face look like a pumpkin.

"Oh yeah?! I love climbing, too. There's lots of great climbs back in Maine. I have difficulty with the knots though. I always had my wife tie them. I could never tell the difference between a figure eight and a barbell," I comment.

Mary sips her coffee concoction, looking at me with intense intrigue. "Figure eight knots are easy. Maybe I can show you when Bobby and I go to the YMCA."

Since I made up barbell knots and she didn't catch it or say there was no such thing as barbell knots, I now know Mary Clifton a liar, at least on the subject of climbing and maybe more. Worst of all, I think she knows that I know she is lying. She creeps closer to Bob, and I look away to watch the poetry readings on stage. Student after student goes up, nervous voices squeaking but determined. I pull out the iPad I use for sheet music, studying my selection and ignoring Bob and Mary.

"What you got there, Logan?" Mary asks with a hint of school girl taunt.

Bob dashes in before I can respond. "That's Logan's addiction. His iPad, he studies sheet music, probably deciding what he and the kid are playing tonight. You decide yet?"

Ulysses and Hannah come over as Bob is speaking. Hannah introduces herself to Mary, and for first time Mary's demeanor changes. It is no longer young and naive; it is now stern and rigid.

"Nice to meet you, Hannah Reyes. Your parents seem to have done well for themselves with this quaint cafe. Are you working tonight?"

"Yes, Ms. Clifton."

"Well, Mr. Nelson's and my drinks are now empty; can you remove them and get us another?" Mary sternly requests, her whole face changing to stone. The table becomes awkwardly silent. A "please" would've been nice, I think.

Bob quickly breaks the silence by coughing.

"Thanks, Hannah, you're the best! Tell your parents great job."

Ulysses and I study the situation and watch Hannah walk away, wearing a peeved expression.

I break the silence further by leaning into Ulysses, "Hey, how about we play this, this and that?"

I swipe my finger over the iPad screen showing him the sheet music to three songs we'd practiced exhaustively for a couple of years. The first was Cat Stevens' "Where Do the Children Play," then The Beatles' "The Long and Winding Road," finishing with Tom Petty's "Wake Up Time." We try to only practice ten songs, so we become really good at just those tunes. We mainly stick to the singer/songwriters of classic rock. Since it's my first performance since Jill died, and the first with Ulysses outside of our condo, I choose songs he will crush.

I hear a cow bell on the patio, signaling sunset, followed by a chorus of people clapping. The bell and applause are a nightly tradition in Somerset. This also signals U and I that we'll be taking the stage in a few moments.

Right on cue, Mr. Reyes mounts the stage again after the final poetic performance. He reiterates thanks to the patrons, this time adding thanks to Mr. James and his poetry class. Applause was thunders through the cafe. I try to get in the last-minute conversation with U throughout his speech but manage to add in my applause at the end.

"I would like to invite the Adairs to the stage. Ulysses and Logan, come on up. They are going to play some acoustic guitar for us," Mr. Reyes exclaims, hissing his words out with exuberance.

Ulysses and I grab our nearby guitar cases and take to the small circular stage where two fragile looking chairs stand waiting for us. Keeping them company are two tall, metallic, vintage Dynamic microphones. I set my iPad on a music stand for both of us to view.

I look at Ulysses with enthusiasm, "You ready, big guy?"

He nods with a grin, "Let's rock and roll!"

We unpack our guitars. Mine was a thirty-year-old satin black Gibson that Jill's parents had bought me on my thirtieth birthday. Jill would play the piano and I would play my Gibson to the early cold mornings by our wood stove back in Maine. Ulysses was not so lucky; his guitar was a twenty-year-old Harmony. A hand-me-down from my college days. His was traditionally stained natural. Ulysses always plays the rhythm, and I play lead guitar. He looks nervous but confident. One light shows down on us, illuminating even the dust, while about 150 students, teachers and Somerset residents stare in anticipation. Bob is grinning while Mary has her head on his shoulder looking blankly at me.

I nod to U, and we begin the Cat Stevens classic. When we finish, we are proud of no mistakes. Ulysses ran through the chords perfectly, and best of all, our voices didn't crack. When we finish our first song, the audience goes nuts.

Before starting the "Long and Winding Road," I speak to the audience, "This next song goes out to my late wife, Jillian Adair. We'd often play songs by The Beatles, and every time Ulysses and I play these songs, a little piece of Jill comes back to both of us. So this one's for Jill."

Everyone ferociously begins clapping; Bob even wipes a tear away. I see Hannah do the same, her eyes and Ulysses are locked on each other, glistening in the loud lights. Aww, young love. When we finish, we continue right through the next applause to "Wake Up Time." By the time we are done, people are on their feet, clapping and whistling. Mr. and Mrs. Reyes come up and emphatically hug both of us. Hannah also kisses Ulysses.

Ulysses turns to me and says, "Mom would be so proud!"

"Yeah, she would!" And I rub my hand through his puffy hair, and we both bow to the crowd. While bowing, I see Bob and Mary slink out the front entrance. I hope you know what you're getting into there, big guy.

CHAPTER 14

- ULYSSES -

PIZZA, DRUGS, BASKETBALL, AND TRACKSUITS. OH MY!

Last night was truly lit! Hannah and I are an item! Maybe we'll get a cool celebrity name mesh like Uannah — nah! Everything is going awesome! Dad and I rocked and got a standing ovation last night. I feel great. My only trouble is Conrad. He didn't show up at Penny University last night. I've sent him snaps, texted him, called him, but no luck. Dad says not to worry, he probably has a lot of stress. Mangrove High's men's basketball team is playing Everglades High later tonight. I am a little concerned; it's not like Conrad to not contact me. He usually at least sends me a pic or an emoji.

Dad and I are cruising over to Penny U to pick up Hannah, jamming out in the car to some Amos Lee. It is only five o'clock, but we need to get some dinner before the game. Dad is watching the door at the game tonight, to make sure nobody enters without a ticket.

We pull into the parking lot where Hannah is outside waiting. She yells into the cafe before bolting down the stairs towards our car.

"Who's ready for some b-ball!?" Dad obnoxiously bellows as I switch to the back seat, and we are on our way.

Hannah, also a little corny, encourages him, "I am! Let's send Everglades High back to the swamp! Give me a WHAT! — WHAT!"

"WHAT! WHAT!" Dad echoes back.

"Hope you don't mind we're meeting Mr. Nelson at Somerset House of Pizza. Why didn't you want to eat at Penny U?" I softly speak so Dad can't hear.

"I worked there until 11:00 last night and woke up at six, on a Saturday, to set up for today's breakfast crowd! I have the next three days off, and if I'm there, they will put me to work."

"That sucks, no worries," I reply and kiss her on the cheek.

Dad spouts quickly and semi-sternly, "Whoa, whoa. I'm still getting used to you guys dating. Friends is one thing, but now it's something totally different. Also, I'm Hannah's teacher, so cool the lovey-dovey stuff around the old man, capeesh?"

Hannah giggles, "Capeesh, Mr. Adair."

"Jeez, Dad, it was just a kiss on the cheek!"

"Capeesh?" Dad repeats.

"Capeesh, Daddio. Really, Dad, is it your role in life to bring back every dorky word ever used in the English language?"

"Damn Skippy!"

Hannah and I laugh and talk about school, her

parents, and my concerns about Conrad. When we arrive at the Somerset House of Pizza, both Hannah and I are starving. Our stomachs do a rumbling drum beat as we walk inside and catch the scents of oil, bread, and spicy tomato sauce wafting through the air. We see Mr. Nelson at a table, already looking anxious, in a silver tracksuit adorned with white racing stripes. Emblazoned on his right chest is "Coach Nelson, Mangrove High School Athletics." He looks nervous. His usually dark skin appears pale, his cheeks red, and he is twisting his hands together awkwardly. When he sees us, he tries to put on a game face, but Dad sees right through it.

"You okay? You look a little white."

"It's that bad?!" he quickly responds, shocked either by being too nervous or too white. Both sound equally distressing to Mr. Nelson.

"Both Terry Lewis and Jack Lipton have been suspended."

Hannah and I look at each other in amazement. Terry and Jack are Mangrove High seniors and Mr. Nelson's best basketball players. Dad's mouth literally drops.

"I shouldn't be talking about it, but it's too awful! What chance do we have at beating Everglades High now?"

The waiter approaches; everyone is too stunned to acknowledge him except Dad. He knows we are on a time crunch, so he orders two pepperoni pizzas and two pitchers of Coke.

"Is that alright, Hannah?" he asks.

"Sure, sure," she replies, still shocked by the news, while the waiter retreats to the cash register.

"What the heck happened?" Dad loudly inquires.

Mr. Nelson hesitates, wringing his hands. "I got a call around noon from Principal Barron. He said an anonymous tip came to him that both boys had drugs in their locker. So he called the parents and the boys into the school while Mary — Ms. Clifton — and Deputy Diaz searched their lockers." Mr. Nelson is practically squeaking out his words. "They found several ounces of marijuana! They now have to serve a forty-day suspension, not to mention no — basketball. We were going to destroy Everglades High! But — now!"

"So you're two students down, you guys should still be fine!" Dad tries to reassure Mr. Nelson, but his anxiety is spreading. "I had both Terry and Jack in American history. Both of them are good kids, with bright futures. Why would they be dealing with drugs?"

"They profusely deny everything. They even said they'd do a drug test. Maybe it will come back negative; either way it won't be done by tip off!"

I am starting to think Mr. Nelson cares more about this game than the innocence of his two players.

As we sit in a gloomy silence, our sodas and pizzas arrive, hopefully bringing our spirits back. Mr. Nelson's appetite is not affected by his current dilemma. He eats one of the pizzas practically by himself, leaving the rest for the other three people at the table.

Dad whispers to Mr. Nelson, "Where did you and Mary go off to last night?"

Hannah's eyebrows shoot up as our eyes meet during this intriguing adult conversation.

"Nowhere special. To be honest, as soon as we

left, she told me to drive her home. So I did. Just like all my dates, no action and quick." Hannah and I simultaneously choke on our soda. "I don't know what I said or did to her. It's like she got something she wanted from me and moved on."

"How did she act on the ride home? Was she still bubbly?" Dad asks.

"No, actually, she became cold and stern. She had me drop her off at the Whispering Winds Condos, which was a totally different place than I picked up from. Weird! Right?" Mr. Nelson finishes speaking and resumes his sulking once all the pizza had been consumed.

CHAPTER 15

-ULYSSES -

WHO KNEW BASKETBALL WAS MURDER!

We arrive back at Mangrove High, just in time before the sky does its summer tropical rain routine.

"I feel bad for Mr. Nelson," Hannah relates to Dad and me as we walk into the gymnasium.

"I know," I interject, turning to Hannah but then quickly asking Dad, "What do you think will happen to Jack and Terry?"

Dad shakes his head, a little confused. "Nothing good. I would never have suspected them for drugs; they never seemed like the type. Mr. Nelson will be fine. I've got to go watch the door. Why don't you guys take a seat?"

We watch as Dad sits in a metal seat near the front door as droves of Mangrove and Everglades high students and fans start to file into the gymnasium. Hannah and I sit on a bottom bleacher on the Mangrove side, near the entrance.

Mangrove is wearing their customary bright white uniforms with turquoise trim, while the Everglades wear black with white trim. They shoot around to music, classics by Queen, Aerosmith, and newer rockers like The White Stripes blaring out. I am tapping in rhythm to the music rather than paying attention to the players warming up.

Hannah and I start to fill the time by chatting about her friends and her parents, until I see Conrad take the court. He looks distant and disheveled, which is already his look, so it told me how bad off he truly is. His blonde hair looks unwashed, and his skin appears waxy and pale. Hannah and I look at each other with concern.

Hannah yells over to him, "Hey, Conrad! Good luck!" I wave and smile in agreement.

"He looks like crap," I blurt out to Hannah.

Her eyebrows rise up on her forehead. "Is that what you say to a friend in need? He looks a little sick. I hope he's okay. We should speak with him after the game," she says, correcting me.

"That sounds good. This place is really filling up. You sure can tell everyone knows about Jack and Terry. People keep whispering and pointing to Mr. Barron and Ms. Clifton."

I point, too, showing Hannah where they are standing. Both administrators stand like rigid soldiers under the scoreboard, both scanning the crowd, wearing deep frowns.

"I think you're right. Our side looks like we've already lost," Hannah comments as she sighs and puts her head on my shoulder for the rest of the warmups.

Basketballs thunder on the parquet floor, beating like drums as the teams warm up, swishing their shots into the nets. Hannah and I try our best to follow each of the Mangrove shooters until the Mangrove High band starts to play the national anthem.

As the anthem is playing, I look over to Dad. I am surprised to see Conrad's dad, Mr. Wright. This time he's wearing a fancy black striped suit fitted to his large frame. He stands at the entrance of the gymnasium and then quickly slips behind Dad. He glances over at Conrad and then, to my surprise, opens the door right behind Dad, labeled "mechanical room." I don't think Dad notices him because he is too engrossed in the anthem.

"Mr. Wright just snuck in and went into the mechanical room!" I relate to Hannah.

Hannah looks at me like I have two heads. "The mechanical room?"

"Yeah, I don't think he paid either," I jokingly add, smiling back at Hannah as we take our seats after the anthem and the tip-off starts the game.

I took out my phone and quickly texted Dad, *"Con's Dad wnt n mechanical r%m Bhind you!"* Hopefully he could read it. Dad has difficulty reading text message lingo. I look up to see him reading his phone. It looks like he has to read it a couple times because he looks puzzled. He meets my eyes, shakes his head, and starts typing.

"Ok. I'll keep an eye on it," Dad texts me back.

Hannah excitedly pulls my attention away, "Conrad's starting! Might be why he looked so crappy before the game. He was probably was just nervous."

"I thought that's not what a friend needs to say?" I say.

"Your words, not mine," Hannah says winking

back at me. "Let's go Mangrove!" Hannah cheers at the top of her lungs.

I look back at the administrators. Mr. Barron appears a little nervous as he keeps looking at his watch and tapping his foot like he has to go somewhere. Ms. Clifton looks attractive, wearing a powder blue pants suit, staring either at Dad or the mechanical room door. I quickly bring my attention back to the game when I hear Mr. Nelson squeak at Conrad.

"Conrad, hustle, rebound! Come on, man!" Mr. Nelson's voice cracks, yelling through the gymnasium.

Mangrove isn't doing so hot. We are down twenty points, and it isn't even halftime. The ten players rush up and down the court as Hannah and I watch, like a tennis match, with our heads going from left to right as our sweaty, beleaguered Mangrove boys are getting trounced by Everglades High. I continue to keep an eye on the mechanical room door, and Mr. Wright still does not come out.

"Come on, Mangrove! Take a shot! Pathetic call, ref!" Hannah booms out next to me, now standing. "Ref, you need glasses!" I believe that is what she said because it was in Spanish, and my Spanish is really weak. She sits down in disgust as I look amazed.

"What?!" she asks innocently.

"Nothing." As I stop studying her and throw my eyes toward the ref, I add, "Yeah, get some glasses, ref!"

I aim my dimpled grin at her, but she just shakes her head saying, "Gringo."

The halftime buzzer pulsates through the

gymnasium, and all the fans quickly make for the concessions and bathrooms. Hannah and I make our way over to Dad.

"Ulysses, are you sure Mr. Wright went in through this door?"

"Yeah. He was wearing one of his expensive suits."

"That door is always supposed to be locked. I think only the custodians and Mr. Barron have a key. How did Mr. Wright get in?" Dad is about to try the handle but hesitates.

"Should we let Mr. Barron know?" Hannah chimes in.

"I'm pretty sure both Mr. Barron and Ms. Clifton saw him go in during the anthem," I include in my report.

"Weird, that Mr. Barron didn't do anything. If he doesn't come out by the end of the game, I'll let Mr. Barron know," Dad says worriedly. "Why don't you guys take your seats? The game is about to start up. It looks like Mr. Nelson did have reason for concern. We're getting blown away by Everglades High."

"Those awful refs don't help out; they couldn't see a foul if it was right in front of them! They suck!" Hannah comments passionately, adding a few Spanish words I don't recognize.

Dad and I raise our eyebrows. "What?" she adds.

"Nothing," we both say at the same time as I hurriedly walk back to our seats and Dad resumes his door duties.

The game plays on. Conrad looks distracted. The whole Mangrove team looks like zombies while Mr. Nelson keeps shaking his head, his tracksuit jacket sleeves are rolled up and he looks as pale as Conrad. Our side of the gymnasium is quiet as Everglades High starts to rack up the points.

I look over to Mr. Barron and Ms. Clifton. Mr. Barron looks increasingly nervous, while Ms. Clifton looks happy that Mangrove is losing. Mr. Barron looks at his phone and then looks up sharply. He quickly says something to Ms. Clifton and then speed walks down the side of the court. We watch him as his short body passes us. I can see sweat dripping down his face and his dark tan skin was now becoming bright red. He heads for Dad. I see Mr. Barron pull out a large key ring and wiggle the lock on the mechanical room door. Dad says something to Mr. Barron as he opens the door. Probably how I saw Mr. Wright duck in there earlier and the door was unlocked. It appeared that Mr. Barron shakes his head and laughs it off, then proceeds into the mechanical room.

I quickly turn to Hannah, "Let's go."

"What! Go where?"

"Let's follow Mr. Barron!" I grab Hannah's hand and quickly lead her to Dad's position at the front entrance. I see Dad catch the door before it closes behind Mr. Barron. He looks up at me as Hannah and I arrive.

"What are you doing, Ulysses?"

"I'm interested in seeing what is going on. Like you, Dad! That's why you're holding the door; you were going to go in."

"Yeah, but not with you two."

"I love creepy stuff like this. If there are any problems, I'll protect you guys!" Hannah adds. "I have a black belt in karate."

Both our mouths drop with this little piece of information. I knew she went to lessons but a black belt? Damn, girl!

Dad grunts, "Okay, let's go."

We all enter the mechanical room. Dad stops us before the heavy metal door can close behind us. He examines the door lock. "There's duct tape on the locking mechanism, preventing the door from locking. That's what the burglars did in the Watergate break-in."

"Really, Dad? — A history lesson!"

"Didn't you see *All the President's Men*?"

"No," Hannah and I chorus, shaking our heads confused. "Did Mr. Wright do that? Why would he break into a mechanical room?"

"Let's find out, come on. Be quiet — stay close," Dad whispers before leading the way.

The door opens to a long hallway with bright flood lights. The lights are bright, exposing puddles on the worn cement floor. Several of the pipes have condensation and are dripping, making loud ping sounds with every drop. On all sides of us are large HVAC pipes making hissing sounds. It is hard to hear anything other than the pinging sounds of water droplets. We continue walking, the air becoming increasingly damp with humidity the further we travel, making the place feel eerie and damp. The gymnasium feels like a hundred miles away, but we can still hear thuds and the murmurings of the crowd noise.

"Creepy," Hannah whispers as she clings to my arm, wrapping hers tightly around mine. Dad walks cautiously in front of us.

The heat and humidity are becoming oppressive

as we follow the pipes to the end of the chamber. We are all sweating profusely now. Sweat droplets drip down my face. Hannah's arm is now wet against mine, but we continue onward.

We finally emerge from the tunnels lined with pipes, and we come upon a huge opening with large HVAC power units making loud electrical buzzing sounds. In front of them stands Principal Barron. He is frozen with his back to us and is unresponsive to our entrance.

Dad cautiously says, "Mr. Barron, are you okay?" On my left is an emergency exit door with a smear of what looks like blood on its handle. I am about to tell Hannah and Dad when Mr. Barron turns to face us and we all see what caused him to freeze.

Lying crumpled on the ground, still and surrounded by blood, is Mr. Wright! Mr. Barron's face is bright red and lined with horror. He continuously professes, "I didn't. I didn't. I didn't do this," in a low whisper.

Mr. Wright's body is contorted with his head thrown back in an open-mouthed expression, while a black curved handle of a knife protrudes from his chest. Large smears of blood cover his white shirt beneath his dark suit. The light above him spotlights the entire scene.

Hannah and I gasp. Hannah crosses herself and whispers, "Oh my God, oh my God," while clutching the silver cross around her neck. She tries her best to shield herself against the reality of the gruesome scene in front of us.

Dad puts his arm around both of us, like he is trying to either comfort us or protect us from the scene. He meets my eyes with a grave frightened face, turning to Barron and asking in a shaken voice, "Mr. Barron, what happened?"

My chest is heaving. I am having difficulty grasping for air. I blurt out, "What the hell happened to Mr. Wright?! Mr. Barron, did you kill him?!" I feel a little sick but can't take my eyes of off Mr. Wright's dead body.

Dad is taking in the scene, staring all around us.

Mr. Barron looks at Dad in a shocked, daze expression, "I didn't, I didn't do this."

"Ulysses, I don't think Barron killed him. He only entered a minute before us, and Mr. Wright appears to have been dead for longer than a few minutes. Also, there's blood on the exit door; Mr. Barron doesn't have any blood on his hands."

Dad looks back at us sternly and says in a take-charge, rapid voice, "You two go to the front entrance and call the police. The cell reception is poor in this room. Wait for them up there. Tell them everything that has transpired. Barron, stand in the corner and don't touch anything!" He takes the key ring off of Barron's hip.

"Which key opens this door!?" Barron points at the long key with a bold, black 20 written on the base of the key.

He shows me the key. "Unlock it for the police when they come in. That tape on the lock may not hold. Keep things on the lowdown: Don't say anything to anyone but the police. Are you okay to do this?"

We both nod nervously and quickly walk out the way we came, leaving Dad and Mr. Barron with the murdered body of my best friend's dad.

CHAPTER 16

- LOGAN -

THE 1% MURDER

I look up and stare hard into Barron's eyes as Ulysses and Hannah run off to call the police. He looks sick and worried. His tan, leathery skin is dark in the terrible lighting of the mechanical room.

"What hell happened here, Thomas?!" Since moving south I have never referred to my boss by his first name, but the hell with etiquette.

He looks at me blankly and shakes his head.

"I swear to God, if you say 'I don't know,' I will punch you! Look! I can help you, but you need to be honest with me," I bark at him, moving into the corner as I take a few steps away from the dead body of Mr. Wright.

"Okay! Okay!" he grumbles loudly. He lifts his slumped, short stature to its full height. "Donald Wright and I go way back — we used to be business partners," he stammers. "Before I was an educator."

"What kind of business partner?"

"Logan, this is none of your concern!"

"None of my concern?! It doesn't look good for you! Ulysses told me about your spat with Mr. Wright yesterday in the office. And now you stand over your dead ex-partner — that's enough for an arrest warrant and the school board to suspend you. I can't help you unless you come clean with me. Were you two being blackmailed?"

"How did — " Barron swallows his words and looks at me with a surprised expression, even his leathery skin gave that one away.

"The argument Ulysses overheard for a start, and then I took a stab in the dark, but you just confirmed my hypothesis. How did you know to come here?" I ask.

It looks as if he is about to tell me the details, but we then hear murmuring of voices coming through the tunnel. That was fast! The deputies must have been near the school because of the game. Barron walks down the tunnel to meet them. I turn quickly to Donald Wright's body, pull out my iPhone, and start snapping pictures of the crime scene; first of the body, then the exit door. They are almost at my position, so I quickly slip my phone in my pants pocket and step away from the body.

Deputy Diaz comes in huffing from lack of good air while Ulysses and Hannah trail behind him. Jose Diaz and I are close friends. Jose often joined Bob and I at the bar or when we played in our adult soccer league. Jose immigrated to the United States, from Venezuela, when he was twelve. He's been Mangrove High's campus resource officer for several years now. He looks down at the body, and then at Mr. Barron, with a very depressed, shocked expression.

"Did the kids fill you in on what happened?" I ask.

In his still-present Venezuelan accent he replies, "Yes." Sounding more like "jes." "So you all found the body?"

"Yes," we say in unison.

He leans over Mr. Wright, while putting on rubber gloves. "I have deputies stopping the game and starting to take statements. Mr. Barron, maybe you should go out and assist them, but please stick around. Our detectives will be arriving shortly, and I'm sure they will want to hear from you."

Mr. Barron leaves immediately, not wasting a second more. Diaz raises his eyebrows.

"We touched nothing. I found tape on the door, preventing it from being locked," I share with Jose.

"And there's a blood smear on the emergency exit door," Ulysses adds.

"How did Barron know this rich guy? A principal had a strong enough beef with a parent to do this?"

I lean into him and whisper, "I don't think he committed this murder, but he's involved somehow; he's hiding something. The victim is Conrad Wright's father," I add.

"We will need statements from all of you. Why don't you three go out to the gym? It's too gruesome to wait in here. The detective can take your statements from there," suggests Deputy Diaz.

I gather Ulysses and Hannah and proceed back to the gymnasium, leaving Deputy Díaz and other deputies to secure the crime scene.

We sit in the gymnasium for an hour, watching deputies and crime scene investigators flow in and out of the mechanical room. Most of the deputies are done interviewing the crowd and the gym is practically empty. I don't see Bob.

"Dad, how much longer?"

"I don't know, but I'll ask one of the deputies if we don't hear something soon. Hannah, did you get ahold of your parents?"

"Yes, Mr. Adair. I told them everything. They were shocked, but I told them you were with us and they cooled off. Poor Mr. Wright."

"I saw the deputies swiftly take Conrad away," Ulysses comments.

"It must be so awful," Hannah puts her head on Ulysses' shoulder.

"Here, this looks like a detective."

I see a tall, thin man with an old looking navy plaid suit stroll up to us. His face looks emaciated and he wears thick, black rimmed glasses probably weighing more than he did. He reminds me of a scarecrow with a vision problem.

"You Adair?" he said in a deep Southern drawl, either from Louisiana or Mississippi.

I stand. "Yes."

He gestures for me to sit. I hesitantly agree. "This - Ulysses - Adair, your - son?" he asks in a staccato speech, like he is afraid people won't understand his deep Southern drawl if he speaks too fast.

"Yes, and this is Hannah Reyes. My son's friend. We, along with Principal Thomas Barron, found the body."

"My name is - Detective - Lieutenant - Jaxson - Brute. I am in charge - of this - investigation. Did - y'all know - the deceased?" His Southern drawl was irritatingly slow. Pausing after most words.

Believe it or not, we don't get too many Southerners with thick twangs this far south. They say the Deep South ends at Orlando. There are too many transplants south of that point to maintain that Deep South culture. Confusing? Yes, I know. You sometimes encounter Floridians north of Orlando who have thick accents, but nothing like this guy.

"Detective Brute, nice to meet you. Yes, we knew the deceased. Mr. Wright's son, Conrad, is my son's best friend and a student of mine. I teach here and was watching the front entrance for tickets. Can we give a statement tomorrow? It is getting late and..."

The detective put up his long hand again, giving us a muted face. Brute's flat affect maintained his scarecrow-like demeanor. Crows would definitely be scared of this guy.

"Y'all - can go - when I say - so. Mr. A-dair - did y'all see anybody - enter the mechanical room?"

"No. Sir. My eyes were not on that door; I was mostly watching the front entrance. My son saw only Mr. Wright enter."

"That's right!" Ulysses chimes.

"Hm. I hear this man is - some kinda a rich fella?" He turns to a deputy standing behind him for a pen, clicks it, and licks the tip, while his long fingers take out a thick black notepad. "Let's start - this up - alright - boys and girls. Which - one of - y'all - is wanting - to go - first?"

I volunteer first. "Yes, to answer your question. I believe Mr. Wright was a very well-to-do corporate attorney. He's got a large mansion on the beach."

Detective Brute's eyebrows are thin and arched high when I mention this. He writes everything down while I review the entire night's events. He often interrupts me, and I am forced to restate what I said. He is quite an irritating man. He writes as slowly as he speaks, his sharp elbows making wing movements as with every stroke.

Ulysses and Hannah tell of how they saw him enter the mechanical room and U mentions the argument with Mr. Barron yesterday in the office. With this news, the scarecrow puts his boney fingers to his long chin, rubbing the stubble that is growing there. Mr. Barron is sitting on the other side of the gymnasium, with deputies writing down his statement, looking hollow and beaten down.

"So - why did - Principal," he checked his notes, "Barron go into - the mechanical - room?"

"We don't know. Why don't you ask him? It looks suspicious to me!" Ulysses chimes in.

"I - will, son." Detective Brute replies bluntly.

"Can we go now?" I ask, irritated.

"I have to get home. My parents will be so worried!" Hannah adds dramatically.

"Y-e-s." He makes yes longer than it was ever intended to be spoken. "I - need to - speak with - the principal. But I'd appreciate - y'all-comin - down for a full statement - tomorrow - morning." With that, Detective Brute's long legs glide over to Principal Barron for additional questions. By now Barron's tanned face is its natural pale white. I shake my head at him as we leave the gymnasium. He tries his best to not acknowledge me.

As the exterior doors of gymnasium burst open to Florida's balmy humid air, we find a wave of reporters and bright lights that follow us to the car.

"What do you know about tonight's murder?"

"We have nothing to say," I reply.

One reporter yells, "Did you know the victim?"

I could hear one of the news anchors turn away from us and report back to her live camera. "This is Helen Ross, reporting live at the scene in Somerset at Mangrove High School, home to the rich and famous, where successful corporate attorney Donald Wright was murdered tonight at his son's basketball game. According to the sheriff's department, they have no suspects as of yet but are following several leads. We will continue to investigate and report back with more information."

Her voice trails off as I shield the kids from the cameras, slipping them into the Prius, hopping in myself and driving away from Mangrove High.

"What a night!" Ulysses is the first to speak. I am so pissed that he and Hannah had to endure tonight's events.

Hannah follows, "How did they know so fast?"

"Probably the deputies," I respond. "Ulysses, have you tried calling Conrad? Poor kid, he's going to need you more than ever now."

"Yeah, I know, I've been trying, but it goes straight to voicemail."

"So gruesome. So awful," Hannah slumps in her seat in disgust.

"So you don't think Principal Barron killed Mr. Wright?" Ulysses asks me.

I think for a hard minute and turn to him sitting in the back with Hannah.

"No, I don't, but he's definitely hiding something. I tried to get more information from him while you guys were getting help, but he wouldn't budge. I think he is genuinely scared for his life. He did say that he and Donald Wright were once business partners, before he got into education."

"How is the Gallant house Mr. O'Leary's renovating involved with it all?" Ulysses adds.

"That's the mystery," I reply.

We then sit in silence before dropping off Hannah at Penny University. We both walk inside and speak at length to Hannah's parents, once again retelling the entire night's events before tiredly dragging our exhausted bodies back home to our welcoming beds.

CHAPTER 17

- ULYSSES -

A CAFFEINATED WAR ROOM?

Penny University is sparsely populated as we take up positions at a large picnic table on the back patio. A large shading structure keeps the blazing mid-morning fall sun off our weary heads. Below the patio, large yachts and sailboats rock to the rhythm of the green-tinted Gulf Coast waves. Many different breeds of tropical birds sing in unison, filling the air as the smells of café con leche, scrambled eggs, tostadas, and fresh fruit loom over the patio where we sit devouring our breakfasts after yesterday's long, brutal night.

It is nearing early afternoon on Sunday. Dad, Hannah, and I have just finished giving our official statements at the sheriff's station where Detective Brute continued to repeatedly ask the same questions in a continuous loop. Mr. Reyes invited us back to the cafe for brunch and to decompress after the events of the past few hours.

Mr. Reyes breaks our focus from our café con

leches. "Do the police have any suspects?" He says, over pronouncing his words in his heavily accented English.

"No, Papa," Hannah interjects.

"They almost arrested Mr. Barron. If we weren't there to give him an alibi, he probably would've been arrested," I add.

"Maybe that is what the killer intended," Dad comments, looking unshaven and worn down. The death of Mr. Wright is probably resurrecting the feelings from losing Mom. Dad continues to mull over his coffee as he blows over the rim of his cup to make it cooler. "Maybe the killer wanted to frame Principal Barron."

We all look at each other nervously.

"So if we didn't follow him into the mechanical room, he would have been framed for Mr. Wright's murder?" Hannah asks, looking at me intensely.

"Well, we spoiled that, didn't we?" I add half jokingly.

"I'm just glad you're all safe. Thank God!" Mr. Reyes says as he crosses himself. "I have to get back to help tu madre in the kitchen before the lunch shift begins. Hannah, you take the day off. You've been through a lot; look after your friends."

"I already have it off, Papi," Hannah says dejectedly.

Mr. Reyes smiles reassuringly, throws a hand towel over his shoulder, kisses Hannah on the forehead, and gingerly touches Dad's and my shoulders as he fades away through the glass garage door entrance to the cafe.

"Who would have benefited from Mr. Wright dying and Mr. Barron being framed for his murder?" Dad thinks out loud, not realizing Hannah and I are intently listening. "Sorry, kids."

"I think Mr. O'Leary did it!" I blurt out with anger.

"Why, because he kicked you out of class?" Hannah says with a huge grin.

"No, because of the Gallant house Mr. Wright and Mr. Barron mentioned in their argument and of what you overheard. The Gallant house is the big white house Mr. O'Leary is currently renovating and flipping," I add with a serious face to Hannah's fading smile.

"O'Leary is no killer!" Dad asserts.

"He wasn't at the game. Where was he? Did he have an alibi?" I sure hope not, I thought to myself.

"What about Ms. Clifton? Our great — new assistant principal," Hannah says sarcastically.

"I saw her all night standing at the far end of the court with Mr. Barron," I interject.

"Yeah, I saw her there, too. What would she have against Wright and Barron? No. It wasn't her unless she can be in two places at once."

Hannah shrugs. "Who then? What did Mr. Wright do to deserve this?"

I put my arm around Hannah.

"We shouldn't guess. Let's just leave it to the police. I'm sure they're more than capable," Dad says unconvincingly.

"Oh yeah! Like Detective Brute! He's no Colombo, Dad!" I add wittily, hating the idea of that guy being in charge of the investigation and knowing Dad thinks the same.

"I know, but we don't need to get involved any more than we currently are. Alright?" Dad adds.

"Your dad's right; we should be there for Conrad,"

Hannah says, as she gently takes my hand.

"I'm going over to Mr. Nelson's house, to see how he's doing," Dad says. "His two best players were suspended, they lost a game they should've won and one of his player's fathers died. I've got to be there for him. He also may know when the funeral is." He finishes his coffee and gets up. "Ulysses, you want me to swing you back home?"

"Nah. I'm going to hang with Hannah."

"How about I pick you both up later and I can make dinner for all of us tonight?"

Before I can think of a reason to say no, Hannah answers for us, beaming her enchanting, childish smile at Dad. "That sounds great, Mr. Adair!"

Dad proudly admits, "I make a wicked good spaghetti and meatballs! How about I come back through here around six?"

To be honest, they are wicked good. They are homemade and ginormous! We sometimes give Ortiz one as his meal.

"Sounds good, Dad." As I say this, he exits the stone patio and heads off toward his Prius.

"I think we should check out the Gallant house," Hannah says eagerly. "It may be connected with Mr. Wright's murder."

I do a double take. "You want to check out the house owned by Mr. O'Leary? Are you crazy?! What happened to not getting involved and agreeing with my dad?"

Hannah shrugs. "We should investigate. Our friend's father is dead. We should bring that person to justice. For Conrad," Hannah says unsurely. "You're always reading those mysteries, and now you're in one and you want to sit it out?!"

"No. But I don't have a death wish either." I'm not sure if it is the caffeine running through my body or adrenaline. I can't resist Hannah's smile. She is now pushing her loose brown hair behind her ear, thinking these moves would work on me — she'd be right. "Okay — but we need to be careful! What's your plan?"

CHAPTER 18

- LOGAN -

THE COACH NEEDS A NEW PLAY

I pull into Bob's condo complex. The sun is shining, but some unfriendly clouds are moving in. Bob lives in one of the new posh complexes near the Somerset city limits, closer to Bonita Springs, named Vanderbilt Greens. You can always tell you are in Somerset because all the condo communities have rich, douche names.

How could Bob afford a place like this? One reason is he is a bachelor, another is he often mooches off of us, so he doesn't have many expenses. He often gets a home-cooked meal from Ulysses and I, joining us for dinner four to five times a week.

The building is designed with whitewashed stucco siding and Spanish tile roofing, making it look like a frosted wedding cake. I park the car and ride the birthday cake's elevator to the fifth floor. I knock a few times until Bob slowly answers the door in a faded, ripped Orlando Magic t-shirt and boxers plastered with tiny red hearts. He looks like he has just woken up. Bags hang under his eyes, making his pumpkin head look more like a decomposing jack o'lantern. It is weird not seeing him in a tracksuit, too.

"Hey — Logan." When he spoke, it came out in a depressed shrill.

Empty pizza boxes and beer bottles rattle the floor as he walks back to the worn black leather sofa that forms around his frame. I feel a little sorry for Bob. No pictures hang on his walls, and only a couch and a club chair sit in front of a wall-mounted television, which is too big for the living room. He doesn't have a kitchen table, just two old stools under a breakfast nook. A typical drab bachelor pad.

"Hey buddy. How we doin?" I interject.

He sinks further into the couch and stares at his ceiling fan. "Well, let's review! My two best players are suspended for drug possession. My only good replacement just had his father killed, and I was just told by his supermodel mother that he is going back with her to New York City! Oh, and we lost to a team that we should have beaten! I'm not doing goood, Logan!" Most of this was still in a whiny shrill, but when he said "good," he extended the o, making it sound like "goood."

"Conrad's moving back with his mother?" I exclaim.

"Yup. New York City!" Bob practically screeches. "So now I'm down three players! Logan — you got to help me!"

"What the hell can I do?"

"I think there's a plot to destroy my basketball team," he hysterically adds.

I laugh. "Bob, the world is not out to get you;

nobody is out to get you. You just have a few bumps in the road. You'll be fine. The team will be fine."

"Not if I keep losing! Mangrove wants a winning coach. Mr. Barron will surely fire me; he doesn't like me that much anyway. Rumor has it you found Mr. Wright's body and Mr. Barron killed him."

"I did find the body, along with Ulysses and Hannah, but only right after Mr. Barron found it. He does need to answer some hard questions from the police, but I don't think he murdered Mr. Wright."

"Ah — I was hoping for him to be guilty, so my job wouldn't be in jeopardy."

"Bob, you are a piece of work."

"I know, buddy. I know," he shakes his pumpkin head, honestly agreeing. "Wow! Mmm, hmm!" He continues to shake his head and put his hands on his head. "Nasty business. So that's crazy! Right? How's U and Hannah?"

I look at him, puzzled at how weird Bob could be. "They seem fine, but you never know with teenagers. They shouldn't ever have to see a dead body." Quickly thinking of Jill but blocking it from my thoughts.

"So, can you help me? Please!" His whining now becomes irritating.

"Help with what? Conrad's going to NYC with or without this murder being solved," I add.

Bob clasps his hands together in a praying position as I sit on the edge of his club chair.

"Not the murder, bro; the police got that locked down. I'm talkin 'bout the drug charge on Terry and Jack! I know they don't do drugs," he pleads at me. "Terry goes to Bible school for Christ's sake!" (No pun intended, I think scoldingly.) "Jack may get a scholarship to Gulf State University, and we wouldn't want to jeopardize that. If you prove their innocence, then I would get them back on the team and we would win again, and I would keep my job!"

"You're not being selfish at all!" I sarcastically retort. I don't know how to investigate. Sure, I read a lot of mystery books and I can be hyper observant, but I am just a teacher!

"What the hell can I do? I'm just a teacher like you!" I yell out my thoughts.

"Bro — come on. I know you can see things others can't, what do you call it — de-suction or something? Deduce! Deduce the crap out of this! Please!" Bob now practically begs and looks even more pathetic.

"I shouldn't get involved. We could both be suspended or worse, we could both lose our jobs!"

I did feel obligated to help Bob. Even with all his faults, he has been a trustworthy friend, especially at a time when I really need one.

"Yeah, but everyone is investigating the murder; they won't notice you and me snooping around this unrelated crime," Bob adds, moving his eyebrows up and down in a flinching motion, saying, "Please! Please!" over and over again. If this is how Bob begs, there is definitely a reason why he's still single.

I hesitate a long moment, looking at his face contorting in grief. "I'll look into it."

"Logan! Thank you! Thank you!" he says as he gets up and hugs me vigorously, which feels a little awkward since he's only in his heart-covered boxers.

"No promises! I am just looking into it," I reiterate,

already regretting my words. I see Bob relax a little, but he still looks exhausted. "It's Sunday, nobody is at the school except custodians. You got your keys to the school, right?"

"Yeah, but won't the police be all over that place? They are investigating a murder, inside the school!"

"Yeah, but only in the gymnasium. You want to investigate — right? Then we need to get on the computers at the school office and take a closer look at their lockers, too. But first, let's start by meeting with Terry and Jack. You have their phone numbers?"

"Yeah, why?"

"I want you to call both of them. I want to interview them for myself. If we do, this we may get muddy doing it. We've got to be careful. Have them meet us outside Somerset House of Pizza in an hour."

"What you gonna ask them?" Bob looks confused.

"I don't know yet!" I say sternly. "They must know something. They may know if and why they were framed. That is, if they are innocent," I add with little to no confidence.

CHAPTER 19

- ULYSSES -

KNOCK, KNOCK AT THE GALLANT HOUSE

I really don't know how Hannah talked me into this. I am thinking how manipulative she has been, as I perform covert maneuvers through the dense conservation land that abuts Mr. O'Leary's new house.

The house, known as the Gallant house, is known to us because Hannah overheard a conversation between Principal Barron and Mr. O'Leary. A house that Principal Barron was very interested in, asking Mr. O'Leary to notify him if he found anything in his renovations. This alone would be nothing, but during Friday's fight in the office between Principal Barron and the now-murdered Mr. Wright the word GALLANT was spoken. Coincidence? I think not!

A tall thicket and tall grasses are concealing my movements. They are enough to conceal me, while I dash from one bush to another, making wild bunnies reveal their hiding spaces and scurry away to safety.

I am less than fifty yards from the large Gallant house. It is massive and was probably a beautiful Floridian colonial home at one time. It has a wide wraparound porch, making it look like an Antebellum plantation home, reminding me of the homes Dad and I visited Louisiana.

The outside is untouched by Mr. O'Leary's renovations. Everything looks lost in time. Vines grow in every direction while dirt, grime, and soot from the nearby freeway attach to the siding and roof. The windows are partially boarded up; the outside paint peels like a sunburned tourist caught without sunscreen.

Hannah and I think Mr. O'Leary is only living on the first floor. This floor has newer windows, and through careful inspection, we noticed lights and furniture set up, giving a lived-in appearance.

We went back to my place to get my bike and ponchos. Hannah devised a plan, and I reluctantly approved it. Hannah explained her plan like this: "I will stay on my bike at the street, keeping an eye on your bike hidden in the bushes. I will keep out of range, maybe thirty to forty yards away. When he leaves, I will text you, and when he returns I will text you again. Easy — right?"

Easy for her, safely at a distance, while I break into a possible murderer's house.

I look at her in surprise when we finish reviewing the plan. I can't help but think of what could happen if Mr. O'Leary catches me — what he'd do to me. I shiver as I picture a locked-up torture room scene, like something out of the movie *Saw*. Hannah, on the other hand, thinks she is a genius and just smiles and nods up and down in a freaky overzealous confidence, not realizing my fear and dread from the danger she was putting me in.

"What happens if I get caught?"

"We'll think of something. We have our phones, silly." Her smile sold it for me. I am probably more scared of what that smile could get me into in the future.

Of course, Mr. O'Leary has to live in a creepy place like this. "Probably haunted," I gripe to myself. I have been sitting in the tall bushes for a couple of hours now, frustrated as hell. I can't see Hannah from my position, so I sit in silence, only a few yards from the decrepit fence separating me from the conservation land.

I am starting to get eaten by bugs and notice black rain clouds hiding the afternoon sun. An old, creepy, little doll is half buried by the conservation's overgrown vegetation. The doll is looking up at me with a face smeared with mud and worn by decades of the Florida sunshine. I look back down at the doll with disgust.

I am just thinking about giving up when I feel my phone vibrate. I take it out. It's a text from Hannah. I opened the phone, '*Os gone, Go. B Safe!*' That was all I needed!

I leave my hiding position in the conservation area, freeing myself from the dense vegetation and creepy doll. I swing my legs over the broken, old fence and make my way towards O'Leary's back porch.

As I land in O'Leary's backyard, I notice mounds of dirt everywhere. I stop and take a look around. The mounds were all obscured from my line of sight because of the long grass and fence, but now I can see more clearly.

O'Leary's backyard is covered with dug holes. Some are filled in, others not. His backyard is enormous, probably an acre, and it is covered by at least twenty dug holes. A few look big enough to bury a body, others are small, making the scene similar to a cemetery. Why the hell is O'Leary digging?

Between the black clouds, the scary doll and now this homemade cemetery, I am freaking out. I'm trying not to think of horror movies as I make my way for the large, old, empty house but am failing miserably because Michael Jackson's "Thriller" is now playing loudly in my head. Vincent Price, please shut up! I take pictures of all the holes with my phone before moving into the house.

I continue onto the back porch of the house, knowing I do not have a ton of time. Of course, O'Leary's house has a wooden screen door that creaks when I open it. What other horror movie cliché will I find? My skin has goosebumps, with the humidity in the air, and a rush of coldness strikes my body and continues up my spine. I nervously try the door. It is unlocked. Either O'Leary is trusting, or we live in Somerset, and why rob this place when you could go to the mansions and give them a try?

The door has peeling paint to match the rest of the house — probably lead paint. I already feel like I'll need a tetanus shot after stepping foot in this crazy home. The part of the house I enter is not renovated yet. Dust, dirt, and cobwebs fill my line of sight. Scaffolding platforms are constructed all around the room; it looks like O'Leary is going to start the refinishing process in here next. I creep in the house at first but remember the time crunch and that O'Leary is possibly a murderer, and I hurry through the house.

I walk through another door with peeling paint, heavy and cold to the touch. The air is thin and musty. The house is very warm, especially compared to the freezing cold of a typical Florida home. I see the living room and the kitchen are both renovated nicely.

O'Leary is clearly taking up residence in the living room. A worn-out cot is set up behind an ornate couch. The kitchen looks immaculate, like something off of the home design channel Dad always watches. I look around, but there is nothing there. I'm not sure what I am looking for, but nothing incriminating is present.

I continue to the front of the house, toward a large foyer. A large ornate chandelier hangs twenty feet in the air. A winding staircase stands prominent in the middle of the room, and I travel it to the top rather quickly but suddenly think I hear something. So I freeze. Ulysses, it's nothing. Hannah would've texted if O'Leary had come back. Unless she doesn't have reception, or her battery ran out! My mind is playing tricks on me while I am frozen on the steps. Calm it down, Ulysses, I keep telling myself. Worst case scenario, you get murdered by your friggin' math teacher, best case you get arrested for breaking and entering. Right then, frozen on the step, I feel something at my ankle, and my body stiffens even more. Sweat starts to run down my forehead. What is behind me? I slowly turn and look down.

A fat black cat lies pawing at my leg. I take a deep breath. That must have been the sound. Just as soon as I feel a relief wash through my body, a crack of thunder strikes outside. BANG! The fat cat hisses at me and scurries down the stairs. I am so startled — I lose my footing on the stairway and skid down a few steps. Just then something piques my interest on the wall of the staircase in front of me.

Several old pictures are tacked to the wall, buried in dust and cobwebs. I take a closer look at them, wiping the dust and cobwebs from their frames.

They were definitely taken a while ago; the colored pixels look faded compared to the crisp high definition pictures of today. I can make out a date on the bottom of one of them. It read the tiny red lettering on the corner, 6/2/90. Twenty-eight years old.

In one picture, a blonde man is posing with his wife and two children, they look happy, and, based on their clothing for that time period, they look wealthy. Another picture on the wall shows the same two small blonde children being held by a different woman, not pictured in the other photos. She is joined in the picture by the woman in the first photo, presumably their mother. The mother is very beautiful with short blonde hair. The two women looked to be in their early thirties. The mother is prettier than the other woman, who had a darker, flat face with long black hair and intense green eyes. The two children look like twins, one girl and one boy. They have the same platinum blonde hair, like their parents, and appear to be about three years old. Everyone looks happy.

"This must be the Gallant family," I whisper to

myself.

I continue upstairs, checking each of the decrepit bedrooms, all looking old, dusty, and practically pitch dark, since no new lights had been installed yet. I use my flashlight on my phone sparingly to find my way around. I don't want to waste its battery, which is already a little low, so I place it back in my shorts pocket.

I'm not finding any evidence of Mr. Wright's murder or his argument with Mr. Barron. "Why am I here?" I ask out loud in frustration. Maybe Mr. O'Leary is not a murderer. It's probably just a coincidence that the name Gallant came up in two of Mr. Barron's conversations. Or I may have misheard it. Maybe it was, "I like ants," or something crazy like that.

As my mind wanders, I look outside into Mr. O'Leary's backyard. At this height I can see his entire yard. The holes and dirt piles look like an archaeology site — or a graveyard. It has started to rain. Damn! That means Hannah's out in the rain. I better go, I think before doing a double take, and my stomach finds its old companion in my feet again. As I look back out the old smeared window, I see a person in the backyard!

"What the hell!" I blurt out loud. Someone is down in one of the holes!

It is the hole closest to the conservation area, near the fence line. The sky is growing darker by the minute, with rain blurring my line of sight. The smear on the window pane, neglected for decades, doesn't help my vision either. I can see the figure, dressed all in black, even a black ski mask. In this heat, that was not smart. The figure is furiously digging, for what — I don't know.

Just then I feel my phone vibrate. I take it out from my shorts pocket, reading the display. It reads six missed text messages — from Hannah! How did I miss these! My hand starts to shake and a knot in my stomach starts to twist as I open my phone and quickly read all of Hannah's messages. Each text was a warning that O'Leary was coming back! Each text becomes more and more urgent and desperate. The last one says, '*HE'S COMING IN — GET OUT!*'

CHAPTER 20

- ULYSSES -

IT'S A HOLEY ESCAPE!

I must've not felt the vibration of my phone in my shorts between the cat scaring me and noticing the pictures on the wall. I quickly text her back, '*B 2 u soon! Masked man in the backyard!*'

I hear a door slam downstairs. "Damn," I gasp in a hushed whisper. I was out of time! It's O'Leary! HE'S BACK!

My eyes almost pop out of their sockets. I think, quickly looking around for a place to hide, trying to find anything promising — nothing! Not good! I am out of ideas, alone in this dark creepy room — about to be murdered!

I cautiously tiptoe to the door, so I can hear him better. It sounds like Mr. O'Leary is unpacking groceries or hardware store supplies in the kitchen. Let's hope it's groceries and not hardware supplies, I think, envisioning saws and hammers that he can use to attack me in this house of horrors. I swallow hard. My frenetic thoughts are growing, beads of sweat run down my forehead, my mouth is going dry and my face starts to twitch.

I glance outside the bedroom window again. The rain is now coming down in sheets, but the black figure is still digging. It's probably getting hard to shovel when the ground is turning to mud. I can't tell how tall or short the intruder is from this distance.

Thunder blasts around me while the lightning gives me glimmers of light in the darkened room. I anxiously wait in the upstairs bedroom of Mr. O'Leary's house, thinking of my next move. But the only thing I can think of was how Mr. O'Leary was going to kill me!

Crazy thoughts of Dad having to identify my body in the morgue flood my mind. He probably won't be able to recognize it because O'Leary will hack my face off. My breath starts to explode rapidly. How the hell am I going to get out of this house?!

My panicked mind flickers for ideas on how to get out of this house. I creep to the staircase, peering over cautiously. Everything in this ancient house creaks with chalkboard-scratching irritation, so I keep every movement excruciatingly slow. Just then I hear a loud bang. BANG! BANG! That wasn't thunder!

I peer over the staircase just in time to see Mr. O'Leary walk slowly to answer the door, swinging it open in disgust. On the front porch is Hannah! She is wearing a bright yellow poncho drenched in rain.

"Afternoon, Mr. O'Leary," she sheepishly smiles.

"What are you doing here? Ms. Reyes!" he says in a loud, confrontational tone. Even out of school he is a dink.

What is Hannah doing? It is bad enough O'Leary is going to find me and chop me into little pieces, it is another thing hurting Hannah!

Hannah appears nervous but continues on, "Um, I was riding my bike by your house, knowing you just bought this - great place." I can hear the slight sarcasm in her tone. "I could see around your porch, into your backyard. I saw a masked man dressed all in black digging holes in your backyard."

"Him again!" From what I can see from up and behind him, he looks pissed! He quickly yells, "I'll catch him in the act this time! This prankster won't escape me!" He turns away from Hannah and runs away from the door, leaving Hannah in the door frame. For a math teacher, he sure can run. I can hear him burst through the back-porch door, the same one I came through earlier, yelling so loud I can still hear him after the porch door slams shut behind him. He sprints into the pouring rain. "Hey, you! Stop! You're trespassing!"

I take this opportunity to move to the top of the stairs to see Hannah take a few steps away from the door and motion me to come along. Without hesitation, I dart down the stairs, running for my life.

Half way down, a crazy idea to steal one of the pictures off the wall jumps into my head. I don't know why this thought came to mind. Why in the heat of running for my life, away from a creepy house, possibly being tortured and murdered by my math teacher, would I take the time to steal a framed photo from his staircase? I stupidly stop, quickly grab the picture with the two kids and women. I slip it under my shirt and continue my desperate departure. I burst out the front door of the house to meet Hannah on the porch. I grab her hand as we both run back to where we hid our bikes.

It feels like we've run for a mile, but it is only a few yards. I throw on my poncho. My adrenaline is still making me breathe fast and hard. We both hop on our bikes and race like we are in the Tour de France. All the while, I keep the frame under my shirt, tucked tight into the waistband of my shorts. Finally, when we're several miles away from O'Leary's house, we breathe a sigh of relief.

Hannah finally looks over at me, panting from running and then our quick bike ride. Her bangs are soaked to her mocha skin that protrudes from her yellow poncho hood; she looks so beautiful. She breathlessly asks, "You okay? What did you find?"

There is so much adrenaline running through my body; going through all of that made me feel so wired and alive! It was like having ten cups of Penny University's Cuban coffee.

Finally catching my breath, I look into Hannah's eyes, smiling, and reply ecstatically, "You were terrific! I owe you my life!"

With both hands, I quickly grip her wet yellow poncho and pull her into my wet poncho, giving her a long and well-deserved wet kiss.

CHAPTER 21

- ULYSSES -

A NOT-SO-PRIVATE READING NOOK

We arrive back at Penny University, after a long sloppy bike ride, wet and tired. We discard our ponchos and sit at a bistro set in a corner reading nook out of prying eyes. We are cold but are soon warmed by some frothy cappuccinos.

"You stole one of Mr. O'Leary's pictures!" Hannah says, baffled.

"Shh! Keep your voice down," I whisper. "I didn't steal anything! I'm just borrowing it. I don't think this is his anyway. Look at the date. O'Leary is, what, forty-five? The boy in this picture would only be around thirty at the most. I think these are the Gallants. I think the picture came with the house."

I follow by relaying my entire visit at the Gallant house to Hannah. I even tell her about the cat; she thinks that is funny.

She, in turn, tells me about her situation outside. How she couldn't wait any longer when she saw O'Leary's car pull in, sending me several texts. But she couldn't wait around and do nothing, so she proceeded to take the chance of knocking on O'Leary's door. When she walked up, she could see the figure in back digging, giving her the best opportunity to distract to O'Leary, getting him out of the house so I could hightail it out of there!

"Any ideas who the person dressed in black was? Why dig up O'Leary's yard? This must mean he's not a suspect. Right?"

"No, he could've still killed Mr. Wright. The digging could be unrelated. It's probably other students that O'Leary pissed off in the past, and they're seeking revenge by messing with him."

We stop our hushed tones and quickly put the framed picture under the table when Mrs. Reyes peeks around the corner. She brings over two enormous sticky buns, gingerly saying, "Thought you two could warm up with these."

Since I first started dating Hannah, her parents have not stopped feeding me. I've hung out a lot at the cafe before and was never fed. At this rate, I'll be 300 pounds by summer. I don't know where Hannah puts it all; her metabolism is unmatched.

"Thanks, Mama!"

"Thank you! You're such a great baker, Mrs. Reyes!"

"Thank you, Ulysses, that's what we're here for. So what are you guys up to?" Mrs. Reyes has Hannah's same stern, inquisitive look.

"Nothing, Mama!" Hannah replies, giving her a get-lost look.

"Okay, okay."

"Mama, is it okay if I have dinner with Mr. Adair and Ulysses tonight?" Hannah says with a little twinkle in her eyes.

"No problem. You guys have fun."

"We'll give her a ride home, Mrs. Reyes," I say quickly as she slips back to work.

"I finally got a text from Conrad. He said he's doing okay. He and his mom are making all the arrangements for the wake. He told me we could talk more there," I say.

"That's good! Poor Conrad," Hannah says before whipping out her phone and rapidly typing with her thumbs.

"What you doing?" I mumble with a huge bite of the glazed sticky bun filling my mouth.

She cocks her head at my eating habits, rolling her eyes. "I'm searching for the name Gallant," she says confidently. "I've tried several searches, around Gallant. I'm now trying the address and their name."

She freezes and her eyes grow wide as her hands start to shake.

"Hannah, what is it? What did you find?"

"Look — at this!" she says, her voice shaking.

I scoot my chair next to Hannah, and she shows me her phone screen. An article from the Somerset Daily News brightly lights our reading nook. The article is titled, "Hurricane Home Invasion!" It is dated 11/6/90. I look at Hannah, shocked. This is only five months after the picture was taken.

"Read it!" she beckons.

I quickly skim the following: "Late Friday night during Hurricane Luis, the city of Somerset was beaten down, causing millions of dollars in property damage. As the hurricane raged, the Gallant family, led by their patriarch, Toby Gallant, were all killed in what looks like a home invasion.

"Sheriff's deputies report Mr. Gallant; his wife, Samantha; and their twin children, Helena and Hayden, five years old, were all brutally stabbed to death during the peak hours of Hurricane Luis.

"The sheriff's department has no suspects. The sister of Samantha Gallant, Sally Gibbins, who was also the children's godmother, is wanted for questioning but cannot be found... Mr. Gallant was a successful corporate attorney with the GG&W law firm and was one of Somerset's most charitable residents."

The article continues on about Toby Gallant's philanthropy work. We continue reading a follow-up article from the newspaper's archives, which presumes the sister, Sally Gibbins, is dead and no longer a suspect, and it explains the case went cold, with no further investigation.

We look at the picture, pointing at the women.

"Sally was the darker-haired woman. The prettier one must have been Samantha Gallant and the children, Helena and Hayden," Hannah says, slowly pointing and studying each figure in the picture. "How awful! They never found the murderer?" Hannah says in disgust.

"Why did they stop the investigation? They were such a prominent family!"

"Maybe the hurricane washed away any evidence."

"It seems like the investigation just stopped! The follow-up article is only a couple weeks after the hurricane. The police just don't stop an investigation that quickly."

"Another 1% murder," Hannah says nonchalantly, as she puts her head on my shoulder.

I sit up straight and her head bounces off me. "They must be linked!"

"What?" Hannah said.

"Mr. Wright's murder and the Gallant murder must be linked! Both men were corporate lawyers, both wealthy, and both stabbed!"

"Almost thirty years apart — that's a long time between murders!" Hannah quips.

"I know, but both murders have to be connected. There are too many similarities," I eagerly say.

"Should we contact the police? Tell them what we found and overheard?" Hannah says, placing her head back on my shoulder.

"Not yet. We need more evidence. They wouldn't believe two teenagers, especially that tool Detective Brute. I do think we should tell my dad. Mr. O'Leary is somehow involved. Dad will know what to do," I say confidently.

"Ulysses, we may be in danger. What if the murderer finds out what we know? If it is O'Leary, he may already suspect me or even you!"

"I won't let anything happen, but we cannot tell anyone. My dad is the only one I want to bring in right now, until we find more evidence."

I take the picture from the old frame, taking picture of it with my phone. I then find a book to hide it in. I take the dictionary from the Penny University bookshelf behind our table and place the picture inside on the page with the definition of murder.

Just then, I hear something around the corner. Hannah and I look at each other; she looks scared and is staring at me with a blank white face. I quickly whip around the corner trying to surprise any possible eavesdroppers.

Our private nook is in the far corner of Penny University and not many customers come over here in the late afternoon. Nobody is there. I only see the bathroom doors several feet away.

I decide to take the empty frame with me, pretending it is still full, just in case someone saw me take it from the Gallant house. The bookcase obstructed the view of any eavesdroppers as I manipulated the picture, so he or she would not have seen anything then.

I then retreat back to Hannah and the reading nook, breathing heavily, shaking my head back and forth to notify her no one was there. We both look at each other and know what the other is thinking: Someone was there — someone was spying on us!

CHAPTER 22

- LOGAN -

IT'S A TRACKSUIT INTERROGATION

A white BMW convertible pulls into the small parking lot at the Somerset House of Pizza where Bob and I are — not patiently waiting.

Bob is perseverating and I am unfortunately at the receiving end. Bob is asking me every silly question that comes to mind. He can't calm down. "Logan, how much do Walmart employees make?" Or, "Logan, do you think Dick's Sporting Goods is hiring?" Even, "Logan, how long can you collect unemployment from the state of Florida?"

"Jesus, Bob! You're not going to get fired for what these kids did or didn't do. Relax!" I say, irritated.

"Logan, you're right. Man, you're a good friend."

"It's okay, man. We'll get to the bottom of this — no worries. Okay?"

"Okay," he responds, still unsure of the situation.

"Let me do the talking with these boys. Okay?" I say, thinking Bob may end up either throttling them or crying on their shoulders — or both.

"Sure thing, boss; no problemo," Bob says

smiling, which doesn't feel reassuring. He is wearing a new tracksuit; I'd never seen him in this one before. It is bright fluorescent yellow, and in the Florida sun he looks like a big banana. If he thinks we look incognito, think again.

The BMW is nice; it looks new with all the dealer upgrades available. Probably a birthday present from one of their rich parents. In Somerset, I wouldn't be surprised.

Terry and Jack, two seniors who hover at six feet five inches, get out of the BMW like it is a circus clown car, making them look even taller. Both Bob and I hover at six feet and feel very tiny next to these two young men.

Terry is getting out from behind the wheel. He's a strong, strapping, seventeen-year-old with dashing good looks right out of a CW melodrama. Jack on the other hand, has red hair and major acne. He's more of a follower, especially when it comes to Terry. Both come from major money. Terry's parents, I believe, are in pharmaceuticals and Jack's parents are living off an extensive trust fund. They look worn down but still move towards us with that Somerset swagger only teens in this town have. We thought that speaking by the cars would help to make it look like we weren't interfering in a school and police investigation.

Bob greets both of them with an obnoxious fist and elbow bump secret handshake that only Bob could create. I just wave. It takes them a few moments to acknowledge my presence. I once was their teacher, but I definitely take a backseat to their coach.

"What's up, Coach?" Terry starts. "Can't believe

we lost to Everglades High!"

Bob shakes his head in disgust, "We really needed you guys last night. What's the dealio?" Bob's trying to sound twenty years younger, which never helps.

Bob's already talking and asking questions, going against what we agreed on.

Jack finally speaks up, "Coach, you got to believe us, we're innocent!"

"The school set us up!" Terry adds in disgust.

"Why do you think the school set you up?" I ask, concerned.

"We're innocent. They found some bags of marijuana in both of our lockers! It wasn't ours! I swear," Terry blasts to both of us.

"Calm down; I think we can help, but we need to hear everything," I add.

"The lab results just came back. My dad has a friend in the county lab and sped up the results. We both tested negative!" Terry proudly confirms.

"But they are continuing on with the suspension, and we have an expulsion hearing this Thursday. They are trying to peg us with possession with the intent to distribute," Jack says, choking back his nervousness.

"Take me through what happened. Don't leave out anything," I instruct.

"Why? Mr. Adair, what is in this for you?" Jack quips.

"Mr. Adair is on our side. He wants to exonerate you guys," Bob defends.

"I'm getting a feeling your suspensions are connected to Conrad's father's murder."

"Damn!" Jack exclaims.

"How? Why?" Terry adds.

"I don't know. It just is too many incidents and coincidences around that basketball game. I don't believe in coincidences. Tell me what you know," I add.

Terry looks at Jack. They both shrug.

Terry starts, "There is not much to it. We both got a call at home on Saturday morning."

"It was Principal Barron," Jack adds with a glance back at Terry.

Terry looks irritated at being interrupted and continues on, "He asked for my parents and me to come down to Mangrove High. Explaining they got an anonymous tip we were selling drugs out of our lockers. Which is absurd! I've smoked some weed in the past but never would during the season, Coach! You believe me, Coach?"

"I know, man, I know. We believe you," Bob interjects.

I look at Bob, frowning.

Jack continues the story, "When we both arrived, that new hot assistant principal, Ms. Clifton, and Deputy Diaz both waited for us. We showed them our lockers. Ms. Clifton had us open them." Jack stops as he gets a little choked up.

"They found several ounces sitting on top of our folders. I don't know how the hell it got there!" Terry finishes for Jack.

Both boys look nervous and worn down.

"My parents were so pissed! First at me, but then, when I tested negative for drugs, they called their lawyers. We are going to sue Mangrove for all it's worth!" Jack says in a vicious voice.

I did not think him capable of such malevolence.

"Why would we be dealers? We have a five grand monthly allowance!" Jack adds.

Bob whistles loudly and looks at me with a confused face. My face also looks surprised. Jack's right. What would be the purpose of dealing? They would have so much to lose and nothing to gain.

"Do you guys have any enemies? Anyone that wants you two to fail?" I ask.

They both shake their heads.

Bob adds, "Everglades High! They may have done this to make sure we lost to them."

"I doubt anybody there would go to this length to frame your two best players."

"Did anyone have your locker combinations? Past girlfriends, other players, anyone?" I add.

They take a few moments. "No, only the office," they both say in unison.

"Are you absolutely sure?"

They both nod after thinking for a few more moments.

"Coach, Mr. Adair, can you help us? We only have until Thursday. Our hearing is set for Thursday; they will decide then if we can graduate this year. We may have to finish our credits at home with a private tutor!" Terry says.

"If anyone can help, it's my man Adair," Bob reassures them.

I look surprised. "One last question. After your lockers were searched, what happened next?"

"Deputy Diaz and Ms. Clifton marched us into the office. Deputy Diaz took us into the office to meet with Principal Barron while Ms. Clifton left," Terry answered.

"It was only the deputy and Principal Barron?"

"Do you think you can help us, Mr. Adair?"

I think for a long moment and look at Bob, who gives me a puppy dog face, making his eyes wide like he wants a treat or a scratch behind his ears. "I'll try my best. Don't mention our discussion with anyone! We both can get into trouble investigating this."

Both boys shake their heads in agreement. They shake my hand vigorously, then they do their secret fist and shoulder bump with Bob again before zooming away in the BMW.

"What are you thinking, Logan? I know you got something brewing!" Bob says, making his huge forehead wrinkle with excitement.

"Nothing yet. I've got to investigate more. I've got a couple of scenarios in my head, but I cannot prove them yet. We cannot make assumptions without more data!" I add.

"Okay. Where to next?" Bob says as he gets into my Prius.

"Mangrove High. I want to check something out."

"Won't it be crawling with cops investigating Mr. Wright's murder?" Bob looks at me, continuing his wide-eyed expression. If he keeps this up, his eyes will pop out.

"Why would Terry and Jack sell drugs? That's the real problem that's getting hard to swallow," I say. "Like they said: They get a huge financial allowance. They drive a sports car. Sports scholarships are in their future. It just doesn't make sense!"

Bob grunts in agreement, "Mmm, hm," as we zoom over to Mangrove High in my Prius.

CHAPTER 23

- LOGAN -

THE DETECTIVE IS A REAL BRUTE

Bob and I slowly pull into my parking space, 221, at Mangrove High School. We can see a couple of the sheriff's deputies parked at the other end, near the gymnasium. Hopefully, we go unseen.

"Logan, what do you expect to find here? If we get caught, we could be pulled in for questioning. Dude, we'd be fired, guaranteed!"

"Calm it down, Bob!" My Maine accent is starting to come through with my frustration at Bob, so calm sounded more like "Caaalm." The parking lot is empty except my little silver Prius. I turn to Bob in the car. "I know it sounds crazy, but we need to get into the office today, while nobody is there."

"Why the office?" Bob asks inquisitively.

"We need to look at the personnel records." When I say this, Bob only looks more puzzled.

"Logan, why do we need to look at the personnel records? Terry and Jack don't have any files in there. It sounds like a waste of time."

"I want to look at Principal Barron's personnel file.

He said he was a business partner with Mr. Wright. Something in his file could provide more information about this."

"He did? When he say that?" Bob asks, feeling a little out of the loop. I proceed to tell Bob everything from the fight Ulysses overheard to Barron's conversation with me before the deputies arrived at the mechanical room.

"Say what!" Bob is dumbfounded.

"I also think the frame job of Terry and Jack is linked to the murder last night of Mr. Wright," I add to Bob's confusion. His face squinches, visually expressing his confused state, until it looks like it is going to blow from overload. "Call it a hunch, but things haven't felt right since Friday. Things have been weird. Something in my bones is telling me to look into the files in Mangrove's office. I don't know if it's Barron or something else."

"Okay, but breaking into the office? We may get caught!" Bob's voice squeaks. "I don't want to go to prison, Logan. NOPE! — NOPE! I can't help you!"

"Come on! You're the one who got me involved in the first place," I plead.

"I got you involved to help clear Terry and Jack, so I can win again. I mean, we can win again! I didn't sign up to break into the office while the damn sheriff's right there!" Bob says pointedly, while throwing his arms about in convulsions.

"Bob, I think the two incidences are connected. I think Barron played a role, and worst, I think this is about something bigger. I need your keys to get into the school."

"I'll give you my keys, and I'll sit in the car!" Bob adds. Meanwhile the Prius is being blanketed with huge raindrops, and claps of thunder echo in the distance.

"If I get caught with your keys, it doesn't matter where you are, you will be implicated along with me in the break-in. And it's not a break-in if we use keys. Also, I don't know the combination to the alarm system," I add, hoping he would fall for the lie. "Come on, buddy. I'll buy you a six pack of your favorite beer."

"Mmm, mmh," Bob grunts. "Okay, okay. In and out, right?"

"In and out — I promise."

We quickly vacate the Prius and speed walk in the rain that was starting to lessen, making our way to the front door of Mangrove High, hardly incognito with Bob's bright yellow tracksuit. It could probably be seen from space. We can see the deputies' cars, but they are about a hundred or so yards away. Bob pulls out a huge key chain from his tracksuit.

"What are you, a custodian?" I chide.

"It's called being a big dealio," Bob quips as he hums the *Mission: Impossible* theme song.

We hide in the front entrance of Mangrove. Large bushes block the view of the deputies off in the distance as Bob flips through his keys, frustratingly slow.

Something just pops into my mind all of a sudden, like lightning striking in my brain. I move my hand to my temple in a brainstorm gesture. "Bob, do you have a key to the mechanical room off of the gymnasium?"

"Dude. I got key to every door." As soon as Bob says it, he freezes. "I won't be a suspect, will I?"

"Bob, you were coaching in front of hundreds of

people. But who knows that you have all of the school's keys?"

"It's not like I go around bragging about it!" He moves his head in a fast counter-clockwise motion, giving me attitude. I know full well that Bob is a huge bragger.

"Do you have that key now?"

Bob carefully examines his chain, looking at each key, telling me the purpose of each, "This one opens the locker rooms, this one the front door, oh this one opens my office." He did this for about twelve different keys, never mentioning the key for the mechanical room.

"Bob! You never mentioned the mechanical room key!"

He nervously looks at his keychain again. He goes through them again and again. "Logan, it's — it's — it's not here! Does that mean the murderer has my key?" Bob says gulping.

"I don't know, buddy, but we need to report this to Detective Brute. He's in charge of Mr. Wright's murder investigation. Bob, do you know who else has keys to the mechanical room? You know that the detective is probably already asking that question to Mr. Barron."

"Well, it's hard to say. I don't think too many. The custodian, Pedro; Principal Barron, of course; and definitely Jose." Bob was referring to our friend Deputy Jose Diaz.

"Would anybody else in the office have one? Like the new assistant principal?"

"Nah. Not a key to HVAC. They don't like giving those out. I only got one because I have to sometimes go in and mess with the A/C during after-school practices or weekend events. The gymnasium's temperature is finicky," Bob adds before opening the front door and quickly disarming the alarm.

We briskly walk the dark corridor to the office, not wasting any time. The halls are empty, but the darkness quickly fades as the sun shines through the skylight.

We get to the office door; Bob fumbles through his keys again, trying what he thought was the correct one, but it doesn't work. I gesture with my hands to move it along, but he only nods his big head up and down.

"Ah hah! This is the right one!" he shouts as I hiss, "BE QUIET!" through my teeth, just like Mrs. Ryan, media specialist. Back when I was in school, she would have been called a librarian, but since students rarely use books anymore, instead relying on garbage they find on the internet, the term has been changed to "media specialist."

When we finally get through the office door, Bob once again has to key in the code to another alarm. "How do you know the codes?" I whisper.

"Barron gave them to me last year. When I have Saturday practice or when we have late night practices, I sometimes need to use the walkie talkies to contact the bus drivers or the phones to call parents," Bob whispers back loudly.

I quickly make for the giant gray filing cabinet between the office doors of Principal Barron and Deputy Diaz. This office usually has bus scanners blaring, loud typing, and whining teenagers. Having no noise is disconcerting. I grab two paper clips off of Mrs. Simmons's desk, bending them into the lock picks I need to get into Mangrove's personnel files.

"Logan, where you learn to do that?" Bob asks as I am laying the paper clips over each other and attempting to persuade the locking pins to open.

"YouTube, now go out in the hallway and be a lookout?" I respond as the lock pops and I open the cabinet drawer. I skim fast now to the B's and find Barron's personal file, pulling it out to take pictures of each page, while trying to skim for anything important as I quickly turn each page.

I read Barron's resume, learning that prior to becoming a principal he worked as a science teacher here at Mangrove for fifteen years. Prior to teaching, it states that Barron worked as a pilot.

"A pilot?!" I blurt out softly.

He also listed a GG&W law firm as one of his references, along with a professor from Rutgers University where he went to school, and another pilot from Somerset Airport. I quickly finish snapping pictures. I am just about to finish and close the file cabinet when I get an idea. I quickly flip through all the files again. Flipping to the C's, I find Mary Clifton's file. I don't know why I suspect her; she seems clingy, but harmless. Her file is very thin since she's had no observations conducted. In it I find her application, resume and references. I quickly snap pictures of each page, reading as I snap. Nothing out of the ordinary.

All of a sudden, I hear, "pst, pst," from Bob who's standing in the office door.

I quickly close the file cabinet drawer and rush over to him. He points silently up the staircase. We can both see flashlights bobbing around and low voices. I grab Bob's arm and point to my classroom.

We close the office door behind us and dash for my classroom, across the hall by the end of the massive staircase. I pull out my key, quickly putting it in the lock as the voices grow louder as they approach the stairway. I move faster before they catch us in the act of sneaking around. I crack my door open, allowing Bob to squeeze through, and I follow behind, gently closing the door behind us just as the voices descend the staircase.

Bob and I are both panting now, completely out of breath as we tuck below the window in my classroom door, crouching in pure fear of being caught. I hold a finger to my lips as a flashlight penetrates the window of my classroom door. I look at Bob, who has sweat running down his forehead. We hold in our position, frozen for what seems like an eternity.

The voices can now be heard clearly as they make their way towards the office after passing my classroom. I recognize one of the voices as Detective Brute, slowly speaking his Deep Southern drawl. The other voice is our good buddy Deputy Diaz.

Detective Brute says, "Someone at this school - murdered Mr. Wright - I know it."

"No way, Detective! Good people work here. I can't imagine anyone here committing murder," Deputy Diaz retorts.

"No imagination - Diaz! That is why- you're a deputy - and I'm a detective! You have - no - imagination."

I roll my eyes at the last comment. So, Brute thinks it was an inside job, too. He may be smarter than he looks; he's still an ass though. They are both searching the school methodically, trying all the doors. Hopefully they won't get an idea to come in here. It doesn't get more incriminating than Bob and I hiding in a classroom on a Sunday afternoon.

We hear them try the office door and then move down the corridor to the science wing. I wait a couple of minutes more, draw in a big breath, say, "You ready?" to Bob, and we are out of my classroom in a dash sprint for the front door. I've never seen Bob run so fast. His banana tracksuit would make the whole situation comical if we weren't running for our freedom. We bolt through the door and rearm the alarm. We then look down the long length of the building, making sure the coast is clear. We wait a few seconds before we start our sprint for the Prius, beeping to unlock with my key fob as I run.

I start the silent engine of the little car, putting it in drive and heading out of my parking space for the exit gate.

"We made it!" Bob prematurely bellows.

As soon as he speaks, we see a deputy squad car at the gate, directing us to pull over.

The deputy talks into his walkie talkie as I explain to him that Bob and I teach here, and I wanted to grab some of my students' papers to grade.

He nods in disbelief rasping, "Y'all are goin' to have to wait for Detective Brute."

Bob's leg starts to shake uncontrollably and his face starts to twitch. "Logan — I can't go to jail!" he hisses in my ear, spraying me with his spit. "Do you know what would happen to me in prison?" Bob squeaks.

"Be cool, Bob," I hiss back.

Several minutes later, Detective Brute and Deputy Diaz pull over to us, rolling down the passenger side window and speaking loudly between both cars.

"Mr. A - dair!" Brute drawls condescendingly. "My - my this is a - pleasure. Who's your - little friend?"

I think to myself that Bob has probably never been called little in his life. He's probably thinking this is more of a compliment.

"I'm, um, Bob Nelson, the basketball coach and gym teacher," Bob answers nervously.

"Yeah, we were just trying to get into my classroom. I've got some papers to grade."

"Really? On - Sunday?" Brute says unconvinced.

I hit the palm of my hand to my forehead. "I can be quite the absent-minded professor sometimes."

"I can vouch for these guys; they're good people," Deputy Diaz adds to the conversation, while Detective Brute shoots him a disapproving look.

"Have you found any connection between Principal Barron and Donald Wright?" I ask quickly, trying to change the subject from.

"Is there one?" Brute asks, puzzled.

"I'm not a detective, but I believe they must have had a connection if they were getting in shouting matches the day before Wright turns up murdered. Something is going on there. Something maybe from Barron's past. Don't you think?" I respond.

"Mr. A - dair, why don't you keep policing - to the police - run along - go sharpen your pencils," Brute says grinding his teeth as he rolls up the window and drives back to the school. The other deputy at the gate waves us forward, and the Prius is free.

"Damn, Logan. That was close! I don't want to do

that again. Didn't you want me to tell the detective about my lost key?"

"Not yet. We'll hang on to that one for now. It was all good! Like I said," I say, smiling at Bob. Bob shakes his head in disbelief; we both know that did not go as planned. "Dinner at my house? I'm making spaghetti and meatballs! Hannah is coming over, too," I add, smiling.

"Dude, you know that's right!"

CHAPTER 24

- ULYSSES -

IT'S A MEATBALL CONCERT

"Hey, Dad! What's up, Mr. Nelson?" I say as Hannah and I squeeze into the back of the Prius.

"Ulysses, you and Hannah can call me Bob. We see enough of each other outside of school," Bob says.

"I don't know, Mr. Nelson," Hannah responds.

"Yeah, we don't want other students to think we're receiving any favoritism," I add.

"I gotcha. I gotcha," Mr. Nelson says as he turns back to us, giving me and Hannah fist bumps.

"You guys have fun, hanging out at the cafe?" Dad asks.

I look at Hannah nervously. Hannah returns the look. Dad must have seen one of our expressions because he knows something is amiss, right away.

"Dad, you're going to be pissed," I explain nervously.

"Why?" Dad curiously asks.

Hannah interrupts, probably thinking Dad couldn't be mad with her, easing the blame from me. "Mr. Adair, we went to the Gallant house. It wasn't Ulysses' fault. I convinced him! It was all my fault."

Hannah proceeds to relay our little adventure in its entirety to Dad and Mr. Nelson. Including everything from the mysterious holes and the guy dressed in black, to me swiping the picture that hung on the wall. She even includes the online article about the Gallant murder and how we thought we were being watched back at Penny University. Although we can't corroborate this last part.

Bob turns to Dad pursing his lips together, "O'Leary? Like math teacher O'Leary? Gallant? What they talkin' about, Logan?"

Dad reminds Bob of the fight between Wright and Barron that mentioned the name Gallant, and how Hannah overheard O'Leary was renovating an old house, previously owned by a Gallant family, making Principal Barron very interested in anything he found there.

Dad's explanation takes some of his initial anger away from me and Hannah.

"Ulysses, you know better!" he says as his anger is redirected at me. "Why did you put yourself and Hannah in that danger? I'm disappointed!" Dad says, staring at us intensely through the rear-view mirror of the Prius.

"Like father, like son," Mr. Nelson jokes with his huge Jack O'lantern smile.

"Bob!" Dad barks at him.

"What do you mean, Mr. Nelson?" I ask as I look at Dad's eyes and back at Hannah confused.

"Well — Bob and I did some investigating work as well."

Hannah and I lean closer to the front seat as Dad relays his earlier adventure with Mr. Nelson at Mangrove High School, taking pictures of the personnel files and having to hide from Detective Brute.

"Do as I say, not as I teach. Right, Dad?" I say sarcastically. Both Hannah's and my eyebrows raise sternly, as Dad looks at us through the mirror.

Dad coughs, clearing his throat before saying, "You're right. I was wrong to judge. I just can't lose you. I don't like the idea of you creeping around, especially at your math teacher's house!"

"I know. But I think Mr. O'Leary had something to do with Mr. Wright's murder. He wasn't at the game last night. What's his alibi? He's connected somehow, maybe even working together with Mr. Barron," I add.

"What's with the dude digging holes in his yard?" Mr. Nelson adds. "That's just messed up! You know?"

"I'll try and bring that up during our carpool tomorrow morning. I can tell him the truth. Hannah Reyes mentioned it to me yesterday, and she was concerned."

"So, we are going to team up then?" Hannah adds excitedly.

"What do you mean?" Dad says.

"It means, we're going to investigate this mystery. We'll find the connection between Terry and Jack's frame job and the murder of Mr. Wright. We'll also discover how the Gallant family and their house are connected to it all," I say.

"Wait a minute. We cannot investigate a murder. Bob and I could get fired, and you kids could get in harm's way. You already said someone was eavesdropping on you," Dad cautions.

"All of those mystery books we read are leading us to this path. We should do it for Conrad," I add.

"I'm sure the eavesdropping was all in our imagination. What could happen? Nobody knows we'd be investigating. Also, I don't think Detective Brute is going to solve this," Hannah says.

"This is goin' to end badly," Bob sheepishly predicts.

"Alright, we can do some investigating, but at the first sign of any danger we'll take what we know to Detective Brute. Capeesh?"

Hannah and I smile. "Capeesh, Dad."

"Capeesh, Mr. Adair." Hannah smiles as we pull into home at River Creek. Our old sign is lit up with large flood lights.

We file out of the car, passing the Hernandezes' apartment, hearing their crying baby as we ascend our stairwell. Hannah and I walk behind Mr. Nelson. I gesture her to check out his bright yellow tracksuit, and we both start giggling.

"Hannah, you're going to love my spaghetti and meatballs!" Dad says as we walk over the threshold and Ortiz starts barking.

"They are good! They're the size of your fist; a meal on their own," I add.

"Ulysses, could you get Ortiz out and feed him, please?"

Hannah had never been to our apartment before. Slowly taking in her surroundings, she examines every photo on the wall in wonderment, while I release Ortiz into the living area. Hannah is studying an old picture of Dad, Mom and me at the summit of Mount Washington while we were on vacation in New Hampshire.

"She was very beautiful," Hannah states solemnly.

"We miss her a lot," Dad adds.

Their discussion is broken up when Ortiz finds Hannah, jumping up in greeting.

"Oh, is this Ortiz?" She laughs. "You're so adorable!" She proceeds to scratch his tummy, with his four paws straight in the air in pure enjoyment.

"He likes you. He usually only allows the tummy scratch from me and Dad. I think Mr. Nelson is more of a cat person," I say half whispering. I clasp the leash to Ortiz's collar and Hannah and I take him for a walk, leaving Dad to start dinner and Mr. Nelson to start on his new six pack of beer.

When we come back in from Ortiz's walk, I quickly feed him and then join Hannah at our kitchen table. Mr. Nelson is catching up on sports, watching ESPN. Dad is busily creating his culinary masterpiece.

"Dad, you mentioned you took some pictures of the files. Can I see them?"

"I'm not sure if you two should be looking at your principal's personnel file," Dad says sternly.

"How are we going to solve this then?"

"Kid's got a point, Logan," Mr. Nelson chimes in from the couch between sips of beer.

"Alright, here," Dad says, passing his phone to me.

Hannah moves her seat closer to mine as I wake his phone, find the picture app, and start to swipe to find them. We open to my cross-country victory, followed by a picture of Dad, Mr. Nelson, and Deputy Diaz all sweaty and happy after their adult league soccer match. We smile at this picture, and then swipe again, but our smiles disappear. Hannah gasps because we are looking at a picture of the dead body of Mr. Wright.

I whisper to Hannah, "My dad must have taken pictures at the crime scene."

I quickly recover from my shock and start to examine the picture.

Hannah pleads, "Swipe forward; I can't stand seeing that again."

"Okay — sorry." As I am about to, I notice the position of the knife. The handle was pointing down, not thrust from above or straight on. It was also right at Mr. Wright's heart. Doesn't that mean his attacker was shorter than him? I express this thought to Hannah and then Dad.

Dad comes over from the stove. "I didn't want you to look at those pictures!"

"I know Dad, but look." Detective Poirot and Sherlock Holmes would agree with this assumption, I think to myself.

"I noticed that, too. The killer must have been much shorter than Mr. Wright," Dad says before going back to the kitchen, speaking to me while his head is in the refrigerator. "Remember watching the old movie, *12 Angry Men*? The jurors came to the same conclusion you just did. Good work!"

I smile as I flip to the pictures of Principal Barron's personnel file. Hannah reads out loud, while I read along silently.

"A science teacher and a pilot, that's an odd

combo," I comment.

"No. Most pilots know a thing or two about engineering, so it wouldn't be a stretch," Dad says from the stove, listening to our findings.

As he says this, my body freezes when I reach the end of Barron's resume, where it lists his references. Hannah sees it, too, bringing out her phone and opening the article about the Gallants again.

"Dad! Check this out!" Even Mr. Nelson is intrigued enough by the tone in my voice to come and see what we found.

Hannah shows Dad the article about the Gallant family. How Toby Gallant once worked for a law firm named GG&W. The very same law firm listed in Principal Barron's references.

"Does one of the G's stand for Gallant?" Hannah wonders aloud.

"Why does some pilot trying to break into teaching use a law firm as a reference?" Dad contemplates.

"So that's the connection!" I exclaim, "GG&W law firm."

Hannah quickly starts to Google GG&W. I am pretty sure something will come up on the internet about this law firm, but that hope is dashed when Hannah says, "Nothing! I cannot find any law firm with those initials."

Dad takes his phone from me and searches for the law firm himself but he can't find anything either. Right then the oven timer goes off. "We'll have to put a pin in this investigation; dinner is served."

Hannah loves Dad's cooking. She is so impressed he can cook so well. Mr. Nelson tells stories of his college basketball days, keeping dinner very entertaining. Dad makes Hannah feel very welcome. Ortiz even gets a taste when I share a bite under the table.

When we finish, Hannah and I both offer to do the dishes. Mr. Nelson finds another beer and turns on the Red Sox; they are in Florida playing the Rays. Dad, of course, goes into his bedroom, coming out with his old banjo. Yes, he has that old of a soul, he owns a banjo.

Dad sits on our lanai, first tuning and then finger picking several tunes while Hannah and I finish cleaning up in the kitchen. Mr. Nelson mutes the TV, bringing his beer onto the lanai. I recognize a couple of the songs: One was Bob Dylan's "Girl from The North Country."

"That was one of Mom's favorites," I say to Hannah as she puts a hand on my shoulder.

Hannah and I join Dad and Mr. Nelson on the lanai, all sitting on our cheap Walmart camp chairs.

I quickly go back into the apartment to grab my Harmony guitar from my bedroom, resuming my position on the lanai, quickly tuning and then joining in with Dad.

Dad starts playing one of our favorite Mumford and Sons songs, "Not With Haste." We are just about to start the lyrics after the intro but are shocked to the core when Hannah jumps in and starts singing the lyrics — really well! Dad and I sing back up to her angel-like lyrics. Hannah must be a Mumford and Sons fan because she knows the song by heart. I had no idea she could sing — and well, too. I can tell Dad and Mr. Nelson are impressed; they are grinning with sheer enjoyment.

We all finish the song, and Dad pauses before quietly murmuring to himself, "You sound just like Jill."

I nod in agreement, beaming at a blushing Hannah. We all sit in silence for a few more moments. If I didn't know any better, I would swear Dad wipes away a tear.

Mr. Nelson breaks the silence by blurting out, "Well, it's a school night, and this kid turns into a pumpkin if he doesn't get his eight hours of sleep."

I giggle when I hear Bob comparing himself to a pumpkin.

"Alright, let's pile back into the Prius," Dad says, sounding exhausted. "How about we meet back here after your basketball practice, Bob? We can compare notes on what we find out tomorrow. I'll speak to O'Leary about his backyard visitor. Bob, why don't you ask around tomorrow to see if anyone on your team or in your classes knows something about Terry and Jack's lockers being messed with?"

"No problem, buddy," Mr. Nelson says before burping a few times.

"That sounds great! I'm glad you're jumping on board in the investigation," I say enthusiastically. "Hannah and I will investigate that law firm more. There has to be information somewhere, maybe we can go to the Gulf University law library," I add with Hannah nodding in agreement.

"We can make a suspect board like they do in the TV shows," Hannah suggests energetically.

"I'm not endorsing all of this snooping around, but we need to get to the bottom of this mystery," Dad adds before we all leave to take Hannah and Mr. Nelson home.

CHAPTER 25

- LOGAN -

THIS CARPOOL SUCKS!

I run out of the apartment to find Sam James' crossover SUV idling. It is a nice new red one with all kinds of key features my little old Prius lacked. I sit in the back because he has already picked up Bob — who is gleefully sitting in the front seat, happy to have shotgun.

"Hey, guys. It's another lovely Monday!" I say tiredly.

"Did you hear about the murder at Mangrove?" Sam says, glancing over his shoulder at me with a concerned look.

"You didn't hear? Logan found the body!" Bob adds.

I frown at the back of Bobs round head. "Yeah, it was a lot to deal with this weekend."

"I don't have Conrad Wright in any of my classes. Poor kid," Sam interjects as he is pulling on to O'Leary's street.

Sam James is Ulysses' English teacher. Bob and I sometimes hang out with him, getting a beer or a coffee after school, but Sam never hung with us consistently. He is married, and Sam and his husband would always find excuses not to hang with us, promising us a rain check. I blame Bob; he can be a handful. Sam's a good guy, a bit of a gossiper though. It is his turn to drive this week's carpool, and he is definitely fishing for information about the murder.

"Conrad's a good kid. He's a bit of a nervous nelly, but very athletic," Bob adds somberly. "I read in the paper Mr. Wright's wife is holding a wake tomorrow afternoon at their beach house."

"Do they have any suspects?" Sam asks.

Bob is about to speak when I hit him on his arm. "No, not yet," I answer for him. Quickly changing the subject, I add, "Good job Friday night with the poetry readings. The kids did a great job!"

"Thanks! They've been working hard and were a little nervous. You and Ulysses were the biggest hit; the crowd loved you guys! It was awesome! You're scheduled for this Friday, too?"

"Thanks! I think so," I say as we pull up in front of the Gallant house. I can see a little of O'Leary's backyard; several of the mounds are visible from the road. O'Leary is waiting on his front porch, looking as irritable as always.

"Morning, Silas!" Sam says through a rolled down window, very chipper for a Monday morning.

Silas O'Leary is a royal douchebag — oh and now a possible murderer!

Also, what kind of a name is Silas? Do we live in 1850? Well, I shouldn't say anything. I did name my own son Ulysses.

O'Leary's whole demeanor is weird. He wears full

plaid vested suits every Monday, circa 1975, even when the temperature is above ninety degrees — which is most days! Today's suit is dark tan with yellow stripes, straight from Mike Brady's closet on *The Brady Bunch*. I've also never seen him sweat. Never trust a guy who doesn't sweat.

As we pull over to pick him up, he slowly steps down each of his front porch steps, with irritatingly careful steps. He leers into Sam's car with sunken eyes lined with puffy bags. It has always been hard to like O'Leary, mainly because of the constant expression of dissatisfaction plastered on his face. His pursed lips are always pursed, and he's always complaining about something. He never seems excited about anything, and he appears condescending to anyone who does show happiness or excitement. Welcome to the worst carpool!

I was right when I told Ulysses that he reminded me of the judge from *Who Framed Roger Rabbit*; every word O'Leary speaks is in an obnoxiously loud tone, never having an appropriate volume. That leads me to believe he has an unchecked hearing problem.

O'Leary only nods hello to the three of us when he climbs into the small SUV, sitting next to me in the backseat. I am now thinking along the same lines as Ulysses: This guy is guilty of murder.

I shouldn't let my personal opinion and dislike for a guy cloud my judgment. Just like Sherlock Holmes, we need data. I need to investigate to find solutions and evidence of guilt, not come to conclusions without data.

"You have a good weekend, Silas?" Sam asks as

we drive onto Mangrove.

"Fine!" he says sternly.

"Did you catch the game Saturday night?" I quickly ask before anyone can start speaking about the murder.

"No! I do not watch sports!" O'Leary replies in a condescending tone.

"What did you do Saturday night, if you didn't go to the game?" As I ask, Bob starts to squirm in his seat.

O'Leary slowly turns his head to me and narrows his oval eyes, which accentuates their puffy, sunken look. "What does it matter to you?!"

"I'm just making small talk," I add, raising my hands in defense.

"I stayed in and worked on my house. I'm preserving a hundred-year-old home, and it's very time consuming, if you must know," O'Leary says in a somewhat normal tone, at least for him.

"Alone?" I ask.

"What?!" he screeches.

"Were you working on your home alone?"

"Why yes; what do you care?" O'Leary says, now changing to his typical disgusted tone.

"No reason. It seems like a nice house." O'Leary nods like he didn't care. "I heard some Gallant family owned it before you," I say trying to read his face.

"No." O'Leary stops for a long pause, sighs deeply to himself, and continues hesitantly. "If you must know. The last occupants were some family named Gallant, but no one has lived there since. It had been owned by the government for almost thirty years," O'Leary finishes, looking irritated that he had to speak at all during this carpool.

"Oh. The government? Why the government?" I ask.

"I don't know, Adair! Why do you care?!"

"No reason. Ulysses' friend Hannah Reyes mentioned somebody tried to vandalize your yard yesterday. I hope they didn't destroy too much," I say, trying to sound like I cared.

"I know Mz. Reyes! She is a student of mine. As for the vandals, they have caused immense damage to my backyard! When I catch them, they'll wish they had never messed with me!" O'Leary looks at me suspiciously, maybe wondering how much I already know. Or why I'm taking such an interest in him. His alibi can't be corroborated, so he could still be a suspect.

"Why do you think they are messing with your yard?" I add.

"I don't know; why don't you ask your son? I think he did it!" O'Leary spouts.

Both Sam and Bob defend Ulysses simultaneously.

"Ulysses is a good kid!" Bob says.

"You shouldn't throw out accusations, Silas!" Sam adds.

"I don't know where you got that idea, O'Leary! But you can count on one thing, you accuse my son of anything again, either because you don't like him or me, and they'll have to dig a hole for you because I'll put you in there!" I say passionately, knowing full well Ulysses may not have dug up his backyard, but he did break into his house and steal a picture.

"It's funny that your son's girlfriend is at my doorstep right at the time someone is digging holes in my backyard," O'Leary sneers.

"Why the hell would Ulysses want to dig holes? I can barely get him to do his chores! I can think of a hundred better pranks that wouldn't involve strenuous labor!" I sneer back at O'Leary in pure disgust, wanting to perform some of those pranks right now.

"Okay, okay, why don't we all chill?" Bob suggests, trying his best to squash the tension.

I really feel like punching O'Leary, but I know it would exacerbate the situation.

"We're here!" Sam says nervously. While conversing with O'Leary, I didn't realize that we'd arrived at Mangrove High.

O'Leary zips out of the car, slamming his door behind him. He tells Sam he will take a Lyft home after school, saying he no longer wants to be part of this carpool.

"Fine! Nobody wants you in this carpool anyway!" I yell childishly after him as he scurries into school.

"Smooth, dude," Bob says with raised eyebrows.

"What?" I ask innocently.

"O'Leary's got his panties in a twist," Bob says, trying to lighten the mood. Sam and I frown at Bob.

"What was that all about? He sure doesn't like you and Ulysses," Sam says, turning to me as we make our way into Mangrove.

"I don't know; guy's got issues," I say flatly to Sam and Bob. But I think to myself, O'Leary's definitely hiding something! He doesn't have an alibi. The Gallant house is definitely connecting Barron, Wright and O'Leary; just how? Why did the government own the house? More questions to have answered. I'm not sure if I'm closer to the truth or further from it. Let's hope Ulysses and Hannah have better luck with their investigating.

My blood is running hot, but it quickly boils over when I remember Ulysses has O'Leary in class today. Oh boy! I think as I text Ulysses to be extra invisible in geometry today. Ulysses is going to be pissed!

CHAPTER 26

- ULYSSES -

GG&W?

I feel sick to my stomach as we leave Penny University. I had just read from the Somerset Daily News that Mr. Wright's wake will be at his beach house tomorrow afternoon. Thinking of Conrad without his dad reminds me of Mom. I am also over-caffeinated, which doesn't help. Mrs. Reyes used me as a guinea pig for her new coffee and Frappuccino concoctions. This one was called the Dean's List. All of her coffee concoctions have college-related names, but this one had three shots of Cuban coffee, one cup of whole milk, two scoops of coffee ice cream and strawberries. First thing in the morning, along with a banana nut muffin the size of Ortiz's head, and I am rolling my way to school. With the added news of the wake, my brain and stomach are swimming during our walk to school.

I often bike to Penny U and then walk the rest of the way with Hannah. In the past, we'd take this walk as friends, but now she's my girlfriend. These last few days have seemed like an eternity with all that has gone on.

We start our walk to school, and Hannah puts her hand in mine. It is cold; "Cold hands, warm heart," she says after I inquire as to why they were cold. This causes a huge grin that gives my brain the focus I need to think on how we'd investigate this murder.

"Where should we start?" Hannah asks, knowing what I was thinking. "I searched backwards and forwards on the internet last night for GG&W law firm: nothing!"

"I know; I did, too. It could be made up, or no longer in existence after this many years. The only reference we've seen is in the Gallant online article."

"And listed as one of Principal Barron's references," Hannah adds, finishing my thought.

"Mr. Wright was an attorney. He could be the W, in the GG&W," I say halfheartedly.

"Maybe!" Hannah says with energetic hope. "We can't prove it. Maybe we can snoop around at the wake tomorrow?"

I look at her, surprised, as my hand gets hot and sweaty. "You want to snoop around at our friend's father's wake?"

"Yeah, just a little. In and out," she says hesitantly.

"Well, I guess we go where the clues take us," I say as a tropical autumn breeze brushes against me and Hannah, leaving us refreshed for today's challenges.

We arrive at Mangrove High feeling older and less innocent. We have barely been gone two days from this school, but as we enter its hallways we feel a change, a change felt by everyone from student to faculty. The innocence of our school is gone. We had a murder in our beloved school; maybe nothing would ever be the same.

We see groups of kids in the hallway whispering and glancing over to us. They are probably wondering if Hannah and I know anything they don't, especially since we found the body.

Hannah looks at me, concerned, as we approach our lockers right next to the entrance where they film the Mangrove High morning news, *Manatee Live*. It sounds like a nature show on *Nat Geo*, but it was only Mangrove's corny attempt at making school news. It's televised throughout the school on every smartboard and computer screen.

Hannah and I unload the contents of our backpacks in our oversized, turquoise lockers, when out of nowhere the valley girls from hell pop over to check on Hannah: Sarah Flanders and Isabella Cortez, Hannah's best girlfriends.

"Are you 'kay? We were so worried!" Sarah, the tall overly thin blonde says, followed by, "Oh my gosh, you poor girl!"

"We got your message, but we're so worried!" is said by Isabella, the short thicker-set girl. Both adore Hannah, but Hannah is finding less and less time to spend with them. This is mainly because she's working for her parents, has fewer interests with the girls, and of course, she's hanging with me, which made me enemy number one in Sarah's and Isabella's eyes.

"I'm okay," Hannah dryly says as both the girls block me from retaking Hannah's hand.

"We heard you found the body — EWW!" Sarah says, loud enough for the entire hallway to hear. In turn, whispers from kids around us grow as they point toward us.

"How gross!" Isabella adds. The girls play off each other, trying to bring Hannah back into the mix that they know she is falling out of.

"Who knew this was going to be your big news? We heard you and Ulysses are an item now," Sarah says, giggling while leaning into Hannah, grasping her arm. Hannah is having a hard time getting a word in, and I think of how often I'm in that situation with her.

"We can talk more at lunch. Ulysses and I have to get upstairs to geometry," Hannah says, quickly grabbing my hand and escorting us down the hall and up the large winding staircase. Hannah's face looks relieved to get out of that circus. But we both quickly remember we are going out of the frying pan and into the fire, in this case back to Mr. O'Leary's class.

We take our seats and start to watch the morning *Manatee Live*. It is a somber one. Deputy Diaz and Principal Barron are on the show to speak about Saturday's murder. In most of the classes, people look at me and Hannah with curiosity and murmur to each other. Mr. O'Leary, who had been sitting quietly behind his desk, has to use his loud voice to tell them, "Be quiet!"

Both Diaz and O'Leary urge, "Anyone at Mangrove High with information about the murder, please come forward." They also reassure everyone of our safety and how the police think this is an isolated incident. It is pretty much the same message we all got on our cell phones this morning in an "alert now" message. All I can think of is Conrad's empty chair next me. I hope he is okay and can come back to school soon.

The rest of Mr. O'Leary's class goes remarkably smooth. He barely looks at me, or even acknowledges my existence, but — I'm okay with that. This was the case for the entire class, all the way to the bell. But why? I mean, last time I saw O'Leary, he threw me out. Hannah is surprised too, which we discuss as we walk to Dad's U.S. history class.

"Maybe he thinks people are onto him as the murderer," I wonder out loud to Hannah.

"Maybe he's trying to be civil with all this stuff goin' on," she says, sounding more sensible.

As we approach Dad's classroom, we both wave as he is greeting students at the door, looking dressed more to play golf than to teach us U.S. history. He sees us and ushers us into his class, closing the door while leaving everyone else out in the hallway.

Before the bell rings, he quickly relays the carpool findings, that the Gallant house was owned by the government for nearly thirty years and just now went up for sale. Also Mr. O'Leary doesn't have an alibi for Saturday night, but most frustrating, he thinks I'm the mysterious hole digger.

"I thought your text about being invisible in his class was about him kicking me out of class on Friday!"

"That must've been why he was not his usual annoying self," Hannah adds. I frown at Hannah, thinking this took O'Leary's hatred for me to an all-time high. Hannah also tells Dad her idea that the W in GG&W could stand for Wright.

"That makes sense, and it was right in front of our

eyes the whole time. Good work!"

Hannah beams like she got an A in a test.

Before letting his students in, Dad asks, "Did you find out anything more about that law firm?"

"No, but we were thinking about checking the law library at the university before Hannah's shift at Penny U."

We hear the bell and Dad lets in his students for an additional lecture on Breed's and Bunker hills.

The rest of the day goes by excruciatingly slow. Especially after lunch; I don't see Hannah for the rest of the day. All I can think of is the investigation and the connection with the law firm GG&W. Common sense tells us one G stood for Gallant. That was easy, the law firm he worked for, it fit. The W, pointed out by Hannah, could be Wright; that would help to bridge the connection between Gallant and Wright, but where does Barron come into play?

I contemplate this as I wait outside for Hannah. Droves of students continue to look at me when they pass by, whispering to each other. Several classmates ask me crazy questions, like Paul in science, "Did the body smell?" or Rick in Lit class, "How much blood was there?" I had to put up with these lame-o's all day.

My concentration comes to full attention as I see Hannah walk through the front doors. Her slender body is accentuated by her tight black leggings. Her black skull *Goonies* T-shirt says everything about her personality. She is also wearing her thick black glasses. She usually chooses to wear contacts, but today she preferred the glasses. Hannah releases her ponytail, whipping her brown hair down, while waving at me. She looks like she just came out of shampoo commercial. My heart literally skips a beat.

"You okay?" she says as she grabs my arm.

"Yup. I'm fine, why do you ask?"

"You look like someone kicked you in the gut. Nobody kicked you in the gut — right? I'd kick their butts if they did!" Hannah threatens very seriously; people around us are lucky she hasn't started spouting off Spanish words or karate moves.

"I'm fine! I just saw you and couldn't catch my breath. That's all."

"You are so sweet, Ulysses Adair!" And she kisses me quickly on the lips.

We walk back to Penny University to get our bikes, so we can ride to the law library at Gulf University.

"My shift is from four to seven. Remember, on school nights fourteen-year olds can't work past 7 p.m., so I have to start my shift earlier."

"The law library is only a ten-minute bike ride, so we should have plenty of time."

As we start out on our bikes, I realize that this is the first afternoon that hasn't looked like rain for weeks. The balmy breeze feels good as we pass the rows of palm trees and oversized homes to the small private school campus known as Gulf University, which has a small law school and an even smaller law library.

We ride in silence most of the way to make good time, but Hannah quickly breaks the silence.

"We'll ride over to your place after my shift? My parents were thinking about asking you if you wanted a job."

"A job?" I ask dumbfounded.

"Sure, you're there all the time anyway, helping

us all out; we may as well pay you. Those were my dad's exact words. You know, busing tables, taking out the trash."

"That would be lit!"

"It would be awesome working together," Hannah adds. "Check with your dad first, though." As she said this, we arrive at the small campus.

The law library is a concrete, beige stucco building with red Spanish tiles on the roof. If it didn't have the sign saying Gulf University Law Library, I would've thought it was just another mega-sized Somerset home.

After locking our bikes, we stroll in, finding rows of thick green and tan leather-bound books. Several wooden tables, lined with chairs, finish off the room. The library is just one large open room, sparsely decorated with just a few paintings of contributors and deans hanging, stuck in time, on the walls. A bank of computers hugs the corner, while an old woman sits behind a checkout desk. Several college students with headphones and yellow legal pads sit like silent monks, flipping through immense law volumes.

"Where do we even start?" I whisper to Hannah, feeling a little intimidated. I can tell she was too because she took a step back toward the door to retreat. I stop her and grasp her hand. "Why don't we ask the little old lady behind the checkout desk?" I suggest in a whisper.

Hannah nods in agreement.

The woman's tag read Ruth, and she was definitely pushing eighty; her age spots were getting age spots. "Can I help you two young people?" I hate being called "young people."

"Yes, ma'am. We are doing a research project on a local law firm and need to find more information."

She leers at Hannah and then looks back at me with a smile, which is disconcerting. "You can try. We have a database of law firms in the state."

"Can it look nationally?" Hannah asks.

Ruth leers again at Hannah and answers her but addresses only me. "The database does have that feature."

"Great! We are looking for a law firm named GG&W."

"No names?" Ruth asks with an increasing negative tone.

"No names. Will that be okay?" Hannah asks.

Once again Ruth answers Hannah's question but looks directly at me, avoiding Hannah completely. I notice this is starting to irritate Hannah because she sways from side to side and her jaw starts to clench.

"We can try," Ruth says with little confidence. We also ask her to try Wright, first name Donald; and Gallant, first name Toby or Tobias, as possible partner names in the acronym.

Ruth tries all the letters backward and forward. Even adding Wright and Gallant, she is unable to find any law firm with those letters. Or the men's first and last names.

"There is nothing about the men either! No court cases they worked on? They were attorneys; shouldn't they be in your database?" Hannah inquires impatiently.

"Miss, if it's not in this computer, then those two names never tried a case. I cannot find a law firm, or any cases, related to the names and acronym you gave me. Have a good day." Again she answers

Hannah while looking at me.

We walk out and back to our bikes, feeling discouraged. "Why was she so rude to you?" I ask Hannah.

"Because I'm Latina," Hannah says somberly.

"What?!" I exclaim in a loud voice. "I'm going back in and giving her a piece of my mind!"

"You will not, Ulysses Adair! I'm used to it and pissed! Papi always says we should be proud but also rise above their prejudices."

"I'm sorry, I didn't realize; I never think of you as any different."

"I know, Ulysses, because you were brought up to be compassionate and considerate of others!" Hannah quickly changes the subject. "Sooo, we're back at square one with GG&W?"

"It looks that way, time wasted! I'm sorry," I add.

"Hopefully Mr. Nelson finds out something with his investigation," Hannah adds as I frown back at her, and we hurriedly bike back for her shift.

CHAPTER 27

- LOGAN -

PINEAPPLE EXPO MARKERS + MURDER BOARD = DEAD ENDS

Bob and I wait for Ulysses and Hannah in my living room, propping up a whiteboard and an easel I snagged from school.

Bob is sniffing markers. "You got to try this one; it smells like pineapple!" He is wearing an orange tracksuit, so he must have been feeling tropical.

I yank it out of his hand like a parent with a toddler. "Let's focus, Bob!"

I start to print pictures. The first picture came from today's obituary of Mr. Donald Wright, the victim. Next, I print pictures from our school website of Principal Thomas Barron and Silas O'Leary, writing "suspects" in the pineapple-smelling Expo marker under each picture. Bob hands me printouts of Terry and Jack from the newspaper. I put their pictures off to the side, label them "Connected?" and draw an arrow to Donald Wright's picture.

The kids burst in, making Ortiz bark. They come

in to the living room out of breath, telling us of their fools' errand to the law library. They look dejected.

"Maybe it's not a real law firm," I add. I write the acronym GG&W on the whiteboard, drawing arrows to Wright, Barron and then to a pinned picture of the Gallants. Under the acronym, I put a question mark for "G = Gallant and W= Wright," and "law firm."

Hannah draws a picture of a masked man. She is quite the artist. She then drew lines to the Gallants and O'Leary, adding a little house between the Gallant picture and O'Leary's name, then labeling it "Gallant house" and in parenthesis "federally owned."

We all stand back from the board and stare at it for a long time, our faces blank. "This is definitely easier on TV," Ulysses says.

Bob lets out an "Mmm..." and then, "Anyone hungry?"

It is eight, so I order a couple of pizzas from Somerset House of Pizza, while we sit and stare at the board.

"Oh, I never shared what I found!" Bob says enthusiastically. We all turn to him sitting in one of my club chairs. "See, you guys thought I wouldn't find anything; y'all don't have any faith, but I did."

"Spill it, Bob!" I demand.

"Why didn't you share with us sooner?" Ulysses asks.

"Um — I forgot," Bob says sheepishly. "Alright, so I interviewed my players; they didn't know nothin' about Terry and Jack using drugs or how someone could get into their lockers. Nobody knew nothin'," Bob reiterates, now more energetic and sharing with his usual animated arm gestures. He moves to the edge of the chair, leaning closer to us, "I put my feelers around, to my students."

"Your feelers?" Hannah asks.

"Let me tell you somethin', I know Mangrove, the students, and how they operate." Both Ulysses and Hannah roll their eyes at each other while I signal him to hurry up. "Well, the students, they knew nothin'."

"So, your feelers failed?" I said.

"Mmm," Bob grunts, "Yeah, until I spoke with Pedro."

"The custodian?" I ask.

"You know that's right! Dude's been there since day one. Pedro knows when anything is out of order; dude knows when light bulbs are out before they go — you get me?"

"Yeah, we get you; what did you find out, Bob?" Just then the doorbell rings, and Ortiz howls and growls, running to the door ready to protect us from the terrible pizza man. I tip the delivery man, put the pizzas on the coffee table, and we all dive in, still looking for Bob to finish. "So?"

"Well, Pedro informed me that only two people got the codes to the lockers." Bob takes a large slice of pepperoni pizza, curving the slice in one hand before shoving it in his mouth. He starts to talk with a partially full mouth, "Only two people have the combination to any school locker. The student gets it on day one, the only other person is..." Bob chews his slice, adding more dramatic effect, which I know he loves. He then takes a huge swig of the beer he has been nursing. "According to Pedro, who says he can't open the lockers, the only other person with all the students' combinations is ..." Bob pauses again.

We all sigh in unison. "Okay, okay. The assistant principal! Mary Clifton — my ex."

"She's not your ex! One date does not mean you were an item!" I explain to Bob, slightly frustrated.

Bob finishes by adding, "I'm counting her as an ex! Anyway, Pedro said they keep the combos in a three-ring binder in the safe in the assistant principal's offices. They only take it out to get combos when kids forget them."

Ulysses stood up to the board. "So if Terry and Jack are telling the truth, the only other person that could get in their lockers is Assistant Principal Clifton?" As he said this, he wrote her name on the board and drew an arrow to Jack and Terry.

"She can't be the murderer. She was in the gymnasium in full view of everyone the entire time. Why would a new assistant principal want to frame two seniors on her first week, or at all?" Hannah says, standing up and going over to the board with Ulysses.

Ortiz takes advantage of their distraction, popping his head up on the coffee table to lick the grease and cheese from one of the partially empty boxes before I shoo him away.

"You make an excellent point. She does act strange, but that is not a reason to kill Mr. Wright either. She has the perfect alibi, too, and what would be her motive?"

"I don't know, but she digs me," Bob adds, smiling and taking another piece of pizza.

"I feel that we're missing something right in front of our faces," I say, staring at the board. "I know there is a connection somewhere." I look over at the time. "This war room is over for tonight. It's ten o'clock on a school night."

"Tomorrow's the wake for Mr. Wright. That will be a good time to find some clues, maybe his connection with Principal Barron and the Gallants," Hannah says doggedly.

"We haven't seen Conrad either; I hope he's doing okay," Ulysses adds.

"I haven't had the chance to tell you yet: Bob says Conrad has to move back to New York with his mom." With this news, Hannah puts her head on Ulysses' shoulder.

CHAPTER 28

- ULYSSES-

WAKE, WAKE, DON'T TELL ME

"What's the big dealio? I've worn clothes other than tracksuits," Mr. Nelson says as we all give him weird looks while Dad drives us toward the wake at Mr. Wright's beach home. We all laugh at how well Mr. Nelson suits up. Dad and I have rarely seen him not wearing his trademark tracksuits. Dad and I wear simple ties, but Hannah is wearing a long black slinky dress, almost too sensual for a wake.

Mr. Wright's beach house is a white stone Art Deco block sitting on the edge of the Gulf of Mexico. It sits sterile and cold, perfect for a wake, I think. We all pile out of the little car, struggling to smooth out wrinkles and not look like we've just woken up. A dozen other cars are jamming the side streets and double parked by their gated driveway. I can see Conrad and his mother greeting visitors as we walk up their expansive driveway.

"Wow! Mmm, mmm!" Mr. Nelson utters to Dad when he sees Conrad's mother. He told me she was a runway model, sometimes showing me pictures, but somewhere in the back of my mind I thought he was lying — not anymore. As we approach Conrad and his mom, Bob shoves in front of Dad, sticking out his hand and straightening his tie. "I'm so sorry for your loss," Mr. Nelson casually says with Conrad's mother's hand in his, "Miss?"

"Ms. Thatch. Vanessa Thatch. And you are?" she replies with a little disdain.

Conrad speaks up, "This is Mr. Nelson, my gym teacher and basketball coach."

"Prefer physical education teacher," Bob says, then gets an elbow from Dad. "Gym teacher is fine."

Conrad finishes the introductions, "Mr. Adair, my history teacher, and Ulysses Adair, my friend and his son." Almost forgetting Hannah, "Oh, and Hannah Reyes, my other friend."

"I've heard so much about you. Thank you for befriending my son. Welcome," Ms. Thatch says somberly.

"We are very sorry for your loss," Dad adds to Ms. Thatch's kind words.

We walk into the foyer of Conrad's home, a place I have been to many times, but it was the first time for Dad, Mr. Nelson, and Hannah, so when they enter, gasps, oohs, and aws are exclaimed. I can always relate to Conrad being nervous in this place; even the dust looked expensive, if the place had any dust.

Hannah and I turn to Conrad, who has momentarily broken away from his mother.

"Hey man, sorry about your dad," I say, not really knowing what to say, and remembering all the trite things people said to me when my mom died. I can't remember anyone saying anything meaningful to me the day we laid her to rest.

Hannah hugs Conrad, "We hear you're moving to New York City. Is this true?"

"Yeah, Mom's got a big place in the Dakota Building. You know that's where John Lennon lived. Yoko still does," Conrad says, almost lost in his thoughts.

Hannah hugs Conrad again, holding back her tears. "Wish you could stay. We are going to miss you so much."

"Do you know why someone would do this?" I boldly ask.

"No. I don't know who would stab my dad, Ulysses! Sometimes I wish I had. He was a jerk."

"Conrad, you don't mean that!" Hannah says, wiping away tears.

"Why not? I lived under his thumb my whole life, and now..." He didn't finish the sentence because he started to cry himself, pushing his blonde, wavy hair away.

I notice Dad and Mr. Nelson drift toward the food while I give Hannah a look. "Conrad, is there somewhere we could talk? Privately."

"Yeah, sure." Conrad leads us through two sliding doors, adorned with samurais in red and black, that open to an expansive black and white tiled floor. Black leather couches and a large chrome desk fill the space.

"It's my father's office, was my father's office," he corrects. "What's up?" he asks, confused as to why we need privacy.

Hannah relays our entire experience the night his father was killed. I include parts of the office fight, which produce a confused look on Conrad's face.

We tell him everything, including how we, Dad, and Mr. Nelson are investigating and how his dad's murder may also be connected to Terry and Jack's suspension.

"What!" is his only response; his face looks stunned.

"Why weren't you answering our messages and why did you act weird the night of your dad's death?" I ask.

Conrad continues to look stunned, trying to find words to respond. I think everything is hitting him hard because he looks like he may faint, swaying in place. The floor looks hard, so Hannah takes him by the hand to one of the black leather couches. Conrad puts his hands to his head.

"Take a deep breath, man. Sorry we sprang this on you at your dad's wake."

Conrad finally looks up. "No, I really appreciate you guys caring about this. He was a jack off but didn't deserve to be killed. I was standoffish because my dad told me right before my game that he was going to move overseas and I was going off to New York to live with my mom."

Shocked, Hannah blurts, "Why was your Dad moving overseas? Where?"

"I don't know, but either way, dead or alive, I was moving to New York. That's why I was a little standoffish. I didn't, don't, want to leave you guys."

Hannah and I sit on either side of Conrad. We both give him a big hug.

"Conrad, can you remember anything your dad did or said that could link back to his murder?" I ask.

"That Detective Brute asked me the same thing. I told him I do remember seeing a blue piece of paper with cut-out letters glued to them, you know like in the movies."

"What'd it say?" I ask eagerly.

"I only remember bits. I saw the word *MANGROVE*, that caught my eye for obvious reasons, but I also saw the word *GYM-MECHANICAL* and *JEWELS*. There were a lot of other words, but I couldn't see them all because the font was too small. I only saw those words because the person who made the letter used really big print for those words."

"Jewels! Anything more? Did he look more angry than usual?" I ask, trying to process this new information.

"Ulysses! You know my dad. He was always a jerk. Hated me and hated basketball. He even hated that I attended a public school."

"What is the connection to your dad and Mr. Barron?" Hannah adds.

"I don't know," Conrad says, shrugging.

"Your dad pushed him and argued about this Gallant family. Does a law firm called GG&W mean anything to you? Did your dad, as lawyer, work with or against this firm?"

Conrad looks up quickly, making his hair whip back. "Yeah. I mean, Dad would refer to it as his firm, GG&W. I have heard him speaking on the phone to people in New York about GG&W — I think."

"The W does mean Wright!" Hannah confirms.

"Yeah. Look over here." Conrad leads us to his dad's desk. It looks like a desk of a super villain with the black metal and chrome.

"Yesterday, Mom and I were going through his

things in here. I was messing around with his desk. Sitting in his chair, playing with his things. Knowing he'd kill me if he were alive. Then I found this."

Conrad proceeds to act out what he did yesterday, sitting in his dad's chair, when he reaches for an ornate, jade paperweight statue of a roaring lion. He pulls the lion toward him, and we hear a tiny click sound in his father's desk, revealing a secret compartment.

"Wow!" Hannah and I chorus in unison.

Conrad opens the hidden compartment on his dad's desk. In the small compartment of the drawer is a series of business cards.

Conrad picks one up and hands it to me. I take the card and flip it over. In the middle of the card is a large crest. The crest includes an old British lion climbing the back of three bold cursive letters; **T**, **L**, and **M**. The letters are raised off the card, making it look very ornate. The card itself is made of thick, soft paper. Below the crest, in bold script, are the words **GIBBINS, GALLANT AND WRIGHT**, listing an address in New York City, with a phone number also in New York.

"Wow!" Hannah said looking at the card; sounding like Mr. Nelson. "GG&W! So Gallant and Wright were in the same law firm. Who is Gibbins? Why does that sound familiar? And what does this have to do with Barron?"

"I don't know," I reply, thinking we now have more questions than when we started. "Conrad, do you know what these letters stand for?"

"I have no clue. That's all I really know," Conrad responds, parting his blonde hair again, looking exhausted. "Dad never spoke about work. He kept everything from me, and I never cared to ask."

"Can we keep this? My dad and Mr. Nelson have got to see this," I question energetically.

"No worries," Conrad responds. We both give him more hugs before moving on to find Dad and Mr. Nelson.

Hannah and I push open the doors of the study, leaving Conrad with his memories. As we are leaving the study, we both bump into what feels like a brick wall, looking up in our haste to find an irritated Ms. Clifton.

CHAPTER 29

- LOGAN -

REDHEADS AREN'T FUN AT WAKES

We both look at the food table. Bob is practically drooling, but I also never pass on a free meal, especially when it is catered by the rich and famous.

"Dude, they got lobster tail! Now that's what I'm talkin' about!" Bob, not using his indoor voice, might as well have shouted, "I don't belong here!" The smell of lobster brings me back to my childhood in Maine. We both tuck in, as Jill used to always say in her English accent.

"Do you see anyone else from Mangrove?" I ask Bob.

"Nah. We the only suckers at this wake."

"Keep your eyes peeled for anything out of the ordinary." I grab some cheese and crackers along with the biggest jumbo shrimp I've ever seen. I start to walk around the huge mansion, leaving Bob to graze. The view is spectacular. The patio doors span the length of the room, making the living area feel twice as big. The blues and greens of the Gulf visually meeting the hues of the pool give the appearance of being right on top of the water. Wow, so this is how the 1% lives. Donald Wright had huge multi-colored blown glass on pedestals scattered all over the living room.

"Great place for kid to be raised," I mumble to myself.

Suddenly the frames on the wall draw me closer. There are several of Donald and Conrad, both looking unhappy. Another picture hangs in the middle of the wall. This picture is hung in a large golden frame. The picture is an eight by ten black and white. Conrad isn't in it, just his dad and six other men. The picture was taken in a restaurant. All six men sat in a large booth with wine and plates of pasta set on a checkered tablecloth. I identify Donald Wright immediately, having met him several times. The others I don't recognize.

"Wait a minute, I know you," I whisper to myself, pointing a finger at a man sitting in the booth. He had what appears to be a dimpled chin and blonde hair. I thought back to the article on Hannah's phone when we read the obituaries of the Gallants. This is Toby Gallant, the head of the murdered Gallant family! What was he doing in a picture with Donald Wright?

"What the hell!" I softly exclaim as Bob comes up behind me. I relay my findings to Bob and take out my iPhone and take several up-close photos of the picture when no one is looking. As soon as I put my phone away, I hear a voice behind us calling, "Bobby, oh Bobby!"

"Damn!" I say out loud to Bob.

Bob and I spin around. He still has his mouth full

of lobster, and the side of his chin is dripping butter.

"Ms. Clifton, what a pleasant surprise," I say raising my eyebrows to Bob.

She rushes over to us, wearing a very inappropriate dress for a wake, especially a wake for a student's parent. It is green and sparkly. A low v-neck in the front exposes too much cleavage. She looks very out of place amongst the one percenters. The length of her dress — well, just using the term length is being generous. Maybe Bob is right — I have become a prude!

"Hello, boys," Ms. Clifton says seductively. "Bobby, why haven't you called?" She pouts, putting her hands on his cheeks, and brings him in for a very tight, long hug. Hopefully she doesn't see the disgusted look on my face.

"Mare." He already has a nickname for her? "I called you, babe, like twenty times. You don't answer Bobby," Bob finishes, in not only a Barry White voice, but he is now referring to himself in the third person!

"Oh baby, I've been so busy, but I've been thinking of you," Ms. Clifton says, pulling his tie closer to her like a fisherman with a line. "It's so sad to have a student's father die, especially under such — tragic circumstances. Principal Barron wanted me to go as the Mangrove representative. Let me get you guys some drinks; it's an open bar!"

"Oh yeah! I'll have a beer m'lady," Bob says, making me almost vomit in my mouth.

"Yeah, I guess I'll have one, too," I say hesitantly.

After she walks to the bar, I pull Bob aside. "Don't you think she is a little insensitive?"

Bob frowns and lowers his shoulders in

disappointment. "Dude, jealousy doesn't suit you."

"I'm not jealous! That woman has a few screws loose. She also could be involved!"

"Logan, Logan, let me tell you somethin', when a woman calls you got to answer, my friend. Anyway, you said it yourself: She was in plain sight the entire night of the murder."

I frown, especially because I know my arguments will be of no use. Bob is smitten. "I've got a bad feeling about her. Be careful!"

"Be careful about what?" Mary Clifton says, coming over to hand us our drinks.

"Nothing. My boy Logan was just saying something about basketball," Bob quickly covers.

"Well, I unfortunately have got to go," Mary says to Bob.

"Girl, you just got here!" protested Bob.

"I know, but I have a long parent meeting in the morning and have some errands to run before then," Mary says, her voice suddenly changing. This voice is cold and stern, compared to the immature, flirtatious tone she typically uses with Bob and me. "I'm sorry, Bob; rain check?" She then, to my shock, gives Bob a huge kiss on the lips and another hug while I look away in pure disbelief. My suspicions are growing with this woman; something is off.

Mary starts to walk away, turning to wave to both of us. I wave back while Bob blows her a kiss. As she blows one back to Bob, a door opens in front of her and Ulysses and Hannah walk right into her. It appears that they banged into each other hard.

Ulysses looks shocked at who it is, while Hannah says, "Oh, Ms. Clifton. We're so sorry!"

Ms. Clifton turns to both of the kids, points her

finger in disgust, and says in a raised voice, "You brats watch where the hell you're walking!" The entire room falls silent after hearing this. She then storms out in disgust.

CHAPTER 30

- ULYSSES -

CUBAN SANDWICHES AND MAFIA CONNECTIONS

We arrive at Penny University after the wake.
"So that was an interesting wake," Hannah says with a smirk as we sit down at a large table near the cafe's merchandise counter.

Hannah and I are starved. We didn't have a chance to eat anything at Mr. Wright's wake. Dad and Mr. Nelson, on the other hand, say they are full, which makes me a little upset. Did they do any investigative work? Or did they do what Mr. Nelson always does around food? Gorge!

Hannah and I order a couple of Cuban sandwiches with a pot of coffee in a large French press for all of us to share. The sandwich hits the spot, and it is even better washing it down with some hot coffee.

"What did you guys find out that you couldn't tell

us in the car?" Dad asks as Mr. Nelson flags down a waitress. Feeling left out, he orders a Cuban sandwich, too.

Hannah tells Dad and Mr. Nelson everything Conrad said to us at the wake, handing the business card over to Dad. Mr. Nelson leans over to read it with Dad. I see their eyes widen at the same time.

"The law firm GG&W business card was in a secret compartment in Mr. Wright's desk?" Dad exclaims, practically spilling his coffee.

"Gibbins!" shouts Hannah. Realizing her voice was loud and people could be snooping, she lowers it immediately. "I knew we've seen that name." She whips out her phone, "Look here." Hannah opens the article about the death of the Gallant family. The sister," Hannah continues eagerly as the three of us look at her blankly. "Samantha Gallant, wife to Toby and sister to a Sally Gibbins. This can't be coincidence. Maybe she was Toby's partner."

I hug her for this nugget of information while Dad and Mr. Nelson both give high fives.

"Also, the picture I took at the wake; Toby Gallant and Donald Wright are both in it. I know I recognize one of the other men," Dad says, typing into his phone. "Yes, right here. Guss Leoni. I remember seeing him in one of those true crime shows on cable. He is a mob boss working out of New York City. Leoni is wanted for a variety of crimes. I sat up late one night watching an expose about this guy. He is a bad dude."

Dad shows a picture of his mugshot from his phone. It matches one of the men in the picture Dad took from the wake. Guss Leoni was pictured sitting right in the center. His arm was around Mr. Wright.

He had his sleeves rolled up and his curly black hair had streaks of gray.

"There are three other men in that picture. The initials on the business card T-L-M could be other mob ties. Maybe those initials stand for different mafia bosses or associates. The L stands for Guss Leoni; the others must be his accomplices in the photo," Dad says.

"More stuff to put on the murder board!" Hannah says cheerfully.

"Gallant, Gibbins, and Wright. They must have been private attorneys — only working for the mafia. That's why you couldn't find anything at the law library. They must have used the business cards for associates working with them. If they got into trouble with the law, they could make their one phone call to their personal attorneys. We have to find out what the other initials on the crest stand for," Dad says as he looks over every inch of the card.

"Forget about it!" Mr. Nelson says loudly, with a smirk in a very weak imitation of an Italian accent. It actually sounds more like Russian. Nobody laughs.

"Mr. Wright was an attorney for a mobster?" I question, puzzled.

"And this Toby Gallant fella," Mr. Nelson says, chowing down on his Cuban sandwich that just arrived.

"How do you find out who they are?" Mr. Nelson asks.

"As I say to my students: We have the World Wide Web at our fingertips," Dad says eagerly as Hannah, Dad and I wake up our phones and start to search for the mafia members.

"Hannah, why don't you look at the FBI's most

wanted list?" Dad suggests. "Ulysses, check the initials on Google and try a reverse phonebook search using the phone number and address from the business card. I'm going to enter the information into this database I found online. You can browse mugshots in New York. I know there must be thousands, but maybe if we find one, that one can lead us to the others. It's a long shot, but I think it's worth the time."

"What do you think about the piece of paper Conrad saw that said Mangrove, gym, mechanical, and jewels?" I ask Dad.

"Yeah, that. I think someone was blackmailing him. So now this case may involve the mafia and jewels. The note sounds like a meeting place and what to either bring or someone was supposed to bring to him."

"I remember Mr. Wright putting a blue paper into his suit jacket last Friday when he argued with Principal Barron. Does that mean he got it from Barron? Or was showing it to Barron?"

They all shrug.

"I found more information on Guss Leoni," Hannah says gleefully.

"What is he wanted for?" I ask.

"This report says he's a crime boss out of New York City, and he's wanted for smuggling, murder, kidnapping. Wow! You name it, he's done it," she says. Her demeanor quickly changes to gloom. "I just read an update. He's dead. But it does list known associates."

She starts to list them off her phone while Dad and I type rapidly on our phones. Thankfully, Penny University has good Wifi.

"He has two associates listed. First, Michael Taban." Dad and I search Google for a picture.

"I found him!" I proclaim. "Will you look at that. Another match. He's wanted for similar crimes and is also a big crime boss from NYC." Michael Taban was thick looking man with a cue ball head sitting right next to Toby Gallant in the picture.

"He's vile," Hannah expresses. "His other associate listed here is — "

Before Hannah could finish, Dad pipes in. "Gio Mecoli?"

"Yeah. How did you know?" Hannah says shocked.

"I googled Michael Taban and found a news report of him and Gio being murdered two weeks ago. Michael was also wanted for smuggling and was a crime boss in New Jersey and New York."

He points to the picture of an older wrinkled man sitting in the booth on the other side of Mr. Wright. As he says this, we all feel dread seep through our bodies.

"Everyone in this picture is — dead?" Mr. Nelson nervously asks.

"No, not everyone. Who is this last man sitting at the end of the booth next to Toby Gallant with the creepy eyes? It's like they are following you," Hannah says, shaking off a chill.

"I don't know, but these men died recently. Leoni died the week before the other two," I add. "Dad, look! Taban the T, Mecoli the M, and Guss Leoni is the L. The mafia clients of Mr. Wright and his partners Gallant and Gibbins are all dead," I comment wearily.

"Is someone bumping these mob bosses off?

Taking them to the mattresses," Mr. Nelson says, half-jokingly but then soon realizing the reality of his words and swallowing hard.

"Why would three mob bosses be in the same photo with their three lawyers?" I say flatly.

"Why would the three lawyers be working together? And have their own business card?" Dad adds. I can see Dad is working hard to mentally put all the pieces together. I haven't seen him in such deep thought for a while. His eyes narrow, wrinkling his forehead.

"How and why is this happening way down here in Somerset?" Hannah says.

"I don't know. I mean Gallant had a home here in Somerset thirty years ago and now Wright. Or, at least, he did have a home here," I say, trying to comfort her and trying to connect the dots myself.

"It seems like when we get close to answering a question, two more pop up in its place," Hannah says dejectedly.

Dad finally breaks from his trance. "No, I think we are making great strides. We just have a few more pieces to fit together and then this case will be solved."

"What? How? Why don't we go to the police with what we got then?" Bob asks eagerly.

Dad answers in a confident, but cautious tone, "Not quite yet. Soon though — real soon."

"I'll get everyone another cup of joe," Mr. Nelson says, trying to be helpful. As soon as Mr. Nelson gets up from the table, someone around the corner runs away, bumping into our waitress, sending her tray in the air and crashing on the floor.

We all cringe from the loud bangs and sound of

glass breaking. It makes me think of Dad's story of how he met Mom.

I look around the corner, since I was facing that wall. Dad looks over his shoulder, concerned. We both get up, along with Mr. Nelson. We help the waitress pick up her spilled tray.

"Are you okay? What happened here?" Dad asks the waitress. It was Lisa Nance, one of Dad's old students.

"Hey, Mr. Adair. Thanks. No, I'm fine." She sounds a little shaken. "Some woman was creeping around the corner. I think she was trying to eavesdrop on your table, Mr. Adair. All of a sudden, she turned on her heel and ran hard into me. She didn't even say sorry because she continued on out the door."

"Did you get a good look at her?" Dad inquires.

"Yeah. I guess. She had really short brownish hair, mid-fifties — I think. She was wearing big black sunglasses," Lisa says as she finishes cleaning and then leaves us to attend to her other customers.

Dad turns to us with a ghostly white face and nervously says, "I think we may be in danger."

CHAPTER 31

- LOGAN -

I DIDN'T LIE TO THE SHERIFF. I ONLY LIED TO THE DEPUTY

Ulysses looks back at Hannah. They look a little spooked. "Dad, why do you think we're in danger? Because some woman was listening in on us? Come on!"

"Yo Logan, it was probably a reporter," Bob adds nervously.

"That was no reporter! Let's reconvene tomorrow at my house," I suggest before Bob heads home. Ulysses says his goodbyes to Hannah, and we head home ourselves.

The ride home starts off silent, but quickly changes when Ulysses asks, "Do you think someone is following us? Come on, Dad."

"I think so. I don't want you and Hannah looking into this murder anymore. It's too dangerous. If the killer found out we were investigating him, then who knows what would happen to us. Especially since the mafia could be involved!"

"Why give up? I thought you said we were close," Ulysses adds dejectedly.

"I know. I know. But I can't put you guys in any danger. I'm going to bring what we have to Deputy Diaz in the morning. Hopefully Diaz and Detective Brute can make sense of everything and finish the job. Promise me you and Hannah will stop investigating Mr. Wright's murder." Ulysses is about to respond, but nods in agreement. We stay silent as we pull into River Creek.

The next morning is pretty uneventful. The carpool is shorter than usual since we don't have to pick up O'Leary. Bob seems a little rattled. He is probably thinking mob bosses are hiding behind every corner, about to bump him off like in the movies. Sam tries to make small talk, but I'm too lost in thought to join in. I am running through the events of the last few days in my mind.

I can't believe it's only Wednesday. It feels like weeks have passed since Mr. Wright's murder, but it has only been a few days. Terry and Jack have their expulsion hearing tomorrow morning. I know that case is connected to the murder; I just have to prove it. I know I told Ulysses that we would back off this case, but I only meant that he and Hannah should back off, just in case of any danger. We need to get this case solved, and if I hand it over to the police now it would take too much time for them to catch up. I have a couple of scenarios in my mind as to what may have happened, but I have to fill in some of the gaps and verify some facts. That's the true purpose in wanting to meet with Deputy Diaz.

When I arrive at Mangrove High, I head straight into the office. Ms. Simmons is busily typing on her computer and does not notice me approaching the office counter. Ms. Simmons only started here last summer, but she has become a fixture here at Mangrove, always so helpful to the teachers. I don't know why Ulysses can't stand the sight of her. Yes, she is old and frail, but as I explained to him, the elderly just get set in their ways.

Ms. Simmons looks up, startled. She rips her bifocals off, so she can see me better with her large green eyes.

"Ah. Mr. Adair," she says in a frail voice, making me feel a little guilty that she has to do all the duties in the office since Mrs. Lafayette has been out sick with the flu. "What can I do for you?" Ms. Simmons asks.

"I'm here to see Deputy Diaz. Is he in?"

"Oh yes. I hope it isn't urgent! We have had enough drama around here," she comments, making a clicking sound with her tongue.

"Where is the administration?" I notice their doors are open and the rooms are empty.

"Mr. Barron is home sick," she says with the side of her mouth slightly twitching. "Ms. Clifton out on school business," Ms. Simmons finishes, smiling at me, exposing her mouthful of dentures.

I thank Ms. Simmons and walk behind the office counter to Deputy Diaz's office. I knock first, hear him say "Come in," and close the door behind me.

Jose Diaz, a mid-thirties dark skinned Venezuelan, sits in his dark green sheriff's deputy uniform behind a small desk. Files are laid upon his desk in every direction, and more are stacked in the corner by his file cabinet. His office is stuffy, but pictures of his children and his wife personalize the space.

"Logan! How goes it my man!" Deputy Diaz greets energetically, but he quickly remembers the previous day's events, and the black cloud currently around the school, and continues more soberly. "Hey, how you holding up?" he asks, getting up now and shaking my hand.

"Fine," I reply.

"How about Ulysses? Finding a murdered body is something that will stay with you." When he says this, he looks out into a corner of his office and zones out for a minute.

I break his reflective moment. "Jose. I have information about Donald Wright's murder," I say in a hushed tone.

Deputy Diaz shifts in his seat. "Si?"

"I've been looking into his murder."

"What!" Deputy Diaz exclaims, sitting bolt upright.

I put my finger over my lips giving him the universal sign to stay quiet. "I think Principal Barron is somehow involved in Donald Wright's murder."

"How do you know this?"

I explain what Conrad told Ulysses and Hannah, while adding how we found the picture on the wall with the three mob bosses and their lawyers. I also reluctantly add the connection to O'Leary's house and how he was now living in the Gallants' home. I also add the detail about the holes being dug by a person in a black mask.

Deputy Diaz takes in what I say, nodding and making notes in his pad. "So why do you think Principal Barron is involved? Nothing you have told me links Barron to Wright."

I am hesitant to share that I got a copy of his

personnel file, listing the GG&W law firm as his reference. I only let Deputy Diaz know what he had admitted to me on the night of the murder. He and Donald Wright were once business partners. I know I should share everything, but if Deputy Diaz knew I broke into the office and made copies of our principal's personnel file, I'd be fired for sure.

He frowns at me and starts to breathe through his nose more than his mouth, creating a loud, uncomfortable atmosphere. "I have to report this to the sheriff and Detective Brute," he says reluctantly. "You think this was a mob hit?"

"Maybe. It's definitely mob related," I add.

"Wow," Diaz says, shaking his head and leaning back in his chair.

"Question: Did you, by chance, go to the Wright mansion?" I ask.

"Ah — yes. Detective Brute said I should go since I knew Conrad from school. Why?"

"I think you could get a promotion if you do what I say."

"I'm listening," Deputy Diaz says, leaning forward against his desk.

"You could start with the picture hanging in Wright's beach house. You could say you remembered seeing a familiar face in that photograph. You could say you remember one of the men from the picture on the FBI's most wanted page."

"We thought Wright was dealing with shady characters, and when we interviewed Conrad, he did mention the blue letter you just mentioned. What jewels?"

"I don't know." Yet, I add to myself. "If you put this

all together, and report your findings to Detective Brute, they'd promote you in a heartbeat." I also show him Wright's business card. "There are more of these hidden in his desk."

"We did find these and followed up on them. We aren't complete idiots," Deputy Diaz says, smiling.

"What were your findings?" I eagerly ask.

"Less than you found. We didn't find out anything about the initials on the card, but we did trace the connection of Wright to the Gallant family murders. Detective Brute is licking his chops. He thinks if he uncovers Wright's murderer, he may also solve the Gallant murders."

"What did you find out about Gibbins on the card?" I add anxiously.

"We only found out about this woman named Sally Gibbins. She was presumed to have been murdered with the Gallants. Oh, and she was Mrs. Gallant's sister and the children's godmother. Do you think she was also a lawyer to these mob bosses?"

"I don't know, I thought you guys would know. Anything more?" I say.

"No. Nothing. Logan, you know I can't share information from an ongoing police investigation."

"It's not a 'I scratch your back, you scratch my back' kind of thing," I say smiling.

"Ah — no! No more amateur investigating! If Detective Brute found out, he'd lock you up for obstruction of justice. Not to mention your teaching career would be in the toilet."

"I know. No more. I promise. Can you do one more thing for me?"

"Yeah, sure, as long as it doesn't break any

laws," Deputy Diaz says, half-jokingly.

"When you investigate these mob bosses, and dig deeper into the Gallant connection, can you please cross-reference with the people at school? Start with Barron, but it may be deeper than that. I think you should check others that work at Mangrove: O'Leary, Clifton." And I tell him about the lockers of Terry and Jack and how Ms. Clifton is the only other person with the combination.

"Logan, I know some teachers often don't get along with their administrators, but man, you're taking this to a whole new level. I also don't see how you can jump so easily from the drug charge of two students to the murder in the mechanical room of our gymnasium," Deputy Diaz says chuckling.

"Just promise me," I plead.

"Sure, sure, I'm going right now. Don't worry; let the real police take care of this."

CHAPTER 32

- ULYSSES -

PROMISES CAN BE BROKEN — A LITTLE

"My dad said we shouldn't investigate the murder anymore," I say to Hannah, feeling dejected. We have just sat down to lunch and she has inquired as to what my dad believes our next steps should be. "Dad's worried about the mob connections and thinks we should stop and let the police do the investigating."

"I understand that. He's just looking out for us," Hannah responds.

We sit in silence as I pick at my mac and cheese. Mangrove's lunches aren't the most appealing. I guess school lunches across the country are all about the same. School today was a lot like the last few days — blah. Mr. O'Leary was non-confrontational, students are slowly forgetting about the murder and gossiping about me and Hannah finding the body less and less. Things are slowly getting back to normal.

"Your dad didn't say we couldn't investigate

Terry's and Jack's drug charges," Hannah says, breaking the silence.

"I guess. Yeah, you're right. That wouldn't break Dad's trust, and maybe we could find the connection to the murder," I add.

"So, where should we start?" Hannah asks.

"Well, it seems like if Terry and Jack are in fact telling the truth, then we should start with Ms. Clifton. She's the only other person with the locker combinations. I've got an idea!"

We both get up from the table and throw our lunches away. We are too excited to eat anyway.

"Where are we going?" Hannah asks as I take her hand.

"The office. I want to ask Ms. Clifton some questions."

We both head into the office, holding hands. Ms. Simmons sees us immediately and chides, "No PDA!" in her frail elderly voice.

"We're just holding hands, Ms. Simmons," I explain.

She narrows her wrinkling face at us and stares at us with her wide, green, beady eyes. This causes me to immediately drop Hannah's hand.

"How can I help you two?" she asks.

"We were wondering if we could have a chat with Ms. Clifton," I tell her.

"You two are out of luck. Ms. Clifton is away on school business," Ms. Simmons proudly explains.

"What school business?" Hannah asks.

"None of your business, Ms. Reyes," Ms. Simmons retorts in a rude tone, her eyes growing wider. We both leave the office no better off than when we entered.

"Well, that got us nowhere!" Hannah comments. She then whispers, "Hey, your dad took those pictures of Principal Barron's personnel file. He also took pictures of Clifton's. Didn't he send them to your phone?"

"Yeah. He forwarded them to me," I reply, smiling with confidence at Hannah.

We find a bench near my dad's classroom. His room looks empty; he's probably eating lunch with Mr. Nelson.

I open my phone to the pictures Dad took and find Ms. Clifton's personnel file. Hannah puts her head on my shoulder as we scroll through Ms. Clifton's resume and references. "Nothing out of the ordinary," I say to Hannah.

We read that she attended a small college in Georgia. She was a P.E. teacher for eight years before getting her master's degree at the same Georgia college and she interned at the same school. "Peach City High. We should give them a call."

"Why?" Hannah asks.

"To see what they know." A number is listed and I quickly try it, but I get a "beep, beep, beep — this number is not a working number, please hang up and dial again."

"It doesn't work." I try again with the same result. "That's weird," I say as Hannah furiously searches on her phone for Peach City High.

"Maybe they changed their number. I'm going to try this number." She finds the school and clicks on the contact us icon. It is ringing.

"Good afternoon! It's a great day at Peach City High!" The Georgian-accented woman squeals into the phone. "Hello!" The woman says again as Hannah fumbles on what to say.

"Ah yes, this is Hannah — Mangrove," she stutters, not wanting to use her real name. "Yes, hi, we are looking to hire a former employee of yours for an administrative job down here in Florida. Her name is Mary Clifton. Could you put me through to anyone that could give me any insight into her overall job performance?" Hannah says, trying to deepen her voice and keep a straight face. The other end falls silent for a moment.

"Did you say Mary Clifton?" The woman repeats her name for clarification.

"Yes ma'am, her resume lists that she taught P.E. for you guys," Hannah says as she becomes more comfortable in her acting role.

Another long silence takes place on the other end of the line.

"Who is this? Is this some sort of joke?" The woman now sounds suspicious and concerned.

"Why? Can you not put me through to whomever can assist me in providing a recommendation for Mary Clifton? We want to hire her for a job here at our school," Hannah prompts while I give her a thumbs up for doing a great job.

Just then, Hannah's face looks terrified; her mocha skin turns white as a ghost as she lowers the phone. I can hear the woman on the phone yelling over and over again, "Where did you say you were calling from?"

"What did she say? What's wrong?" I ask, feeling a pit in my stomach forming.

After Hannah clicks the end button she looks at me in horror. "The secretary of Peach City High said

Mary Clifton died last year of cancer."

    Hannah grabs my shirt and pulls me nervously away from the bench we were sitting on and into a corner just under our expansive staircase. She looks stunned and almost afraid to ask but does anyway. "What does this mean? Ulysses, if Mary Clifton died, then who is our assistant principal?"

CHAPTER 33

- ULYSSES -

WHO IS THE REAL MARY CLIFTON?

We both are in shock from what we learned from the phone call. Mary Clifton, our new assistant principal, is not who she claims to be.

"What the hell?! She's an imposter!"

"Let's try her references. It may be just a coincidence. Maybe there is another Peach City High School," Hannah says, trying to be optimistic. I quickly do an internet search on my phone and find no other Peach City High Schools; I shake my head in disbelief.

"Ulysses, you call her references. I'll call her college," Hannah adds.

"They won't give you any information unless you have her Social Security number," I say.

"Oh, do you mean — this?" Hannah says, showing me the Social Security number on Ms. Clifton's application.

"Nice!" I add.

I first call a number that Ms. Clifton put down on

her resume as her previous principal from Peach City High. I dial the number thinking I will get Peach City High again, but instead I get a Chinese restaurant in Atlanta, Georgia. I try the next two phone numbers. Both are listed as Peach City High teachers; the first one I call is a pizza place in Atlanta and the last number is disconnected. This is getting strange. I turn to Hannah, who is on hold with North Georgia State College.

"Ah yes. I am trying to request my transcripts. Yes, I do have my Social Security number," Hannah says with relief. "And what address do you have in your records? Yes, that is my current address here in Somerset." She smiles at me as she writes down the information she receives from the college.

"So?" I said energetically.

"They do have Mary Clifton's transcripts. I am thinking they are probably for the Mary Clifton who died of cancer. Our Mary Clifton, or whatever her name is, must've stolen her identity and ordered her transcripts using this stolen Social Security number. I also found out that she has an address on file — which they were nice enough to give to me."

"Awesome! You had more luck than I did. Why would someone list restaurants as references? Wouldn't Principal Barron check those references?" I ask a confused Hannah.

Hannah can only shrug and then asks, "So you think our Ms. Clifton took on the identity of this Ms. Clifton who died in Georgia of cancer? Got her transcripts and faked her resume? You're right, Principal Barron would've checked those references, even if everything else was squeaky clean. Doesn't this seem very devious just to get an assistant principal job?"

"Yeah, but we've proven that she is a liar, though I don't know why. But Terry and Jack could definitely use this information in their trial. How can someone who lies and commits identity theft be leading their hearing tomorrow?" I ask puzzled.

"Okay, what time do we meet your dad and Mr. Nelson?" Hannah asks.

"Well, Dad said after Mr. Nelson's basketball practice, so probably 6:00. Dad said he's going to work late in his classroom, grading. Do you work today?"

"Yeah, but I'm going to cancel. My parents will be okay with it. Wednesdays are pretty slow," Hannah adds.

"Okay. I don't think we should tell my dad. He will think we're putting ourselves in harm's way again," I add adamantly. "We also need to check out this address Ms. Clifton gave to the college."

"It's a few miles from Mangrove High," Hannah states.

"We could bike there after school. She shouldn't be home until later. Administrators usually stay a couple hours late. So hopefully we can be in and out by then," I say.

"What do you expect to find?" Hannah asks.

"I don't know, but hopefully the connection to all this. If Mary Clifton isn't who she says she is, then who is she?" I add.

CHAPTER 34

- LOGAN -

P.E. TEACHERS WORRY TOO MUCH

I sit in Bob's office during my lunch break feeling uncertain. Am I doing the right thing not telling Deputy Diaz everything? We are friends, and most importantly, we could be in danger. Hell, a mafia hitman may be around every corner! I shudder to myself, then look around and contemplate my surroundings — Bob's office. It is a bit much. Old athletic posters are plastered everywhere. Penny Hardaway, Dwyane Wade, even Shaq.

We often eat in my classroom and only occasionally come here. I don't want to be next door to the office with everything going on, so we opt for this place. Bob is blaring Ludacris on his Bose speaker while I eat my traditional PB and J sandwich. He sits behind his desk in a burnt orange tracksuit, chewing on a piece of beef jerky, and reading Sports Illustrated.

"Bob, can you turn that down?" I ask as I flip through my phone, looking for clues.

My thoughts return to the investigation; I just can't give up on it. A murder happened at my school. A student's father is dead; other students are possibly being framed for drug possession. I can't just hand this back to the police. I can keep Ulysses and Hannah out of it, especially if someone is following us.

The mafia! Just a few days ago we were content in Somerset, now our world is topsy turvy. A picture of what happened is forming in my mind, but I need one last puzzle piece before I can fit everything together.

I open my phone to Google, searching for more information about the names we found. I type in Taban, Mecoli, and Leoni, checking to see if any more information could be found. Since all these men are smugglers, it's not a big leap to think the jewels, mentioned in the blue blackmail letter to Wright, could be connected to these mob bosses. Dead end.

I try a search for missing jewels in New York City, using the names of the mafia bosses. I don't find any information about stolen jewels, just paintings. That is until I click on an article titled "Royal Venetian Jeweled Knife Stolen." Bingo! The article was about thirty years old; I start to skim.

"A priceless artifact was stolen from McMasters Auction House on Saturday evening. A knife once owned by a Venetian prince was going up for auction. It was known as the Royal Cinquedea — a cinquedea is a long Italian dagger, adorned with jewels...The guard, or handle, of the knife was solid gold and adorned with Middle Eastern rubies, sapphires, and diamonds. It is valued at $35 million ... Several people linked with the Taban, Mecoli and Leoni mafia families were brought in for questioning but were released.. At this time, the police have no further leads."

"That's enough to kill for." I whistle out loud, gaining Bob's attention. I show him the article and explain that the timing of the robbery corresponds with the Gallant murders. I also remind him of the blue blackmail letter displaying the word jewel.

Bob looks at me from his cluttered desk along with a bobblehead of Michael Jordan, which bobs away as we continue our discussion. "What did Deputy Diaz say? Was he pissed at you?" Bob asks this smiling with a long piece of beef jerky hanging from his mouth. "You told him everything? Right? You're not investigating anymore, right, Logan? Why look up this stuff if you're not investigating? Right, Logan?

"I told him enough," I respond, ignoring the other questions.

"What?! Logan, we may be in danger!" Bob squeals.

"You don't think I know that, Bob? We need to finish this!"

Bob throws up his hands. "What the hell, you goin' get me killed! Mmm, Mmm," he grunts, tearing off another bite of beef jerky.

"We need to do this for Conrad, and Mangrove," I say, almost giving a pep talk to Bob. "Don't forget, you are the one who got me in this. We need to do it for Terry's and Jack's futures, too," I conclude.

"I got you involved to help me keep my job and to prove Terry's and Jack's innocence. Not to solve a murder!" Bob says, frustrated.

I bury my head back in my phone, saving the article about the jewel heist. I start to type in the other names of the people involved. O'Leary, Barron, Gallant, Wright, and, finishing with the biggest puzzle, Gibbins. We had an old picture of Sally Gibbins but nothing else. Google had nothing either.

I open the picture that Ulysses took at O'Leary's house, studying the picture that hung on his staircase of the twin blonde children and their mother. The other woman in the picture was Sally Gibbins. We knew Gibbins was on the business card. Was that Sally? Or a husband? Maybe a brother? We also know she was Samantha Gallant's sister, but nothing more, other than she was the godmother to the twins. I zoom in on the photo from my phone. Maybe by going extremely close I'll find some kind of connection that will bring everything into focus.

I scroll from one side of the picture to the other and then stop suddenly. Something caught my eye in the picture of Sally Gibbins. I think for a few minutes, pulling all the facts in my head together.

"Ah ha!" I exclaim. By now, Bob is looking down at me from his desk. "I think I've solved this case!" I say giddily.

Bob sarcastically comments, "Oh! Okay, Columbo. Sure, you have."

"Oh yeah, check your keychain for the mechanical room key again," I smirk.

"What? You know it's missing. Why check if the key is still missing?" Bob says condescendingly.

"Just check your keychain," I smoothly respond, looking away while he reluctantly reacts.

Bob pulls out his huge chain of Mangrove High keys, looking at each one carefully. Bob finally freezes on an old jagged looking key. At the top of the jagged key is a white sticker. On the white sticker, in small permanent marker, is written "MECHANICAL ROOM." Under the words is a little smiley face.

Bob is shaking. His lips are quivering. "Logan, this key was not here before. I would swear to it. And now it even has a weird smiley face. I didn't put that there." Bob is holding up the key, examining its features. "How did it get back on my keychain? And how did you know it would be there?"

I lean across Bob's desk, examining the key for myself. "I knew it was there because I knew the killer would put it back," I respond in a whisper. "Well, at least one of the killers."

CHAPTER 35

- ULYSSES -

ASSISTANT PRINCIPALS SHOULD NEVER STEAL

"We are going to just break into Ms. Clifton's house?" Hannah shouts to me as we race our bikes to the address North Georgia State College gave her over the phone.

The last address of the fake Mary Clifton. Why would someone perform identity theft to become an assistant principal? This question occupies my mind while we race on the sidewalks. The mansions give way to run-down condo developments. We enter an area known as South Somerset. This area is home to many migrant families who move into cheap condos so they can work for area farmers, traveling and doing work most Americans won't do.

"We are going to have to break into Ms. Clifton's house," I say as Hannah bikes parallel with me. Her face contorts under her pink bike helmet.

"Even if she's lying, that is still breaking and

entering!" she gasps back.

"You were fine with me breaking into Mr. O'Leary's!" I retort.

"Well, you were also almost caught. If it wasn't for me, you would have been."

"That's why my guardian angel is going in with me," I say with my half-dimpled grin.

"Argh!" she grunts while rolling her eyes.

We ride into a large run-down condo community named Bear Falls. The place looks as old as the city of Somerset. The cement building resembles an old motel you would see on the side of the highway that takes cash without any questions. Bear Falls was a two-story L-shaped complex, wrapping itself around a large broken paved parking lot. Our bikes have difficulty riding on the pavement with the sections of dirt and holes.

"This is a pleasant place," Hannah sarcastically comments. "Really think administrators should get more pay if this is all that she can afford."

We dismount and park our bikes behind one of the many dilapidated cars that look like they will never start again. This collection of cars acts as our cover as Hannah and I bob and weave slowly, trying to stay out of sight. Ms. Clifton's place is number 26 on the second floor.

We don't have a ton of time. It is already 4:00, and this was an hour bike ride back from Mangrove High. We finally make a dash for the stairway. The clouds are darkening as we approach the stairway. The stairs are white, at least they once were. They now stand peeling, exposing the rusted metal beneath. As we cautiously climb the stairs, we notice how empty the complex is. Elementary and middle schoolers are just getting dismissed, so that could explain why there are no kids. I also think all the adults must still be at work. We don't have much time before this place starts to fill up and someone is bound to notice two kids breaking into number 26.

When we reach the top of the stairs, there are only three doors in front of us before we reach number 26. We are startled by a siren blaring in the background. This is the only part of Somerset, besides my section, that doesn't exude wealth. They must hear a lot of sirens in this part of town.

"Are we sure we want to be doing this?" Hannah asks, swallowing hard, probably spooked by the siren. "Just because she's lying doesn't mean we won't get charged with breaking and entering," she reasons in a soft whisper.

"I know, but my gut tells me we need to see this thing through. She lied to Mangrove, and she is a criminal. I want to know why and if she is connected at all to Mr. Wright's murder. We've got to do this for Terry and Jack too," I whisper back to Hannah, half convincing her and myself that we need to follow through with what we are about to do.

We approach the door labeled 26. Beads of sweat are rolling down my forehead. I look over to Hannah, who weirdly has beads of sweat only on her nose, covering her freckles. I smile.

"What?" she asks.

I lean in and kiss her quickly. "For luck," I say before trying the handle. The handle is metal and cold in our humid air and proves to be locked. I knock hard, no answer. I knock again, still no answer. "Good, nobody's home."

"You got any hair pins?" I ask, thinking I could

pick it like Dad had shown me.

"No. Only an elastic. Wait a minute — Step back," Hannah says with a big smile.

I do what she says. Hannah backs herself against the railing and takes a deep breath. Her whole body becomes rigid and serious. She brings her fisted right hand to her flat left hand. She breathes in again, but only through her nose, closing her eyes in a meditative state. In next instant, she swings her right leg forward, hard against the door while she is expelling, "HI-YA!" The door jamb splinters in every direction and swings open with ease.

"My guardian angel!" I proclaim to a beaming, red faced Hannah. "We better hurry; someone may have heard that."

We both timidly walk into a very dark room. The open door gives off a little light, but the sun is lost within some serious looking rain clouds.

Hannah closes the broken door the best she can after I turn on a small, dated lamp.

"No wonder she doesn't have Mr. Nelson drop her off at this dump. She must've had him drop her off at a different place and taxied back here so her base of operations could be kept secret," I say while I examine the surroundings.

"We better hurry; those clouds don't look good," Hannah says. "What are we looking for?"

"I don't know, but I'll know it when I see it," I answer.

"Okay?" Hannah worries.

The room is dodgy, as my mom used to say in her London accent. In Britain, dodgy is another word for nasty, and this place is really dodgy.

It is set up like a motel room. The apartment only

has a small kitchenette and bathroom, with a separate sink outside. I always thought that was weird that hotels wouldn't put a sink in with the toilet and shower. The rest of the apartment consists of a small closet and a full-sized bed. Even the bedding looks dusty with faded flowers trying to stay colorful but losing the battle to age and lack of care.

"The best place to look is in her trash. If any of the detective novels or movies I have watched have taught me anything, it is to always check the trash," I say to Hannah as her face contorts again.

"That sounds like a job for Ulysses," Hannah says smiling. "I got us in," she finishes, looking proud.

"Okay, you check her closet," I compromise, smiling and shaking my head. "This place looks like it's been barely used," I add.

I notice a small trash bin near a couple of wooden stools, under a partition in the kitchenette. The trash is filled with energy bar wrappers and scraps of banana peels. The flies like the banana peels. Several of them buzz around the rim of the waste basket.

"She must be a health nut," I say out loud to Hannah as she is moving through the clothes in the closet.

"Ulysses," she says with a startled voice. "Her clothes."

"What?" I say.

"I think they're all stolen. The security tags are still on some of them," Hannah says.

"She steals identities and clothes?"

Deep beneath the trash, I find several receipts that are either torn or crumpled. Most of them are from the supermarket. There is one receipt that is not easy to read because it was torn into quarters. I put them on the counter, arranging them in place. It appears to be a receipt from Home Depot. My stomach sinks to my knees again. The same familiar feeling I felt when I was trapped in Mr. O'Leary's house. The same feeling I felt when I saw a person dressed in black digging holes in the back of O'Leary's home. The pieced-together receipt shows a $14.95 charge for a metal shovel.

"Why would Ms. Clifton, or the person pretending to be Ms. Clifton, rip up a receipt for a metal shovel?" I ask Hannah, knowing the answer deep in my gut.

Before Hannah can respond, her hands start to shake. She is genuinely trembling as she turns from deep inside the closet. "I think we may have found a connection to the murders."

Hannah is holding a pair of black military boots in her trembling left hand, covered in dry mud. But that isn't even the most disturbing part. Hannah's right hand is also trembling as it holds a ribbed, black — ski mask.

CHAPTER 36

- LOGAN -

PRINCIPALS SHOULDN'T LIE

Bob storms into my classroom and stares at me for a good thirty seconds before speaking. It's finally the end of the school day, and he is still perseverating over our lunch conversation, looking pale and confused. Then he starts laughing nervously, saying, "Nah, nah."

I'm not wasting my time on this again.

"I know you've been wanting clarification all day, but I need to find Principal Barron," I say, ignoring Bob's shock.

"So, the killer took my key? Then returned it?" Bob squeaks. "And now you're saying there are two killers?" Bob gulps. He then returns to saying, "Nah, nah," as he shakes his head in disbelief.

"I also think Principal Barron is in danger and he knows it," I respond, heading toward the door.

"What? Why do you think that?" Bob calls as the door closes behind me.

I pop my head back in and respond, "As they say

in the movies, all will be revealed. Just not yet. Meet me back here at 6:00, after your practice. All your questions hopefully will be answered," I say to Bob before leaving.

I walk over to the office door. It is now 4:30. I know I have grading to do, but I put it off. I have a theory about the events that took place last Friday. The events actually have been building for a while, ever since the disappearance of Mr. Peters.

I approach the office door, but it is locked. "Damn!" I say out loud. I notice Ms. Simmons come out of Principal Barron's office, and I catch a glimpse of him working at his desk, so I knock vigorously at the door. Ms. Simmons looks at me with disdain as I knew she would.

"Office hours are over!" she shouts from the counter.

I arrogantly knock again. "I need to speak with Mr. Barron!" I shout. I see him get up from his desk and come out of his office.

"It's alright, Ms. Simmons; you can let Mr. Adair in," Principal Barron states as he gestures to Ms. Simmons. She creeps to the door, leering at me with continued disdain, and unlocks the door.

As I come into the office, she gives me a smile; I do not smile back. I am all business, and I am going to get to the bottom of this affair.

"Mr. Adair, what can I do for you?" Principal Barron asks in his little voice as he extends his stature, failing in an attempt to reach my height.

"It's best we speak in private. I know you're in danger." As I say this, I turn to Ms. Simmons, who is listening intently. "We'd better go in your office."

"Danger! I'm not in any danger," he says with

zero confidence, given away by his shaky, rattled voice.

He proceeds to guide me into his office, closing the door behind me. Barron gestures for me to take a seat. I sit comfortably in a leather chair. Principal Barron sits behind his large intimidating oak desk.

Principal Barron looks like a man on borrowed time. He still retains some of his authoritative demeanor as he addresses me sternly, "What do you mean I'm in danger?" He laughs nervously. "Oh, Mr. Adair. I think you have a vivid imagination."

I sit in silence studying him, waiting to see what he has to say while my phone lays on my lap, recording every word he says. Principal Barron wipes some sweat from his forehead. "You still think I'm connected to the murder of Donald Wright?"

I continue to sit in silence.

My silence must be nerve-racking for him. He starts to move around in his seat. His sweat is now dripping from his tanned head. Barron's salt-and-pepper hair glistens in the recessed lighting of his office. He takes a sip of the water in front of him. My silence is infuriating him.

"Adair, you said you wanted to talk and tell me why I'm in danger! So, talk!" he shouts, hitting the desk with his fist in a fit of rage.

"I know about the Royal Cinquedea," I say, staring him down with a stern poker face.

Principal Barron relaxes a little and looks at me with disbelief. It seems like time stands still. He arranges some pens on his desk, now giving me the silent treatment. "How much do you know?"

"Probably everything. Just a few facts elude me. I was hoping you could fill them in for me," I respond.

"Ha!" Principal Barron laughs. "What do I know? I got out of that stuff a long time ago!" he snarls back at me. Hopefully I'm not backing him into a corner like a wild animal.

"I know you used to smuggle drugs from Florida to New York for the mafia." This comment makes him choke. He takes another sip of his water.

"How did you...?" he nervously starts, unable to even finish the sentence.

"Before you made the leap into teaching, you would fly small airplanes. You were probably approached by one of the lawyers from GG&W. Gibbins, Gallant, or Wright." He flinches with every name.

I throw the GG&W card at him. He picks it up with his tan fingers. He starts to mumble something. "Where did you get this?"

"That's not important. The important thing is you were once a drug smuggler. And you should be in jail, not an administrator at this fine school," I lecture.

"They pressured me into it. They said they would kill me if I didn't cooperate. The mob families teamed up to completely take over the Florida drug market, distributions into New York and New Jersey. I was twenty years old for Christ's sake!" he says as he stands, facing the window with his back to me. "It had never happened before. I mean the Taban, Mecoli, and Leoni families all teaming up. They sent their lawyers to do their bidding. Each lawyer looked out for their individual mafia family. They settled in Florida; their families bought homes and became part of the community," Barron says with a little giggle.

"It wasn't just drugs, it was also stolen art, that they fenced for drugs. I was approached by Donald Wright. He recruited me to use my puddle jumper to make trips back and forth from the Everglades. One of the lawyers even bought a plot of land next to the landing strip I used. They had so much power, they even paid politicians to make my landing strip a conservation area for miles around. This way nobody would catch on to our flying timetables. I would load the plane with the drugs after unloading either money or fenced materials."

This must have been the land behind the Gallant home. Thirty years ago, that was the only house that was near the landing strip.

"Toby Gallant's house," I blurt out.

Principal Barron turns to me with a surprised face. "You really do have it all figured out," he says as he sits down at his desk and takes a long sip of water.

"And the Royal Cinquedea?" I prompt.

Barron turns a little white and hangs his head. "I know. I know it was awful. Toby Gallant and Anthony Gibbins were a family. I mean, a real family not mafia family. Since Anthony Gibbins' sister married Toby Gallant, both of Anthony's sisters were close to him. Both pressured the men to quit this life and move to another country. They got wind of me moving a stolen royal dagger, what you said, the Royal Cinquedea. It was going to sell for millions on the black market. They saw that as an opportunity to steal it and escape; start over somewhere else, somewhere the three families couldn't find them." Barron looks off into the distance as if he is recalling these memories. He starts to cough.

Principal Barron's skin is looking very white and waxy rather than its usual tan and waxy.

Barron takes another drink of water, this time finishing off his glass. Barron continues to cough, though now it's stronger and louder. He loosens his tie and the top button of his shirt. The coughing continues to worsen, causing him fall out of his chair and onto the floor, flipping his chair.

I jump out of my seat, dashing behind the desk. I kneel down next to him, but it is too late. His tongue is protruding from his mouth, turning a weird shade of purple, and sizzling white liquid drips out of his mouth and onto his chin. I feel for a pulse — nothing. I sniff his water glass. It smells of burnt almonds.

"Cyanide?" I consider aloud, looking down at Principal Barron — dead.

I grab my phone, which is still recording our conversation, and start to dial 911, but I'm so focused on what is happening in front of me that I don't hear the door creak open behind me. As I dial the first 1, I feel a hard object strike the back of my head. I drop my phone down to the floor, and everything goes dark.

CHAPTER 37

- ULYSSES -

X MARKS THE HIT

Hannah and I stand in the fake Ms. Clifton's dodgy apartment. Hannah has just found evidence of muddy boots and a black mask, proving that Ms. Clifton is our mysterious hole digger at the Gallant house. I take a picture of the receipt, boots, and mask, texting it to Dad.

"Ms. Clifton has to have duped a lot of people. How were her references not checked by Principal Barron?" Hannah nervously asks.

"If she was able to adopt the real Mary Clifton's identity, then it wouldn't be hard to fake the rest. Schools just ask for a copy of a driver's license, which she could have forged. Teacher certifications, and even college diplomas, can be easily made and printed. If anyone ever traced her, it would be the Mary Clifton in Georgia," I say.

"Unless someone called her old school," Hannah reasons. "It took us fifteen minutes to call and figure this out."

"So why is this woman, pretending to be Ms. Mary Clifton, digging holes in the back of Mr.

O'Leary's house?" I wonder.

Hannah shrugs as she continues to look around the apartment, holding her arms around her chest, shivering. "This place gives me the creeps."

"It has to have something to do with the murder of Mr. Wright. It cannot be a coincidence that she was digging at the Gallant house, a house where the entire family was murdered nearly thirty years ago," I say.

"We gotta get this evidence to the police. Get a CSI crew or something. I think we are in over our heads," Hannah pleads.

"Yeah. I agree. She could be home any moment," I say, but quickly turn my attention to her bed, suddenly remembering one of the best hiding places someone could keep: under the mattress. "Hey, help me with the mattress?"

Hannah reluctantly helps me pick up one side of a very nasty mattress: empty. Then the other side, "Bingo!" A large manila file is stuffed under her mattress.

Hannah and I sit on the edge of the mattress, opening the thick file to examine the clues.

The file is loaded with pictures and police files of the mafia bosses that were listed on the business card, all recently murdered.

"Look! The mugshots of the mafia bosses!" Hannah exclaims. Each mugshot of Taban, Mecoli, and Leoni has a large red X drawn on it.

"Was Ms. Clifton the mafia hitman killing all three bosses?" I contemplate.

"Remember these pictures were taken long ago, maybe twenty to thirty years. All three of these men were now old and past their prime; she could have easily killed them," Hannah reminds me before continuing on. "Ms. Clifton could have also conned her way into their lives, just like she has at Mangrove. Then she would have had the opportunity to bump them off one, by one, by one," Hannah says, getting a cocked eye from me, surprised that she could think so deviously.

"Look here." I point out a part of the file dedicated to Mr. Wright. It too had a red X on his picture. It lists his acquaintances, his address and his business dealings. There are also surveillance photos taken of him in front of his house and even at Mangrove High.

"How? How did she murder Mr. Wright? She was in full view the whole night of the murder," Hannah says in disbelief.

"Unless — unless she was not working alone!" I declare with a shocked realization that there may be two murderers.

"What? This crazy woman may have another person working with her? Oh Dios mio!" Hannah reverts to Spanish and crosses herself.

We then turn to another page containing several cut-out pieces of magazine lettering that fall to the floor. With them is a blue piece of paper. "This must have been how she made the blackmail letter to Mr. Wright. But why is a hitman — I mean hitwoman — wanting to blackmail her target?"

We turn to the last page of the file. It is surveillance pictures of Principal Barron. "What the hell!" I blurt out.

The last page of the file is a picture of Principal Barron, and just like the other pictures, a large red X is drawn through it. "Principal Barron is next!"

As soon as I say these words, we hear a click. The click sounds familiar, like something I'd heard on a TV show or a movie. Startled, we whip our heads around in horror to find Ms. Clifton in the doorway, leveling a cocked black gun at the two of us.

CHAPTER 38

- ULYSSES -

HELL HAS NO FURY!

"You little brats!" she hisses. Her giddy cheerleader voice, which I heard less than a week ago in her office, is now gone. I only hear rage and hatred.

"Ms. Clifton?!" I say, shocked.

Hannah and I cling to each other as we wonder about her true identity. Ms. Clifton looks around the room, seeing her black boots and mask next to the ripped receipt on the kitchen counter. We also have the manila folder sitting on our laps. It doesn't look good. She actually could shoot us now and not be charged because of the "Stand Your Ground" law in Florida.

"What the hell! You two just couldn't mind your own business? Now you'll pay. You'll pay the ultimate sacrifice!"

My mind races for a way out. Maybe if we distract her long enough, we can make a run for it or

Hannah can do another karate chop and disarm her.

Here I go. "Who are you really?"

"I'm not sure what you mean," she says, half smiling at us, not knowing what we really know.

"He means we know you're not Mary Clifton. We called your previous school and your references. We know you're a fake," Hannah says sternly, showing strength. I know she has the same idea I had.

"Why kill those mobsters? We know you did that, too," I add.

"You don't know the half of it," she says, smiling. "So, it's a farewell to both of you. Killing the two of you will be easy. I just have to tell the police that two of my students have broken into my apartment. I felt my life was threatened. You know home invasions are happening everywhere." She says this with a sinister grin.

"Well, you said we don't know the half of it. Tell us, what don't we know?" Hannah says in disgust while Ms. Clifton just cocks her head back and forth, as if trying to decide whether to kill us, when her phone rings. She answers.

"You're not going to believe who broke into my apartment." It must be her accomplice, I reason. "I was just about to kill the both of them. Is he dead? What? You do? Good." She says "good" like a villain from the comic books. Was she talking about Principal Barron? "So, I should bring them to you?" It sounds like she isn't calling the shots. Maybe her accomplice was the brains behind this operation. "We'll have a family reunion. Okay, I'll be there soon," she says, laughing. What did she mean by a family reunion? "Alright! We're going to the school.

Outside both of you!" Ms. Clifton orders. She covers the gun with a jacket, to hide it from any prying eyes.

We walk down the same rusty steps we went up. Hannah is looking nervous and starting to cry a little. I take her hand to reassure her everything is going to be okay. Ms. Clifton walks a few steps behind us, far enough so we can't hit the gun away, but close enough that we also can't make a run for it.

We walk up to an old red Chevy Lumina. Ms. Clifton pops the trunk. Inside is a shovel, gasoline, and a bag of clothes. She tells us to put our phones on the ground and then stomp on them with our feet. We comply with her demand. So much for calling for help. She then instructs us to take the gas can out and put the shovel and bag in the backseat. We comply with this as well, making the trunk empty of anything that could help us to escape. It doesn't even have a jack.

"Get in!" she orders.

We hesitate, and she hits the back of my head with the gun. I feel my legs go a little limp. My head throbs with pain as I fall into the trunk.

"Now you, Ms. Reyes." Hannah first hesitates but then complies.

Ms. Clifton closes trunk behind us.

"Ulysses, are you okay?" Hannah says, taking my head and feeling around for any blood.

"Yeah, yeah. Just a little dazed. Damn, that hurt. I don't think I'm bleeding," I reassure her.

"What do we do? We have no way of calling the police," Hannah says, her voice cracking with fear.

"We see what she and the accomplice have in store and try to make a break for it. I should have listened to my dad. My stupid curiosity got us into this. I'm sorry, Hannah."

"What are you talking about? I pushed you to investigate this. I make my own decisions, Ulysses Adair. I decided to seek the truth right by your side. We're in this together. Okay?" Hannah smiles and gives me a kiss on my bruised head.

The trunk is cramped, and we practically have to lay on top of each other. We take turns looking through the keyhole of the trunk to see what Ms. Clifton is up to. We can see her take the gas can up to her apartment. Several minutes later, she comes out with smoke billowing behind her. Before we know it, the car has started and we are her prisoners.

CHAPTER 39

- LOGAN -

CONCUSSIONS ACCOMPANIED BY SQUEALING ARE NOT GOOD

"Get on your feet!" a voice blares in my ear. The sound of the voice vibrates through my brain. I can't even think. I blink my eyes, but they hurt, too. Everything from my neck up throbs. My head feels like it weighs a thousand pounds, and I already have a pretty heavy head in the first place.

I bring my hand to my head, trying to feel the wound. No blood, that's a good sign. Then I feel a welt the size of Florida on the back of my head. When I touch it, my head throbs louder. I fully open my eyes. They struggle to adjust to the lighting in the room. As they adjust, my head's maddening beat continues its pressure. I am in my classroom, on the floor, near my smartboard.

"Christ!" I call out, as I fully wake and stand with shooting pain at every step.

"I'm glad you're awake, Mr. Adair," a frail elderly voice says from behind me. "You were awfully heavy, to drag next door to your classroom." The voice snickers.

I turn to face my attacker and find a frail looking Ms. Simmons sitting on a desk holding a gun on me and blocking the only exit out of my classroom. "Good evening, Ms. Simmons," I say condescendingly.

"You don't seem surprised! Maybe it is true what you said to Principal Barron; you have figured it out — somehow!" she says coldly and collectedly.

"I knew you would be eavesdropping. Just like you did when Wright and Barron were fighting in the office last Friday. You took pleasure in seeing them squirm as you blackmailed them and plotted your revenge," I say, taking a seat on top of a student's desk opposite Ms. Simmons. "You were the only part of the puzzle that I didn't have. I've known about your accomplice since the start of this charade. I didn't quite peg you as the mastermind until today. During lunch, I looked closer at the picture Ulysses took from the Gallant home on my phone. I zoomed in on the face of Sally Gibbins. I looked into those wide leering green eyes. I said to myself, 'I have seen those eyes on Ms. Simmons, or should I say Ms. Sally Gibbins,'" I accuse her and add, "You have aged poorly." My confidence is building, and this game has gone on too long. "You can give up the act." As I say this, she slowly grins at me and cackles.

She gradually comes to a standing position, stretching out to her full height, her back cracking from the prolonged hunched position. She is now about six inches taller. Her mannerisms even change. Her once frail, old body is now replaced with a much younger, more confident frame. She takes her left hand, the one not holding the gun, and starts to peel her face off. Not literally; she quickly peels away a layer of plastic wrinkles and throws her old face on the ground, never taking her eyes off of me, nor wavering in her aim. She then pulls off her dark grey wig, exposing a short-bobbed hairstyle. Shoulder pads and a small stomach pad are also discarded. She even spit out false teeth, revealing a nice set of white teeth. When everything is removed, a 70-year-old frail woman has transformed into a 50-year-old attractive woman, leering at me with a proud smile and wide green eyes. I slow clap in disgust.

"Yes, Mr. Adair, I am Sally Gibbins," she says, now with a much younger, but still cold, voice.

"You're quite the actress," I coax.

"Well, that was my profession all those years ago. As you can see, I can fool anyone. Especially dumb men like Barron," she smirks, waving the gun.

I am just about to ask her a question when my classroom door bursts open. The door knocks the desk over, sending Sally to the ground. As she falls, a big orange blur comes strolling in like he owns the place. It is Bob!

"Hey Logan, I was thinking..."

But before he can say another word, I yell at him, "Go get help! She has a gun!"

Bob looks down at Sally Gibbins, not recognizing her as Ms. Simmons. She has regained the gun, quickly recovering from her fall, and is about to shoot at Bob. He squeals, "Ah!" and runs out of my classroom for the exit.

Sally stands, aiming the gun at my chest just as I am getting up to follow Bob. Hopefully he can get help. But then I realize that this is Bob and sigh with regret.

Sally shows even more anger now. She quickly takes out her phone and dials a number. "Yeah, that idiot gym teacher saw me holding a gun on Adair. Are you here yet? Good. Stop him," Sally orders into her phone while smiling at me.

CHAPTER 40

- ULYSSES -

AN UNEXPECTED FAMILY REUNION

The car stops abruptly, throwing Hannah and I hard against each other. "You okay?" I ask Hannah.

"I'm good," Hannah says in frustration.

Before we can get our bearings, the trunk pops open. It is now night, but I can still make out the barrel of the gun aimed at Hannah and me.

"Get out!" Ms. Clifton hisses. Hannah and I do as commanded while Ms. Clifton hides her gun under a jacket. "Walk!" she orders.

We are in the Mangrove High parking lot right by the front entrance. The lot is empty except a few cars, one being a silver Prius. Dad! Damn. The pink Mangrove High building looks a little creepy at night. Especially when the clouds in the distance expose bolts of lightning coming our way.

"Where are you taking us?" I ask, but she doesn't answer.

"Shut up and walk!" she snarls again.

As we walk to the front door, Ms. Clifton answers her phone. "Yeah, I'm right at the entrance. Okay.

With pleasure." She smiles as she hangs up and gives me a key to unlock the front door. After we all file in, she quickly keys in the password on the alarm system. She then pulls out a bike chain and locks the front doors.

The hallway is almost pitch dark except for a bright, large orange object running toward us. For a second I think it is a running orange, but no — it is Mr. Nelson in his bright orange tracksuit. He is waving his hands hysterically, out of breath.

"Glad to see you guys! Logan is in trouble! There is a crazy woman with a gun! We need to call 911!" he squeaks, panting and out of breath. Mr. Nelson sees Ms. Clifton standing behind us and collects himself.

"Hey Mary," he says in a deep, cool, collected voice. "How you doin'?" With that, she takes the gun hidden beneath her coat and points it at Mr. Nelson. "Oh man!" Mr. Nelson says, reverting back to his squeaky voice.

"Shut up, you idiot! Give me your phone and get walking," Ms. Clifton says, disgusted. I think she'd been wanting to say that to Mr. Nelson for a while. Ms. Clifton marches us down the dark corridor, past the expansive staircase, and to the front of the office. When we reach the office door, we see another woman, holding a gun on Dad, coming out from his classroom. We all meet outside the office.

"Well, well, well. Isn't this quite a family reunion!" a woman that looks slightly familiar says before yelling, "Get in the office!"

We do as we are commanded. Ms. Clifton closes the shades on the window of the office door and the windows that look out onto the hallway, clicking the door locked behind us.

Hannah gasps and I squeeze her hand tight because we can see into Principal Barron's office, where his stiff body is lying dead on the floor.

"Logan Adair — look, I found your boy and his little girlfriend snooping around my apartment. I think they need a detention," Ms. Clifton chuckles, enjoying her power. "Now they will share your fate. What did they say happened to the cat for being curious? Oh yeah, it died!"

Dad looks at me with surprise. "Ulysses, I thought I told you to stay out of this and stop investigating!"

"I know, but we didn't investigate the murder; we investigated the frame job on Terry and Jack. And you were right, they are linked. Ms. Clifton isn't even her real name. She has conned us all and framed Terry and Jack," I rapidly spit out my words, pointing at the fake Ms. Clifton.

"Oh, Mary. So that's not your real name? Why do I always fall for the wrong woman?" Mr. Nelson squeaks, sounding more desperate than usual.

"You idiot. I only used you to get the key," Ms. Clifton says.

"You mean you're the one who stole my key? And put it back?" Mr. Nelson quips.

"She probably put it back on your keychain at Mr. Wright's wake," Dad reasons.

"Who are you?" Hannah says to the other woman working with Ms. Clifton and now holding a gun on all four of us.

"That is Ms. Simmons!" Dad shares with the rest of us. He also shares that she wore a disguise, and he found out after zooming in on the picture I took from the Gallant home. Dad then reveals her real identity is in fact Sally Gibbins.

"You're little old — Simmons? She's fine now, Logan. Girl, you clean up!" Mr. Nelson says.

We all shake our heads at Mr. Nelson. "Who are you really then?" Hannah asks, looking at Ms. Clifton.

"You're Helena!" I proclaim.

"Good work, Ulysses," Dad adds.

"You're Helena Gallant, the twin sister to Hayden Gallant, and daughter to Toby Gallant. But you were murdered!" I continue, confused.

"I am Helena Gallant," the woman we had known to be Ms. Mary Clifton confirms, putting a hand on Sally's shoulder.

Sally makes us all stand behind the high office counter while both women point their guns at us on the other side near Ms. Simmons' desk.

"What are your plans for us?" Dad asks.

"I was going to frame you for Principal Barron's death, but now I will just have to tweak the story. I am going to shoot all of you and frame Principal Barron for your murders. Can't you see it? Principal kills a group of amateur sleuths investigating Donald Wright's murder and then takes his own life. We even have a suicide note, confessing to Donald Wright's murder." Sally Gibbins laughs at this, while we all gasp. "I want to know how you knew what we had done!" she says, wagging her gun at Dad.

Dad starts to go through all the events. "Well, Ms. Clifton, or Helena as she is really known, never seemed quite like an educator. An assistant principal would have had a giddy school-girl demeanor worn out of her long ago from the stress of dealing with parents and students. There is also her calloused hands, she claimed from rock climbing, but she couldn't answer simple questions about the sport. Then Ulysses said there was a mysterious digger at the old Gallant home, which is now being renovated by Mr. O'Leary. That's a good way to get calloused hands. Ulysses shared the article about the Gallant family murders, and I thought, what if Ms. Clifton was digging at the Gallants' because she in fact was a Gallant. Maybe Helena, one of the twins. Her age matches. And she was searching for something lost all those years ago. I also suspected her when she came on strong to Bob, too. What could she possibly want while being so unprofessional?"

"Logan! Come on, man; help a brother out," Mr. Nelson chimes in.

"Sorry, Bob. Those are all weird coincidences around the time of Donald Wright's murder. And I don't believe in coincidences. Ms. Clifton must have known about the mechanical room from her accomplice, someone working on the inside of Mangrove High. The mechanical room would have been a great, quiet place to kill Mr. Wright and frame Principal Barron. But only Barron, the custodian, and Bob had that key. A custodian would've immediately noticed a missing key and reported it. But Bob only uses that key occasionally. So, warming up to an easy target, such as Bob, with a pretense of stealing that key and putting it back later, was perfect."

"I can't believe I liked you!" Mr. Nelson squeaks before Dad gives him a look to be quiet.

Dad continues on, now pointing his finger at Helena. "You would have needed an accomplice to inform you that Bob had the key and was very susceptible to the opposite sex. Ms. Simmons probably overheard Bob going on about how special he was for having all the school's keys in either the teachers' room or the office. The night of the game was perfect, too. Hundreds of witnesses would see you out in the gymnasium, while Mr. Wright would have a blue piece of paper that said 'Come to the mechanical room with the jeweled knife.' The killer would lie in wait after the mechanical room was unlocked earlier that day. We also found out that the stab wound came from a much shorter person, most likely a woman, about your height."

"Why frame Terry and Jack?" Hannah asks.

Dad continues, "Good question, Hannah! Why indeed? The frame job of Terry and Jack, by Ms. Clifton, to plant and then find the drugs in two high-profile seniors playing that night in the basketball game was just a ploy. She used this as a distraction to get into the school on a Saturday. After framing Terry and Jack, you snuck down to the gymnasium and unlocked the door to the mechanical room, opening the exit door at the end of the tunnel, where Sally Gibbins then waited for Mr. Wright. Helena duct taped the lock on the way out to ensure Mr. Wright had no problems getting into the mechanical room."

"Why did they do this? Revenge?" I ask Dad.

"Revenge, of course, but as I found out today, it's also because of money. Your big revenge problem was complicated by the fact that Donald Wright didn't have the jeweled knife; neither of them knew where the knife was," Dad says, while taking a moment to tell us about how he found out about the jeweled knife, known as the Royal Cinquedea.

"So, you didn't give up investigating either?" I ask.

"Ah — no. Sorry, Ulysses. I guess I couldn't let it go either. But I think this knife is what Helena was searching for in the backyard of the Gallant home. You two didn't count on Ulysses, Hannah, and me following Principal Barron into the mechanical room, providing him the perfect alibi and preventing you two from framing him. How am I doing so far?"

"Fine," Sally responds, grinding her teeth. "Go on."

"I knew it had to be an inside job to allow Helena to con people to think she was Mary Clifton, our new cheerful assistant principal. I also knew whoever was working with Ms. Clifton was also spying on us, trying to find out what we knew and trailing the kids and me to Penny University."

"She was the woman who bumped into Lisa — our waitress," Hannah says with Dad nodding in agreement

Dad continues. "Ms. Clifton, or Helena, saw me take the picture of the photograph at the Mr. Wright's wake. So that is when you both decided to kill Mr. Barron and frame us. Then, as I said, I took a closer look at the photo and saw you, Sally Gibbins, were actually pretending to be the frail unassuming Ms. Simmons. I'm sure if the police check Ms. Simmons' records they would find another stolen identity. As an office secretary, you wouldn't be questioned by a principal when you pushed for the hiring of a new assistant principal. We only needed a new one because one of you killed our old assistant principal, Mr. Peters, so there would be room to hire a new one. An assistant principal that would have access and privilege." When Dad shares this, everyone shows horror, even the women holding the guns on us. "An assistant principal that you would make sure got hired, throwing out resumes of qualified candidates. It would be easy for the principal's assistant to pretend to call references for Mr. Barron. You also made sure Mrs. Lafayette came down with a bad case of the flu so she would not catch on to your devious plans."

"No. No — that wench does have the flu," Sally Gibbins says, smiling.

Dad finishes, "Also, I remembered the faculty meeting when Ms. Clifton was introduced, she thanked Mr. Donald Barron instead of Thomas Barron. I didn't think much of it until now, but I think you were messing with him and he didn't realize it. Donald Wright, his old business partner in smuggling drugs, comes out of the woodwork to say he is being blackmailed!" We all listen with our mouths open to all the new evidence and revelations Dad uncovered.

"Well done, Mr. Adair. I applaud your detective skills," Sally says in her cold voice, staring at him with her beady green eyes.

"What I don't know is what happened the night of the murders twenty-eight years ago," Dad says, cool and collected, to Sally and Helena, who are still both holding guns on us.

CHAPTER 41

- ULYSSES -

THE GALLANT MURDERS

Sally Gibbins leans against the office desk that used to belong to her alter ego — Ms. Simmons. She starts to speak with a creepy, somber voice. "Thirty years ago, we moved to Somerset from New York City. That is, my brother Anthony Gibbins and his business partners, Toby Gallant and Donald Wright, moved from New York, with me and my sister, Samantha. I had been an actress living in New York, living with my brother. Samantha was in love with Toby. They always took care of us."

As she says this, she looks at the ceiling to hold back tears before continuing. "I didn't know what kind of business my brother was in, but I would've followed him to the ends of the earth. I gave up my career on Broadway to follow him to Florida. Samantha eventually married Toby and gave birth to a beautiful set of twins, Helena and Hayden. Life was good! Samantha and Toby built a beautiful house near conservation land. We were so happy."

"You do know that politicians were bought to set

aside that land for their drug-smuggling business, don't you?" Dad sternly interjects.

Sally continues waving her gun at Dad in a gesture that indicates he should shut up. "I know! Toby eventually told Samantha and in turn Samantha told me. He told her everything. How the three families in New York united and sent their lawyers Anthony, Toby, and Donald to lead the business in Florida. They hired a local pilot to fly the drugs and the money back and forth. We first turned a blind eye, but eventually we didn't want to raise the twins surrounded by the mafia and drugs. So, we convinced Toby and Anthony to run away to Brazil. Anthony always said, 'The three families would never find us in Brazil.' Toby got wind of a big fence coming through on one of Thomas Barron's airplane runs. A jeweled knife called the Royal Cinquedea. Toby said it was worth tens of millions of dollars, enough for all of us to live comfortably in Brazil forever. The only problem was that when the Royal Cinquedea went missing, Donald Wright suspected Toby and Anthony. Donald was a ruthless man. He was also loyal to the core to those hideous men in New York."

While Sally is speaking, I notice Dad give me the briefest of looks. He then looks down at the stapler on the office counter. I slowly nod. I am already holding Hannah's hand, so I squeeze it to let her know we are planning an escape.

My attention goes back to Sally's account of the murders.

"We were going to escape the night when Hurricane Luis hit the Gulf. But the day before the hurricane was due to hit, Donald killed Anthony and sent his fingers to Toby in a box. It was a warning Toby didn't heed. So, Donald sent some of his thugs to stop us all from fleeing. They tortured Toby and Samantha before killing them in an attempt to find the whereabouts of the Royal Cinquedea. They cut them deep with a knife until they talked. They never gave up the location, though. Then the thugs killed little Hayden." Her beady green eyes glossed over and grew very wide with this admission before starting again. "Luckily, I was able to get to a hiding place with Helena in a shed, hidden away in the backyard. The others weren't so lucky. The goons must've not been told by Donald about me and another child. We could hear them being tortured from our hiding place, even over the sound of the bellowing hurricane winds."

Helena came over and put an arm around Sally, fighting back tears, "That bastard Donald Wright tortured my family. I remember Donald clearly. He always had a fake smile that everyone knew wasn't genuine. He would always come to the house bearing gifts, like toy trucks for my brother or little creepy toy dolls for me. I hated those damn dolls. I hated him! He pretended to love my family, but he was just a crazy gangster who only cared about money. He got what he deserved! You know I was the one who found them. Just a little kid. I found my whole family sliced up and murdered. I will never forget that night!"

"So that's why you two planned the murder of Donald Wright?" Dad says to them, but looking at me with confidence.

"That's right! That bastard deserved to die. Everything you said about the night of his murder is true. We had waited years. After going into a witness protection program, we lost his scent. Donald Wright went into hiding up in New York, probably changing his name to an alias. His mob connections hid him away from us and the police, probably because the feds were onto him after our statements. But we were thirsty for revenge. We waited for the right time. When Donald Wright retired and separated from the mob, he moved back down to Somerset and used his old name again. The full cockiness of that man!" Sally says, shaking her head in disgust.

Helena continues, "He came back on our radar when we saw his divorce in the newspaper. Because he was married to a supermodel, their divorce went public. He probably assumed we were dead, too. We were presumed dead after the murders anyway. His mob friends also had people in the FBI. They didn't pursue any further investigation, presuming the Royal Cinquedea was lost forever. In Donald Wright's eyes, he was free and clear."

"Girl, you messed up," Mr. Nelson comments under his breath.

Helena yells with intense rage. "They took everything from us! Our home was in the possession of the federal government because the Royal Cinquedea was suspected of still being there. Finally, they sold it in an auction a couple of years ago. Aunt Sally and I didn't have enough to purchase it, and instead it went to Silas O'Leary. We were thinking about killing Mr. O'Leary but thought it would bring too much attention to the house. So, I started to dig in the back and search the house when he was at school but had no luck. My father hid the knife in a safe place. It will probably never be found. We need that money!"

I had forgotten that just a few days ago she sounded like a cheerleader. Now she sounds like a sadistic killer, barely able to control her rage. Sally starts to comfort Helena after her confession, almost forgetting about us.

Dad looks at me, winks, and yells, "NOW!"

I quickly pick up the stapler on the counter behind us, and moving with primal instincts, I throw it at Helena. Simultaneously, Dad picks up a three-hole punch and throws it across the office, right at Sally's head. Both women drop their guns and fall to their knees in pain, screaming profanities.

"Go! Go!" Dad yells.

Dad, Hannah, and I all jump over the counter, followed by a stumbling Mr. Nelson, swearing under his breath while trying to follow us. We race for the office door. Hannah is the first to the door, quickly unlocking it and throwing it open. We all file out rapidly, hoping to buy ourselves a few minutes before Sally and Helena can get up and shoot us. My heart is racing and sweat is pouring down my face. Dad is the last one out, making sure Mr. Nelson gets through after his stumble.

I look back at him and he points ahead saying, "RUN!" As he slams the door behind him and begins to run towards us, a gunshot rings out, shattering the glass of the office door. At the same moment, I hear Dad yell in pain.

CHAPTER 42

- ULYSSES -

A SHOT IN THE DARK—AND YOU WANT TO LISTEN TO QUEEN?

We run down the hallway as fast as our feet can carry us. As we take a sharp right for the science wing, I look back at Dad, who was still running but holding his arm. He hisses, "Keep going!"

We remember the exit was locked by Helena with a chain and padlock when we came in earlier, so we need to find somewhere to hide. I have the idea to make it to the audio video classroom where they film the morning news.

"Let's head to the newsroom," I say in a loud whisper. It is located at the end of the science hallway, near Hannah's and my lockers.

"Why are we going there?" Mr. Nelson asks, huffing and puffing behind us. We all stop to catch our breath.

"I don't hear them following us," Hannah says after a moment of listening.

"Yeah, but they will soon be following my blood trail." Everyone looks at Dad with shocked faces as he shows us his wound. "I think it's just a flesh wound. It stings like no other though. And they'll follow the blood and catch us in no time."

As he says this, Hannah rips off one of Mr. Nelson's orange tracksuit sleeves, quickly tying it right above Dad's wound, just below his shoulder.

"Hey now, Hannah?" Mr. Nelson says in protest.

"We need to stop the bleeding. Your tracksuit should be a good tourniquet to stop the bleeding. This has to be tight, so it's going to hurt." As she says this, my dad winces in pain; she quickly finishes tying the knot. We all look at her, stunned.

"What? None of you guys have taken a first aid class? What would you do without me?" Hannah says, blushing red. "What's the plan?" she adds.

"I texted Deputy Diaz before confronting Mr. Barron. I told him Ms. Clifton and Ms. Simmons were imposters and planning to kill Mr. Barron. I forwarded him the pictures and my research on the Royal Cinquedea. But that was about an hour ago. They may not follow through on my leads and may drag their feet getting here. Especially if Detective Brute is involved," Dad says regretfully.

"Do you have your phone now?" I ask.

"Ah, no. When Sally hit me over the head, it rolled under Mr. Barron's desk," Dad says smiling.

"This is no time to smile — you're shot! Crazy women are after us and our principal is dead!" Mr. Nelson squeaks.

"I left my phone recording. It recorded a confession from Principal Barron before he died, and it's got pretty good range. I bet it got the confessions of those two witches, too," Dad says, filling us in on his tactics.

"We need to hide," I urge.

"Agreed," Dad adds. "And call the police."

"There is a phone in the newsroom," Hannah recalls.

"I got a hiding place," Mr. Nelson interjects.

"What place?" Dad says, holding his arm and wincing in pain.

"The concession stand in the gymnasium. They would never check for us there," Mr. Nelson adds.

"Okay, you guys go there. You're hurt and need to sit down. You've lost a lot of blood. Hannah and I will make it to the newsroom. Call the cops and hide," I say with a newfound confidence.

"We should stick together," Dad protests, but as he says this he leans on Mr. Nelson and is looking a little pale.

"No! Sorry, Dad, this is the plan. We got this," I add.

"Ulysses, I can't. I can't," Dad tries to speak.

"I know, Dad. I love you, too," I reassure him before grabbing Hannah's hand and running toward the newsroom just as we hear rapid footsteps approaching.

We arrive at the newsroom at the end of the science corridor. Hannah bashes the glass window of the newsroom door with a fire extinguisher and unlocks the door by putting her arm through and opening it from the opposite side.

"You're amazing!" I say but am feeling a little intimidated by Hannah. Thankfully, she is on our side.

She smiles while whispering, "They probably

heard that and are coming this way."

"I hope so," I say.

She frowns. "Why?"

"So, they don't follow Dad and Mr. Nelson."

Hannah nods in agreement.

We leave the lights off because the bay windows allow enough light to illuminate the large room. The media room that hosts the morning Mangrove High news actually looks like a real newsroom, with its very own green screen, anchor desk, and large pivoting video camera. The newsroom phone is on a cluttered teacher desk in the corner.

"There's the phone," I say as we run over to it. I dial 911.

A female operator answers with a husky older woman's voice. "911. What is your emergency?"

"Yes. There are two female gunmen at Mangrove High. They have already killed Principal Barron and now are after us," I quickly say over the line.

"Who is this? Son, I don't appreciate bogus calls," the 911 operator says over the line.

What! She didn't believe me! Also, who uses the word "bogus" anymore? "My name is Ulysses Adair. My father, Logan Adair, has contacted Deputy Diaz about Sally Gibbins and Helena Gallant being the murderers of Donald Wright last Friday."

"Nice one, son. You're going to be in trouble for falsely reporting a crime," the operator says in a condescending tone, as only an older person living in 1% Somerset could say.

"Listen to me. We are in danger! They have guns. Principal Barron's body is in the main office of Mangrove High. Send help now!" I say with frustration. A loud shot rings out in the hallway.

"They're here!" Hannah says, pulling on my arm.

"Was that a gunshot?" the operator says in a pathetically surprised voice.

"Yes!" I hiss and hang up.

Hannah and I look around and notice the back door that leads to the chemistry and physics labs.

"We need both of them on our tail, so they need to first find us and then we get away."

"You sure?" asks Hannah, who is looking terrified as they draw closer. "I can hear them."

"If we want them to not find my dad and Mr. Nelson ..." I add.

The benefit of being trapped in the newsroom is we have audio that can be transmitted to all the speakers in the school. I quickly take Hannah by the hand and lead her to the audio board. It is attached to a laptop computer. Luckily, it is already on. The student in charge must've left it on to download music. They often play classic rock songs to open the morning announcements.

"Come out, come out, wherever you are!" We can hear Sally Gibbins chanting in her creepy voice.

It was followed by Helena saying, "We'll kill you nice and slow just like Donald Wright!"

The kid in charge of the morning music had left the computer downloading a new mix. Sure enough, several hundred songs show on the bright computer screen. I turn on the board and flip the switch, making the music go schoolwide. The speakers hum. I quickly scroll the song selection.

"Perfect!" I exclaim and hit play at the same moment we hear their footsteps crunch on the glass after opening the door.

I take Hannah by the hand and run for the back

door leading to the chemistry labs, knocking over chairs and desks to block their pursuit while "Killer Queen" by Queen blasts throughout every speaker in Mangrove High.

    I heard Sally yell to Helena, "They split up. You find the dad and that annoying gym teacher. Ah! I hate Queen!" She says this while firing several bullets that whiz by our heads.

CHAPTER 43

- LOGAN -

A TRACKSUIT REVENGE

Bob and I sit in the corner of the Mangrove gymnasium concession booth, among boxes of chips and candy bars, listening to "Killer Queen." I nod, smiling. "Classic. The kids must have made it to the newsroom. Ulysses must be leading Sally and Helena from us."

"Your arm," Bob says, choking out the words.

I look at the bandaged arm. Bob's orange tracksuit sleeve is now dark red with my blood. Bob rips off his other tracksuit sleeve.

"New fashion trend? Sleeveless tracksuits," I say, smiling.

Bob's face looks concerned. "Logan, how we gettin' out of this?" he says as he ties the new sleeve over the old one, making me wince again in pain. "Your color's not good, and we got mad women running everywhere. Hopefully U got to the phone."

"I know he did. The police should be here any minute," I say, trying to stand. I take a huge swig of water from the bottle I had pilfered from the concession supplies.

"How you holding up?" Bob inquires.

"I'm good, buddy. Sorry for getting you involved in this mess," I say.

"Actually, I got you involved when I asked you to investigate Terry and Jack's frame job. I was so worried about me instead of them. I was selfish and look where we are now," Bob says wearily.

I look at Bob as he hangs his head. "I'm to blame and you're truly the best friend a lonely old man like me could ask for."

"What's bugged me the most is how did Mary, I mean Helena, do all this without any of the Mangrove High internal cameras catching her?" Bob says, standing up next to me in the dark cramped concession booth.

"She was an administrator. Maybe for only a week, but with the help of the office secretary, who has been employed for several months, they could erase or stop those cameras from filming anything incriminating.

Administrators can wield a lot of power, especially if they go unchecked," I reason.

"You know that's right," Bob says in agreement. "You hear that?" Bob whispers as the song ends.

There was a squeak on the parquet floor outside the door of the concessions stand, probably made by a sneaker. I open the door slightly. The gymnasium is pitch black but I can see the silhouette of a figure, which looks an awful lot like Helena, creeping toward our door.

"How she find us?" Bob says in a whispered squeak.

"Like you said — cameras." They must have seen us head into the gymnasium. I look around for a weapon and start to formulate a plan.

"What are we going to do?" Bob whispers.

I point at a wrench on the counter. "Take that and stand behind the door," I direct Bob in a hushed voice. I stand on the far end of the concessions, sitting on a large box of soda cans, just as the door creaks open. Helena creeps into the concession stand, raising her gun towards me.

"I have you now — wait, where's the gym teacher!?" As soon as she says this, Bob jumps from behind the door, striking her on the back of her head with the wrench. Helena crumples to the floor, but in the process, the gun lets off a shot, hitting the side of a large ice cream freezer.

"It's physical education! Crazy lady!" Bob says as he throws down the wrench. "She's not dead, right?"

"No," I say as I rush over. "She's still breathing. Good work, Bob!" I give him a fist bump. "One down — one to go. Bob, do you have a key to that ice cream freezer?"

"Logan, come on, course I do." Bob finds the key and unlocks the freezer. It has barely any ice cream left. We both quickly throw out what is left, except for one carton that Bob devours.

I direct Bob to pick Helena up and place her in the freezer. "She made her own breathing hole with the gun; she'll be fine." I lock the freezer and leave Helena in her temporary cold jail cell.

"Should we take the gun?" Bob asks.

"No, I hate them. Leave it, and let's find the kids."

CHAPTER 44

- ULYSSES -

IT PAYS TO PAY ATTENTION IN SCIENCE

Hannah and I run for our lives. Sally Gibbins is only few dozen feet behind us, very spry for her age. We pass chemistry labs on every side of us, but I am concerned because the corridor is a dead end. We gasp for air as we check every classroom door to see if they are unlocked; we're praying some irresponsible teachers left their classrooms open. We just need a few more minutes before the police arrive. Hopefully the gunshot was enough for the dispatcher to take my call seriously.

Hannah reaches for the door on our left — it opens! We run in, closing the door behind us and sliding over to the teacher's desk to hide.

We can hear Sally trying the doors like we did. She sounds crazier than usual. "I'm gonna shoot your girlfriend first. Then I'm going to take my time with you, Ulysses Adair. Oh, and Miss Reyes, maybe I'll take a trip to that stupid cafe and introduce myself to your parents."

With this, Hannah tightens her fists while I shake my head at her and wipe her tears away. I place a finger on her lips and whisper, "I've got an idea."

I lead Hannah over to a locked, glass cabinet labeled "chemicals" and quickly scan for the right compound. There it is — potassium.

"Yes!" I whisper. I break the glass with a thick textbook, hoping the sound doesn't travel to the hallway.

"What are you looking for?" Hannah says impatiently.

"I remember watching an experiment on YouTube that I'm going to recreate," I whisper.

"Okay?" Hannah says, a little impatiently.

"Potassium in water makes an explosion. We're going to create a distraction. When she is stunned, you bring her down."

"Oh, I got this!" Hannah replies, excitedly cracking her knuckles.

The potassium is in a large beaker submerged in an oil bath to keep it stable. It is a very volatile substance and could easily ignite. I retrieve a metal bowl and a dropper syringe. I dash to the front of the room. I can see Sally is only a few doors away and getting closer. I stick the syringe into the jarred potassium, extracting a large portion. I place the potassium in the bowl carefully and center the bowl right in front of the door. Hannah places herself behind one of the lab counters, shielding herself from the blast. I grab the eyewash water bottle that is filled with water and kept in every science lab, just in case eyes get irritated by chemical reactions. The bottle has a nozzle I can use to spray into the bowl from about a foot away before ducking for cover. I gesture to Hannah to cover her ears. She gives me the thumbs up.

Sally finally reaches our lab door. Opening it slowly, she creeps her way into the classroom. I remember the lesson Dad taught me about the American defeat at Bunker Hill, which was really at Breed's Hill — but I digress. I remember he said the American General Israel Putnam famously said, "Don't fire till you see the whites of their eyes!" I adopt General Putnam's philosophy and wait until she is completely through the door jam. She hasn't seen me yet as I'm hiding behind one of the lab desks. I see her take another step, and that's when I reach around the corner and aim the eyewash bottle at the metal bowl. I squeeze hard before ducking back for cover. BOOM! The potassium and water mixture rapidly creates potassium hydroxide. A large fireball explodes, startling Sally. She screams in horror, falling back against the door, and drops her gun.

Hannah comes out of her hiding place with lightning speed. She first punches Sally in the stomach using her left fist, and with her right she punches her in the neck, causing Sally to gasp for air. Hannah isn't done yet. For good measure, she spins her tiny frame around, whipping her leg and landing a roundhouse kick to Sally's jaw. Sally crumbles, unconscious, to the floor.

I stand with my mouth wide open, gasping for air from shock and exhaustion. "You're amazing!" is all I can say.

"Aww, you're pretty awesome too, Ulysses Adair," Hannah returns, burying her head into my arms before giving me a big kiss.

Dad and Mr. Nelson both appear in the doorway. "We heard the explosion, you alright?" Dad asks.

"I think the kids did just fine," Bob says, looking down at the unconscious Sally Gibbins.

We all form a huge bear hug as we hear the sweet sound of police sirens blaring outside.

CHAPTER 45

- ULYSSES -

HELLO DOLLY!

We are at the sheriff station for hours on Thursday. We find out Dad's phone did record everything. Also, Helena and Sally are so vengeful they cop to everything from the murders of the three crime bosses in New York to our old assistant principal, Mr. Peters. And of course, the murders of Mr. Wright and Principal Barron.

Dad made the trip to the station after they stitched up his wound at the hospital. He was told he has to wear a sling for a couple of weeks and may need some physical therapy, but the doctors gave him the all clear. He stayed overnight for observation, but he wanted to be with us at the station, so he checked himself out early.

Deputy Diaz and Detective Brute had followed Dad's clues and were in the process of raiding the house of Ms. Simmons, aka Sally Gibbins, while Hannah and I were being thrown into the trunk by Ms. Clifton, aka Helena Gallant.

Detective Brute is very thankful for our investigation and closing out six murders for him. He is very forgiving of some of our methods and concealment. He does inform Dad and me in his sternest, thickest Southern drawl, "If you eva - get in the way - of anotha - police - investigation - I will - personally - throw y'all in jail!" Dad and I agree profusely to never again get involved with another police investigation.

Terry and Jack were vindicated this morning and put back on the team, which makes Mr. Nelson extremely happy, especially since he has a game in two days.

But the most excitement today is when we are giving witness testimonies down at the sheriff station and it occurs to me where the Royal Cinquedea was hidden.

I am sitting there thinking about everything that transpired the night before and happy school was cancelled, because much of the school is an active crime scene. Something is gnawing at me about what Helena said to us when she was speaking about Donald Wright. I sit for the longest time trying to think what exactly it was that she said that sparked a memory. Then, while waiting with Dad, Hannah, and Mr. Nelson in a cramped interrogation room with Detective Brute, he has a file delivered to him by a female detective. When she gives him the file, he says, "Thanks - doll." In his drawl. I mean, pretty sexist, but that isn't what made my memory click. Helena hated dolls.

"The doll!" I blurt out.

Detective Brute looks at me like I have two heads. "What - doll?" he asks, confused.

I look at Dad and then Hannah. "I know where the Royal Cinquedea is hidden!" I say, smiling.

"Remember when Helena said she hated dolls but Mr. Wright gave one to her as a gift?"

"Yeah," Dad replies, unsure of where I am going with this.

"When Hannah and I went to the Gallant home, I stumbled across a really old nasty doll right at the fence line abutting the conservation area," I add.

"Let's go!" Dad smiles. We follow behind Detective Brute's police-issued Ford Interceptor with Dad's Prius.

When we arrive at Mr. O'Leary's house, he looks at all of us like we are crazy. Everyone follows me as I try my best to follow the path I took only a few days earlier. I head into the tall grassy conservation area, and sure enough, right by the fence line a decrepit, nasty looking old doll sits staring up at us.

"Yeah, Ulysses. It's an old creepy doll. In a backyard of an old creepy house. It even has an old creepy math teacher living here. No jeweled knife is in that thing," Mr. Nelson says jokingly.

I lean down to pick it up. The doll is heavy. I turn her over and rip open her seam, reaching my hand into the doll's stuffing.

"I think all those years ago Toby Gallant hid the Royal Cinquedea in one of his daughter's cast-aside dolls. He sewed it up with the knife inside and hid it in this field for safety, thinking he would retrieve it before escaping and never tell anyone. He took the secret to his grave," I say before taking a deep intake of air and swallowing hard. In my hands is a hard object, and I pull it out for everyone to see. I hold a shining, gold, ornate Venetian knife, adorned with tiny gemstones and diamonds, perfectly preserved. "I present to you, the Royal Cinquedea!"

CHAPTER 46

- ULYSSES -

NEVER BACKING DOWN

Three weeks have passed and life is starting to return to normal. Me, Dad, Hannah, and Mr. Nelson's names were plastered all over the local and national news. We were celebrities at school, too. We not only solved six murders, while almost dying, but we also found the missing Royal Cinquedea, which came with a sizable finder's fee. Dad and Mr. Reyes say it's for my and Hannah's college funds.

The Mangrove High boys' basketball team is in the playoffs and is expected to go far. With their star players, Terry and Jack, and their fearless leader, Mr. Nelson, the sky's the limit.

Hannah and I are doing great. I got a job busing tables at Penny University Cafe. It's a lot of fun working with her at my favorite restaurant.

It's not all good news, though. We had Conrad's going away party at Penny University. Hannah and I cried our eyes out and hated seeing him move away to New York, but we understood. Conrad and his mother were facing scandal and backlash after his father's crimes and business dealings came to light during his murder investigation. We promised we'd visit and stay in touch.

That wasn't the only bad news: Our school district did a search for a new principal. With all their immense knowledge and wisdom, they chose our new principal — Silas O'Leary. Yeah, that's right! Mr. O'Leary is now running Mangrove High. Who knew he had his administration degree? Dad didn't. He's not happy.

My dad asked me last week if I was okay with him dating again.

"You gotta be kidding me, Dad. It's way overdue!" is what I told him. We both cried at my response. "Mom would be so proud of us," I added.

He told me, "Let's try and not get into any more trouble investigating crimes."

"Dad, there are never any guarantees in life," I said, quoting something Mom always used to say to us.

Dad decided to bring a date by Penny U tonight to meet everyone. Mr. Nelson said he met her when he was in physical therapy. I guess she's a physical therapist helping Dad to get movement back in his arm after being shot, so he could play guitar with me again. Yeah, you guessed it. It's Friday at Penny University. Open mic night!

"You ready?" Dad says to me as we sit down with our guitars, center stage, with a huge crowd around us.

"Oh yeah, Dad!" I reply.

"What do you want to play?" Dad asks.

"How about Petty's 'I Won't Back Down'?"

"Ulysses, that sounds — swell. 1-1-1-2-3-4." Dad winks back at me as he counts us in.

--- THE END --
Look for further adventures with Logan and Ulysses in future installments of:
The Adair Classroom Mysteries
By T.W. Morse

https://adairclassroommysteries.sitey.me/

https://www.facebook.com/Adairclassroommysteries/

1% MURDERS- BY T.W. MORSE

Made in the USA
Middletown, DE
09 September 2025

12890019R00172